CW00541385

Red Skies

Extra Elements Series, Volume 15

T. M. Kuefler

Published by T. M. Kuefler, 2023.

This is a work of fiction. Similarities to real people, places, or events are entirely coincidental.

RED SKIES

First edition. October 17, 2023.

Copyright © 2023 T. M. Kuefler.

ISBN: 979-8223963097

Written by T. M. Kuefler.

Table of Contents

RED SKIES

EXTRA ELEMENTS SERIES

T. M. KUEFLER

GLOSSARY OF TERMS

ALLIANCE: Andromadan Alliance consisting of various factions, including Nordics and Andromadans. They generously extended a helping hand to humanity in order to assist in the removal of the enemy Drako Alliance from their current occupation of Earth.

ANDROMADAN: Leaders of the Andromadan Alliance. Highly intelligent and advanced beings, both technically and mentally. They boast powerful mental abilities and high senses. They tend to be very tall and beautiful with darks skin, dark hair, and bright eyes.

ANTARCTIC PYRAMID: Frozen pyramid under Drako control. The Alliance went in to retrieve a kidnapped Pleiadean and destroy the energy containment machines that the Drako developed. While they were there they found a ley line harness and sacrificial temple inside with carvings on the walls depicting every language known and many unknown to man.

BOSSES: Humans allied with the Drako. Heavily involved in human enslavement and brain washing.

DATA HARVEST: Air-born hacking of the Drako database involving the head of Operations Marko Butcher and hacker River Butcher and first team members Wings and Scope. It was successful despite the group crashing in the Peruvian jungle and being trapped there for weeks.

DIVERGENTS: Shapeshifters who have the ability to change into certain types of animals. They boast extreme strength and heightened senses. So far we have met equine and canine.

DOME ATTACK: Drako attack on the energy Dome protecting the Ranch. This was due to the protection and adoption of Human/Gray hybrid children, Tab and Casper, by Dr. John James and Fain James.

DRAKO: Drako Alliance, enemy occupying forces. Instrumented the pandemic that wiped out 80-85% of humanity that cleared the way for them to attack and take over Earth, enslaving the remaining humans in the process. They experiment and torture the humans under their control and use them in their attempts to breed hybrid beings. They have only been successful twice with Casper and Tab James. As far as we know, they consist of Lizards, Grays, and Insectoids.

THE FIRST TEAM: One of three security teams within the Rocky Mountain Base. The first and main team that is utilized for highly dangerous call outs, Ops, and raids. The team is populated with career soldier's expert in their fields and are commanded by the human head of the Base, Malachi DeMarques. They are also joined by Nordic Alliance minister of defence, Rashnia Hastings.

GRAYS: Part of the Drako, they tend to be very cold and logical, unemotional, and have highly advanced telepathic and mind control abilities. They are tall, thin limbed, grey colored beings with large heads and large dark eyes, pointed faces and delicate features.

HUMANS: Earthlings struggling to hide, survive, and maybe regain their planet from the Drako occupying forces. They have been recently invited to join the Andromadan Alliance.

HUMAN/GRAY HYBRID: Tab and Casper James. They boast the telepathic and mind control abilities that Grays do along with the human capacity for emotion. Adorable with thin limbs and small bodies, pointed and delicate faces, big dark blue eyes, pale skin and dark hair.

INSECTOIDS: Part of the Drako, they are intelligent advanced insect like beings with a keenly carnivorous appetite. They boast thick bodies and long limbs covered in a hard carapace, insect like faces with beak mouths and fly eyes.

LEY LINES: Veins of energy that run throughout Mother Earth. Major monoliths were built by ancient humans on the meeting points of these lines in order to harness that extensive power.

LIZARDS: Leaders of the Drako Alliance. Highly technologically advanced and intelligent beings. They are currently attempting to take Earth over and enslave the surviving humans of which they are using to experiment on and try to breed hybrids. They boast tough, leathery skin, long snouts filled with sharp fanglike teeth. Thick, muscular bodies, long claws, and thick, long tails.

NORDICS: Part of the Alliance, they boast highly advanced technology and slight mental abilities. They are tall and pale in coloration often carrying light, blond hair and pale eyes.

OCCUPATION: The occupation of Earth by the Drako. This was initiated by the pandemic and was continued with the attack and attempted enslavement of humanity. Many humans ran and hid, creating secret Bases and communities in order to survive and, maybe, fight back.

PANDEMIC: A deadly and highly contagious disease that was created and released by the Drako. It successfully wiped out 80-85% of humanity making it easier for the Drako to attempt to enslave humanity and occupy Earth.

PLEIADEANS: Mythical extra terrestrial being of pure energy. Ancient and extremely powerful, they are tasked with maintaining the balance of the universe through a system of juries and Judges. Their humanoid forms boast effervescent skin, colorful hair and eyes, and metallic facial markings. Judges also boast black markings that run over the whole of the body.

RANCH: Originally known as the Skinwalker Ranch and occupied by the Drako. The Rocky Mountain Base and the Alliance took it over and instituted an investigation of the property. In the process they found a buried monolith that was harnessing and changing one of the Earths ley lines. The Andromadan Guardian Coren, with the help of his wide Blaze, was able to release the ley line from the harness and return to its original position. As a gift, Mother Earth now gives anyone who stays at the Ranch advanced healing abilities.

REINCARNATED ANGEL: Andromadan Ancient, Catro Masters, who turned out to be a Watcher, and human Royce Masters. Descended Angels reincarnated into mortal beings with the ability to take on their previous angelic forms. This consists of effervescent skin marked with gold, matte black eyes, extremely sharp cheekbones, and large white wings. They also boast high mental abilities and abnormal strength.

ROCKY MOUNTAIN BASE: A human/alliance run Base hidden deep inside of a mountain somewhere along the Rocky Mountain Range. They are protected by an energy Dome that is the twin of the one found at the Ranch. It is almost fully self sufficient and currently houses 250-300 residents.

SKY WAR: An attack on the Rocky Mountain Base by a Drako mothership. The Alliance won, barely, with the help of advanced technology and mentally advanced beings.

CHAPTER 1

AMBROSE

"Why did they go out there in the first place?" I demanded as I strode around the huge mechanical tent collecting tools, and other things I figured I might need.

I was out at the Ranch doing some maintenance on one of the excavator's that crapped out. The engine was burned out right along with the hydraulics. Some idiot decided that using a bucket that the excavator wasn't rated for was smart. It was not.

The shortcuts that some people came up with just to get a job done quicker honestly amazed me. More times than not those shortcuts came back to bite them in the ass and added at least twice the work to the original job.

Harper, a petite redheaded woman who had once been one of my best Bay mechanics but was now living here at the Ranch with her family was giving me a hand. She was in a triad with Bane, the head of the Ranch, and Bailor, an equine divergent. The three now had a rare set of fraternal twin baby boys.

Bane used to be a Boss owned assassin and definitely looked like he had been in a couple fights. The highly scarred man had white hair with to dark brown streaks and one brown eye. The one he was missing was covered with a black eyepatch that gave him a distinctive pirate vibe. One of their twins, Dominic, clearly took after him with a soft head of fuzzy brown hair and deep brown eyes.

Bailor, on the other hand, boasted a head full of long, shaggy hair that was pale brown on top with dark brown underneath. His brown eyes were interesting with oval pupils that laid horizontally. Sebastian, their other twin had his hair and eyes.

I had been pulling the hydraulics off the excavator when Bailor came racing in to tell us about a broke down jeep that needed emergency help. The issue with this was that the jeep had left the protective energy Dome that covered a good mile all around the Ranch and travelled to the next bowl over in order to collect some samples.

The group in the jeep had consisted of a number of scientists and their assistants along with some security. About eight people in total. And now all of them were stuck out beyond the protection of the Dome.

"We are trying to find out how far the Ley Line's healing influence extends." Bailor stated, watching as I walked around, gathering what I would need based on the information I got on the vehicle and its breakdown.

"I can do it." Harper continued the argument she had started when Bailor first came in as she helped me.

"Fuck no." I denied the tiny, redhead in a tone that brooked no argument.

Lifting the duffle bag full of tools and supplies, I threw it in the back of a two door jeep wrangler before climbing into the front seat and turning it on.

"Wait, you need security." Bailor stated, stepping around to the opened window on the driver's side.

"There is security out there." I pointed out, not worried as there hadn't been any sightings of Drako ships since the mothership attack on the Rocky Mountain Base. That and we had people who needed help. The sooner I got out there and got the vehicle fixed the sooner they would be able to return to the safety of the Dome.

"True." Bailor frowned and opened his mouth to say something else.

I didn't hear whatever that might have been as I threw the jeep in gear and pulled out of the tent.

I drove over the fields to the Dome edge and passed through it before eventually reaching the overgrown dirt road that led to the other bowl. It took me about twenty minutes to traverse the narrow, pothole filled track.

I finally reached a curving part of the road that was surrounded by large rocks and scrubby trees to see the large, four door jeep in question. It was sitting in the middle of the road with smoke pluming from it's opened hood.

Pulling up in front of the smoking vehicle, I left my vehicle running and climbed out to check out the situation. Ignoring the group of sweaty, dirty people that was standing and sitting around the rock strewn side of the road, I walked over and dumped the canister of water I had grabbed over the engine.

It hissed and smoked even more as it cooled. Once the smoke diminished, I bent over to see what I was dealing with to find that the fan belt was completely shredded which would explain why the engine overheated like it did.

I was expecting this due to the information that Ranch security gave Bailor on the condition of the vehicle.

Thankfully, the damage to the actual engine was minimal.

"What's the damage?" Collin, one of the Ranch security personnel bent over the hood beside me.

"Fan belt for sure. It's going to take me about 45 minutes to fix. Why don't you use the other vehicle to take them back." I jerked my chin towards the jeep I left running.

"I am going to stay." Collin denied, turning to join the now standing, watching group.

Striding back to the jeep I drove in, my eyes caught a set of dark eyes staring at me. A very familiar set of eyes that belonged to a very familiar woman. My eyes immediately darted away.

Lux Samaras. The beautiful sister of the bane of my existence, Stella.

The first time I saw Lux, I immediately thought that she was the most gorgeous woman I had ever seen. That still hadn't changed.

She had a slim, delicate build with beautiful bronze skin. Dark brown eyes and silky brown hair. A small, pointed face with delicate features and distinctive cheekbones. Her breasts were a luscious C that were fully on display by the rounded neck of her beige tank top. The cargo pants she was wearing cupped her heart shaped ass beautifully.

But, honestly, the most beautiful part of her, the thing that attracted me the most, was her soul. She seemed to radiate this low hum of pure life. Earthy yet delicate. She was so sweet and gentle, caring and supportive, friendly and funny, but stubborn as hell with a spine of steel.

I felt fury flash through me.

I wanted to yell at her for being out here and putting herself in danger like this. I wanted pick her up and carry her to safety. But I knew she wouldn't appreciate that at all. She wouldn't want my dirty hands on her. She probably hated just being in my vicinity considering she did everything she could to avoid me, even transferring to the Ranch.

See, she had once been my best friend, the one person I actually cared for in this fucked up world. Right up until I fucked everything up by betraying her friendship and sleeping with her narcissistic, manipulative, nymphomaniac sister.

The morning after I fucked up, I had tracked her down in order to be honest and tell her what I did. Only, she already knew. I desperately tried to apologize, to fix the heartbreaking wrong I did, but she didn't want to hear it. As broken and destroyed as I had been, I could see the agony in her eyes, so much pain. Pain that I caused.

I could do nothing but what she requested and exit myself from her life. That beautiful, gentle soul deserved nothing less.

I left behind a big chunk of my being, my character, maybe even my soul. I went from the caring, fun loving guy I used to be and turned into an uncaring cynic. I did my job, I went back to my suite, I hate fucked my punishment when the bitch tracked my ass down.

Beyond that, I had nothing.

Pushing back the tornado of emotions swirling through me, I grabbed the duffle bag out of the back and returned to the engine. My clenched jaw worked as I started pulling out tools and got to work. I chewed on my lip and did everything in my power to ignore the woman who I could practically feel staring at me.

Collin once more bent over the engine beside me. He patiently waited until I tipped my questioning eyes up to him before he started speaking. "There isn't enough room for everyone so three of us are going to have to stay here."

"Fine." I grunted in agreement.

Collin backed away and thirty seconds later the other jeep drove away.

"Can I help?" A dark complexioned male asked as he joined me at the jeep.

"Nope." I denied, knowing that he would only slow me down.

The man nodded and tapped on the side of the jeep before backing away.

I got the belt off and started to put on the new one. I had both hands in the engine when Collin appeared once again, this time with a cold water bottle in hand. "Water?"

"Thank you." I nodded at him and took the bottle, sucking back a number of cool, refreshing gulps.

With the intensity of the sun beating down on me, I was dying of heat and sweating up a storm. After years of living within a mountain that was far to the north, I wasn't used to the blazing heat of the Ranch and it always got to me.

Handing the bottle back, I returned to my work, ignoring the trickling lines of sweat that uncomfortably slid down my body and gathered in irritating places.

I had the belt half on when a low hum hit my ears. I knew that hum and it did not bode well. Pausing mid motion, I slowly pulled my hands out of the engine and lowered the hood to see exactly what my pounding heart had been telling me I was going to see. A large, circular Drako ship was moving over the edge of the bowl that was less than half a mile away.

"Move." I hissed out quietly, drawing the attention of the three people sitting around, waiting for me to finish.

"Fuck." Collin snarled when that ship stopped moving, floating ominously like a dark shadow.

Collin scrambled to the back of the vehicle and began to dig only for the dark complexioned man to yank him back. "No time. Run."

I stumbled backwards, my eyes still locked on the ship, when a small hand caught my arm and pulled at me. My gaze finally released the craft to look down into a set of familiar dark brown eyes.

Terror hit me like a sledgehammer to my chest.

Lux was still here.

Why the hell was she still here? I needed her away from here, I needed her safe. Spinning around, I started running, pushing her in front of me.

The other two men had already disappeared into the brush around us. Taking a cue from them, I caught Lux around her stomach and lifted her against my chest as I stumbled sideways, straight down into a small ravine that was mere feet from the road.

I clenched my teeth and caught her hand in mine as we ran over rocks and through snarled trees. Ignoring the sound of the humming that was practically right over our heads, we continued along the ravine in hopes of either finding a place to hide or out running the ship. A slim chance but that didn't mean I wasn't going try.

A blinding white beam of light slashed down in front of us causing Lux to scream and me to scrambled backwards, yanking her with me. We spun around, desperately tearing up the ravine, through the brush around us.

I knew that there was no hiding now. There was only running, and even then our possibilities of escape was practically nonexistent. We hit the road and started full out sprinting. I kept her in front of me, my feet hitting the ground a second behind hers.

My hair rose on end as the light chased us, playing with us. The ones controlling the ship were obviously enjoying our fear. Eventually though, they clearly set that enjoyment aside in order to finish the job.

The light slashed forward to center right over us and my body was torn apart. I couldn't even scream the pain was so intense. Burning, ice cold. I felt myself being broken down to my smallest atoms. My mind screamed what my mouth wasn't able to.

By the time my body was recombined, I was dizzy and nauseas and seconds from blacking out. My weak legs collapsed to a metallic floor as my stomach ejected everything inside of it.

Once I was done heaving, my glazed eyes finally focused on the unconscious body beside mine. Lux.

"Lux." I croaked out, reaching for her with a set of shaking hands. "Noo!" I screamed when hard clawed hands caught my neck and violently yanked me away from her, dragging me down the halls of the Drako ship.

I gurgled around my cut off airways as I punched at the muscular hand of the Lizard gripping me. The creature snarled down at me with a flash of deadly fangs as it gave me a hard shake. Pain shot up my back and neck at that harsh movement causing me to stop fighting.

I groaned in pain when I was thrown violently into a large cell, crashing off the back wall to fall to the floor. The Lizard slammed the cell doors shut and stepped back.

Wheezing my breath in, I rubbed my bruised neck and eyed the other Lizard that came clomping in behind the first one with Lux draped over its shoulder. The creature dropped her into the cell beside mine and the two of them left the room.

I slowly pushed myself up and looked around the large, shadowed room. The low lights gleamed off walls filled with extremely disturbing metallic instruments. Throughout the center of the open room there was a metallic table, what looked like an exam chair, and a number of shackles hanging from the ceiling in various places.

Yeah, we were in deep shit.

Pushing myself forward, I felt around the bars holding us, looking for a lock. I was slightly disappointed to find that the lock was high security that needed DNA to open.

I needed Lizard DNA.

And in order to get Lizard DNA, I needed a Lizard.

With a snarl, I spun my ass around and began to slam my feet into the thick metal bars. The loud clang of the bars was mixed with my bellows to be let out.

"Owe." Lux's lyrical voice breathed as she began to shift. Her head lifted and her eyes looked around, slowly filling with more and more horror. "We are in the ship, aren't we?"

"Yup." I paused in my bellowing and kicking to confirm.

"Fuck." She whimpered, her head dropping back down to the floor. She laid there for a good minute, obviously attempting to get control of her fear. Eventually, she sat up and curled her arms around her cocked up knees and looked at me. That fear still there but now contained. "What do we do?"

"We break out." I snarled, angry and frustrated, still kicking the bars with violent precision.

"How the hell do we do that?" She hissed at me, her voice stiff with worry.

Instead of answering her, I darted my hinting gaze over one of the five cameras I spotted throughout the room. If they had visuals they also had listening devices.

She sighed, the intelligent woman taking my hint. Her chin fell to her knees as she watched me. Both of us froze, turning to the door when it opened once again. My body tightened in preparation.

My heart dropped when the Lizard that handled me walked in carrying yet another unconscious body. This one boasted bright red hair and effervescent skin. The Lizard was dragging the unconscious man by the shackles that locked the man's hands behind his back. He was wearing a light gray t-shirt that was splattered with blood on the one shoulder and back along with a set of jeans similar to the ones I was wearing.

Blood covered the back of the man's head, dripping down his three inch long hair to splatter over the floor.

"Hey, you ugly motherfucker." I yelled, once again kicking at the bars.

"What are you doing?" Lux hissed at me, her face tense with anger and worry, her eyes darting between me and the Lizard.

The Lizard sneered at me as it clomped towards the cells, pausing to assess which of the two cells to toss the man in.

"Right here, dipshit." I called in a mocking voice. "Or are you scared of one itty bitty human?"

"Would you shut the hell up?" Lux demanded loudly, slapping her hand on the floor.

I ignored her and watched the Lizard press its thumb to the DNA lock on Lux's cell, opening the door and tossing the redhead inside.

"Holy fuck!" I crowed as I laughed maniacally. "You are scared. That is fucking hilarious."

The Lizard slammed the cell shut as it glared at me. I grinned in amusement and kept mocking it, pushing it. I needed it to open my cell, to come at me. Out of the corner of my eye, I saw Lux maneuver herself over so she could check on the unconscious man.

"Shit." She whispered when she saw exactly who she was now sharing a cell with.

I once again ignored the shocked look she sent me as I continued to goad the Lizard.

"Weak assed fucker too scared to take on a mere human. Your friends should call you chicken not a Lizard. Do you squawk every time you open your mouth? I bet they make you lick their feet. Do you enjoy the taste of your friend's toes? Do you like the feel...?" That did it, the Lizard hissed out in its language, clearly threatening me as it stomped over and ripped open the cell door.

Within seconds, my heel shifted against the bar I had been kicking. The blade hidden in my boot slid out just as I used my braced arms to twist my body towards the incoming Lizard and kicking out with fast stabs.

The unsuspecting Lizard snarled and squealed in pain as my knife grated through its leathery skin to seat deep into its unprotected abdomen. I continued kicking, over and over again until it's squeals finally stopped. As soon as it collapsed to the floor, I finished twisting the rest of my body until I was standing over it. Meeting its glazed eyes, I could tell that the fucker knew he was done for. One last kick to its head finished it off.

"I told you, weak." I snarled, my heel shifting and the knife sliding back into my boot.

Stepping out of the cell, I strolled over to the wall of torture instruments and pulled down a wickedly sharp, curving blade type weapon. I palmed it and a short length of metallic rope before racing towards the door, sliding to the side of it just as it opened for the other Lizard to clomp into the room.

With a deep, bracing breath, I gathered my courage and launched myself onto its back, looping the rope around its neck and tightening it down. The creature snarled as it threw itself backwards, slamming me into the wall. I groaned in pain at the extreme force that I was honestly surprised didn't break my ribs. It did, however, steal my breath.

Dizzy and breathless, I stubbornly held on to the wildly bucking Lizard and started punching it with the curved blade fisted in my other hand. Blood sprayed as the Lizard screamed. In a desperate attempt to get me off of it, the Lizard violently slammed me back into the wall. Over and over again.

It failed.

The Lizard thankfully started to slow from the copious amount of blood it was losing. I kept punching even as it stumbled around. I rode it as it eventually sank to the ground, standing over it and delivering one last punch to its head before leaving it dead on the floor.

Using the blade, I sliced off one of the Lizard's fingers before retrieving the rope. I tucked the rope into the back pocket of my jeans and walked over to the cell holding Lux and the now awake male. Lux was staring at me with a set of wide, shocked eyes while the Pleiadean male watched with dazed red eyes.

I used the Lizard's finger to unlock the cell door and stepped over to attempt to use it to unlock the shackles locking the man's hands behind his back.

"It's not working." I hissed when the finger didn't work. "It looks like there is a code that has to be inputted."

"Fuck." The male snarled, yanking on his arms and causing the shackles to clank. "I can't use my abilities. Something in the shackles is stopping me."

"They could be made from the instructions of the confinement cells that were destroyed." I noted, gripping the man's arms and helping him up to his feet. "How the fuck did you get caught?"

"I was at the Ranch, visiting with Grayson when the call came through about you being abducted by the Drako's. I came up here to check on you only to somehow end up knocked the fuck out. I have no fucking clue how the bastards got the drop on me, but they did." The man explained, swaying slightly.

"Come on." I growled, holding the man's arm at the same time I reached a hand down to help Lux up. My mouth tightened when she ignored my hand in favor of standing on her own.

I should be used to the pain of her denial but I wasn't. I didn't know if I ever would be.

CHAPTER 2

LUX

I nervously tucked my hair behind my ears as I followed Ambrose and the Pleiadean male out of the room of terrors and through the Drako craft to the cockpit.

Every time I saw Ambrose, I was reminded of how gorgeous my ex best friend was. Dark blue eyes. Short, blond hair. Dark blond brows. Tall with wide, thick shoulders and arms, and a slim waist. His face boasted a sharply squared jaw with indented cheeks. His nose was long and straight, his plush lips dry as if he had been chewing on them.

Because he had been.

That was one thing that Ambrose consistently did when he was nervous or deep in thought.

As for the Pleiadean. A tall, devilish looking man with the metallic Pleiadean markings on his face accenting his rectangular jaw, sharp cheekbones, high forehead, and smooth, pillowy lips. Then there was his demonic coloration. Red. Bright red hair that was about three inches long on the top and short on the underneath. Bright red eyes made his pale, effervescent skin seem to almost glow. Although that was intensified by the blood coating the side of his face.

My eyes moved from the extremely attractive Pleiadean back to the man who was once my best friend. My mind travelled back to the last conversation we had, a couple of weeks ago.

"Lux." The low masculine voice had me looking up to the heartbreakingly familiar blond haired man who was pacing the width

of the hall in front of my suite. My heart twisted painfully just as it always did when I caught sight of him.

"Ambrose." I greeted softly, not knowing what to say.

We had been friends. Good friends.

When the pandemic hit and Stella and I lost our parents, he and a handful of others had helped us hide from the descending Drako's while we all made our way to the hidden Base that we had only heard about. I remembered how sweet yet strong he was at the time. We would spend hours talking and, to be honest, I felt myself falling in love with him.

He made me feel safe and actually able to trust someone for the first time in a long time. I shared with him about my sister and how she ruined relationships and lives, especially mine, because of her narcissistic nymphomania. He was even there when she slept her way through his friend group. He knew that if he went that way with her, I would walk away from our friendship. And he knew why. I shared with him how damaging it was when she slept with my friends or the one boyfriend I brought home, how she used and abused them, and how they eventually took their anger out on me, blaming me for all of it.

Then came the soul destroying day I found out that he had slept with her, my sister. The one person who she knew would break me.

When he tracked me down he looked absolutely wrecked. He sound desperate as he attempted to talk to me about it, claiming that he didn't mean to do it, how I was really important to him and he didn't want to lose our friendship. As broken as he looked, my torn and bleeding heart knew that I had to protect myself from further pain. I had been through this very scenario before and had been burned, badly. I told him that I wasn't going to do it again. I couldn't. Especially not with him.

So, I walked away.

My heart was broken, my trust was broken. I was done with him, with her, with all of it.

Now that Stella was gone, he was back and I could feel all of that anger and heartbreak rising all over again.

Why did he pick her?

Why didn't he pick me?

He claimed to care about me. But he didn't, not enough.

"Can we talk?" He asked, his hands awkwardly tucked into his grease stained jeans.

"Why?" I sighed wearily, pressing my palm to the security panel and unlocking the door to my bachelor suite.

A small single room with a small, attached bathroom. Cupboards and shelves ran along the wall with the bathroom door. A queen sized bed was set against the back wall and a tiny kitchenette and dining table was against the other wall. A couch was set facing the shelves that held a TV. Then there was the small end tables, nightstands, and the coffee table that was distributed around the suite.

"Stella's gone." He stated the obvious, following me into the suite.

As much as I hated having him here, in my space in a way that I knew I would forever visualize, I didn't want to hash this out in the hall where everyone could hear.

"Believe me, I know." I cringed, remembering the amount of people who found out that I was Stella's sister and tracked me down.

Other than one very nice couple, all the rest blamed me for her actions or assumed that I was just like her. The comments I was getting on a day to day basis weren't kind. This was why I stayed as far away from her and her actions as possible.

"I stopped it. In the end. As much as the drug was affecting me, I still stopped it." He spoke softly.

"That's good." I nodded, not really knowing what else to say. As much as I was happy that he was able to finally break free, it didn't change anything.

"Not that the drugs did anything but, uh, intensify things. After all, that...shit with her started long before she started, uh, using." He scoffed self derisively, chewing on his bottom lip.

I nodded again, waiting for him to say what he came here to say.

"I am sorry, Lux. I really am. I don't even know how I could've let it happen, I just know that I did. And I have regretted it. Every single day." He apologized, his dark blue eyes shining strangely.

"And yet, you continued to do it." I very accurately pointed out, watching his eyes squeeze shut.

"I did." He confirmed, his voice hoarse. *"After, uh, after you walked away, I felt like I had nothing else."*

"Nothing else." I bit out angrily, shaking my head slowly, blinking my tears back. *"That's absolute bullshit."*

"You walked away, Lux. You wouldn't even listen to me." He exclaimed, gesturing wildly. *"You just dropped me as if I meant nothing. So yeah, I kept fucking her because I had nothing else, I was nothing."*

"You had nothing? I have nothing. Because she took everything from me. Everything. I was falling in love with you, Ambrose. And it took you what, maybe a couple of months to fall into bed with her." I yelled back, pounding my fist against my chest.

His eyes widened in shock when I admitted that.

"Yeah." I confirmed with a nod. *"You were my only friend, my best friend, and I was falling in love with you. And you fucked my sister. You claim that I walked away, that I didn't listen to you, but you did it first. You knew how I felt about her. You knew what she caused. And you still did it."*

"I was fucking drunk that night, Lux. Blitzed out of my fucking mind and not thinking straight. She came on to me and the next thing I knew we were fucking. I regretted it the moment I woke up that morning." He shared for the first time, his voice loud and cracking.

"Yeah? And how many times did you fuck her in your drunken state, Ambrose? Because the way she bragged about it the next morning it sounded like a lot. All night long. And not once during that whole time did you put a stop to it. Not once." I pointed out angrily, those memories stabbing painfully.

Ambrose froze when he heard that, his eyes taking on a look of disbelief.

"What? You didn't know about that?" I mocked him. "How the fuck do you think I found out? For fuck sakes, Ambrose, how many times did I tell you how she likes to brag about her conquests to me? What made you even remotely think that she wouldn't brag about fucking my best friend? I told you."

"I didn't..." He began, his eyes haunted, pleading.

"But you did, Ambrose. You say that you were drunk, blitzed out of your mind. Yet, how did you get in that state? Why was she even there? Where was I?" I brought up the questions that I asked myself over and over again.

"It was me and the guys in James' suite. We were playing cards and drinking, having a guy's night. Then she showed up and they invited her to join in. Poker turned into strip poker which turned into something else entirely. Somehow we ended up in her suite and in her bed." Ambrose frowned as he described what happened that night, his brow furrowed in heartbroken confusion.

"James' suite? Let me guess, it was you, James, and all of the guys who already had a piece of her. Your so called friends fucked you over just as much as she did." I rolled my eyes. I had never liked his friends. They were misogynous assholes who only seemed to think that women were good for one thing, fucking.

On the plus side, most of them were now gone, all of them accept James who worked in the Bay with Ambrose.

"Believe me, I know that. I cut ties with them the next morning when I woke up and realized how they set me up." He sighed sadly.

I nodded, feeling tired, drained. "I am sorry that happened to you. It sucks."

"Yeah." His eyes studied me intently, as if trying to see what I was thinking.

"But it doesn't change anything, not for me. I was so fucking stupid, desperate. And the man I was falling in love with clearly didn't feel the same. I should've seen the signs but I didn't. That is something I have been forced to come to terms with. It took me a long time and is not something I want to repeat." I blinked back the tears that pinned my eyes, desperate not to cry in front of the man who had already been the cause of so much of my pain.

"You weren't stupid." He denied, taking a step towards me as if to comfort me.

I held up a hand to stop him while backing up a step. "But I was." I whispered, my gaze lifting up to his. "Goodbye, Ambrose."

His agonized eyes dropped and he drew a deep breath in before nodding his bowed head. "Ok, Lux. Ok." He turned and walked to the door, pausing with his hand on the handle. "But just so you know, you were, are, the person I...uh...care for most in this world. I fucked up. And believe me, I have paid for it. Everyday that I didn't see you or that you ignored me was pain. I just wish that you could've forgiven me."

"I do forgive you." I whispered, feeling that in my heart. "It doesn't diminish the pain and mistrust. It doesn't stop me from feeling inconsequential, worthless, when it comes to you."

His head turned to mine, his eyes carrying the same wet shine that mine did. "I never wanted to make you feel that way."

I gave him a sad smile, my throat working in an attempt to swallow my tears back.

"Goodbye, Lux." He whispered, opening the door and walking out.

As soon as the door shut, I felt those tears break free. It wasn't closure. There was no closure when it came to Ambrose. Loss and pain and confusion and so many other emotions, but not closure.

Pulling myself together, I headed for the shower.

It was time for a change.

My sister Stella was a nymphomaniac who enjoyed sex and did everything she could to get what she wanted. Including drugging men with a pheromone that caused them to be uncontrollably attracted to her and, for some, made them believe they loved her. This was exactly what she did to Diad, Ech's man.

I would love to say she did the same with Ambrose but that would be a lie. They started sleeping together years ago, back when we first arrived at the Base. Needless to say, our friendship stopped the moment she gleefully told me about the night the two of them spent together.

That broke my fucking heart in way that I never truly healed from.

As for Stella, she decided that she wasn't getting enough sex, so she got her hands on a pheromone masked as a perfume. That pheromone was designed to affect the male mind and libido and was unfortunately highly addictive. When the Base found out what she was doing, they immediately charged her and transferred her.

For which I was extremely thankful for. Although, I was apparently still coming to terms with the fact that my sister was no longer around to ruin any relationships I may or may not wish to develop with the opposite sex.

After that conversation with Ambrose, I put in for a transfer to the Ranch. Luckily, two botanists were looking for an assistant so my transfer was quickly put through.

Ice Smith was a tall, dark complexioned male with mocha skin, dark hair, and dark eyes. He had wide shoulders and slim hips, a pointed jaw, pouty lips, and a straight nose. Strayde Young had dirty blond hair, pale blue eyes, and darkly tanned skin. A chiselled jaw, wide nose and mouth, and a heavy brow. He had a thick, wide torso, muscles upon muscles.

Ice was friendly and funny while Strayde was quiet but charming. Both men carried an overprotective bent that was honestly starting to drive me a little crazy. Case in point, when there wasn't enough space for all of us in the jeep that Ambrose showed up in, I volunteered to stay behind only for Ice to immediately volunteer right after me.

I wasn't surprised about that, but I was slightly annoyed because I knew exactly why he did it. Not that his attempt to protect me even helped in the end as Ambrose turned out to be the one saving my ass.

My time out at the Ranch actually helped me heal from my Stella trauma and come to a number of realizations. All of them centered around Ambrose and my friendship with him. To be frank, I was happy to see him step out of that jeep, I had been wanting to contact him and honestly was just trying to gather up my courage.

And then there he was. And stupid Ice was right in my way.

But now wasn't the time to dwell on that.

My overwhelmed mind was still reeling from watching Ambrose take those Lizards out. He wasn't a fighter, not by nature. But I also knew that when he was forced to fight, he did it fast and dirty. So, seeing him once again fighting like that was a keen reminder of when we first met and struggled to make our way to the safety of the rumoured Base we heard about.

That was then, this was now and a blood splattered Ambrose was currently helping the Pleiadean male lean against the wall so that he had both hands free. Ambrose dug the severed finger out of his pocket and used it to open the locked cockpit. I immediately looked away from the high disturbing sight of that dismembered digit.

Ambrose's fingers worked over the handle of the wickedly curved blade as he crouched low and darted his head around the corner. I winced and swallowed back the sharp rise of nausea when the blade whipped out, landing somewhere inside the room with juicy sounding thunk.

It seemed almost too easy.

CHAPTER 3

LUX

We walked inside the cockpit to see a dead Lizard in the pilot's chair. Its body was slumped down the seat with its head sitting above the blade that was sunk deep into the back of the chair. My mind shuddered at that sight while my body moved on autopilot.

Ambrose helped the Pleiadean over to one of the other two chairs in the room. Those chairs were set behind a long control table that was near the front of the room facing the wall length view screen.

I cringed, avoiding the stomach churning sight of the separated body parts as I walked over and attempted to pull the blade free only to find it really stuck. In the process, I inadvertently jiggled the head enough that the damned thing rolled right into me.

"Fucking yuck." I gagged, frantically kicking the head away from me before once again reaching for the blade.

Before I could touch it, Ambrose's long fingered hand appeared and with one hard yank, pulled the blade free. At the same time, his other hand gripped the Lizard body and threw it out of the seat.

"Do you know how to fly one of these things?" I asked, breathing away my nausea, watching as he sat down.

"Nope." He shook his head, his head bent to examine the small control table next to the pilot's seat.

"Ok." I nodded slowly. "So, brace for a crash."

"Yup." He grunted, pointing sharply to the only seat left.

I shook my head and walked over to take the seat beside the worried looking Pleiadean. "We are going to die." The male mentioned in a strangely calm voice.

"Probably." I nodded in agreement, feeling almost numb after everything that happened.

"Lovely." He sighed, his head dropping back to the head rest.

I jerked slightly when a set of energy belts circled my body and pulled me back to the seat, holding me.

When nothing happened, I turned my head to look at a frowning Ambrose. "Ambrose?"

"Just..." He frowned at the controls as his finger's tapped over the small table. "Fuck." His eyes darted up to the view screen when an alarm started going off.

"What the fuck is going on?" The Pleiadean demanded.

"They changed their system." Ambrose snarled, kicking violently at the table. "Just by attempting to take over the controls without authorization, I fucking set off a self destruct."

"They don't want us getting our hands on another one of their ships." I braced myself, knowing that this was going to be very bad. I knew things had been too easy. "What now?"

"Now, we crash." Ambrose growled, scrambling over to the long control table and using the blade to pry it open.

"Humans really are fun." The Pleiadean groaned, watching as Ambrose threw the heavy top aside and dug into the electronics underneath.

"Right?" Ambrose shot the Pleiadean a knowing look as he chuckled.

"Is there a reason you want to crash the ship?" The Pleiadean asked while Ambrose ripped wires out and twisted them together.

"It's better than exploding in midair and falling thousands of feet to the ground. We have a slightly better chance of survival if we crash." I explained Ambrose's thinking.

"Exactly." Ambrose waved his pointer finger in my direction.

"Fucking hell." The Pleiadean growled and began to shift around in his seat.

Ambrose kept working as he followed wires and talked to himself, untwisting and trying different wires together. I yelped when the ship abruptly slowed and I was almost thrown forward. Thank God he was able to activate the energy straps.

"Yes." Ambrose hissed and did one last readjustment before scrambling back to the pilot's chair. When he was about halfway there the ship began to sharply descend. He reached the chair and pressed something on the small control table, locking himself in as the ship descended at a sharp degree.

"Ambrose." I called back to the man, needing to let him know that I was the wrong one, not him. I knew that now.

"If this is some sort of deathbed confession, Lux, I have to say that your timing is phenomenal." Ambrose growled.

"No, well, yes it is but not the way you are thinking. I just wanted to tell you that I am sorry. I was the one in the wrong, not you." I stared at the alarm filled screen in front of me, my heart racing with terror as my horrified eyes watched the countdown that had started. "Spending time away from the Base and all of the memories of Stella, it made me realize that...I was a shitty friend. I abandoned you the moment you showed me that your feelings weren't the same as mine, right when you needed me most, and that isn't what friends do. I am sorry that I wasn't more understanding and a better friend. I am sorry that I left you like that."

"Fuck, Lux." Ambrose's voice vibrated with the speed of our descension. "I never blamed you. I mean, you warned me. I just wished..."

"So did I. But I have come to realize that we can't change the past, we can only do better in the future." I shared with him.

"Lux.." His voice cut off when the ship came to an abrupt stop with an ear piercing screech of metal.

I cried out when the force yanked at my strapped down body, readjusting my organs in very stomach turning way. The lights blinked off as walls, lights, mechanics tore free, crashing violently around us.

Thankfully, one of the remaining lights flickered back on to show the ultimate destruction around us. The ship was sitting at a severe side slant. The cockpit had basically exploded in masses of wires and electronics.

Since I was fully locked down, my body didn't move an inch. The side wall, however, did. It was crumpled inwards until it was inches away from the side of the Pleiadean's seat.

"That really was fun." The Pleiadean chuckled softly, poking at the wall with the shackled hands he somehow maneuvered to lay in front of him.

"Yeah." Ambrose breathed shakily.

"Can you?" I gasped breathlessly, pulling at the energy straps in an attempt to get free.

"Give me a minute." Ambrose stated before once again sighing. "Uh, we may have another issue."

Twisting my head around, I saw that the pilot's control table was now gone.

"Ok, uh, let's see." The Pleiadean turned to the opened table in front of us.

He reached his shackled hands into the table and began to play with the wires. It took a good twenty minutes of being stuck at a very uncomfortable slant before the straps finally released.

I yelped when I suddenly fell free and ended up sliding down to crumple between the table, the Pleiadean's feet, and the indented wall.

Ambrose's groaning grunt had me looking over to see him in a similar condition, having slid straight down into the wall as soon as the straps released.

"I never should've woken up this morning." He used the strong length of his t-shirt covered arms to push himself up and start crawling along the angled wall towards the cockpit door. "If I had just stayed in bed I would not be here."

"And you would still be in bed." The Pleiadean added with an acknowledging nod, his strangely cold hands catching the arms left bare by my tank top and helping to untangle me at the same time I helped him from his chair. My skin goosebumped under his touch, strangely sensitizing.

My foot slipped on a piece of loose mechanics and we ended up butting into one another.

"This is..." He grunted, weaving back and forth in an attempt to keep his footing under the press of my body.

"Awkward." I finished, reaching around the hard muscled man to catch the arm of the chair, bracing both of us until we were ready to try again. My eyes met his devilish ones, a penetrating red that I couldn't seem to look away from. My eyes caught an interesting flash of something I wasn't able to define deep within their depths. Something that had my body shivering with heat.

"It looks awkward." Ambrose's voice noted from the bent door he was trying to pry open, effectively breaking the hold the other man's eyes had on mine. Ambrose had the curved blade shoved into a small crack and was using it as a lever.

"Thanks, man." The Pleiadean stated sarcastically, rolling his eyes. I gestured for him to go first and helped brace him as he turned and carefully climbed around the chair. Making liberal use of my hands, I slowly followed him along the wall.

"Anything to help you boost the self confidence." Ambrose snarled with the effort he was using. That snarl ended with a yelp when the blade slipped free and sent him sprawling backwards.

"I see that am not the only one who needs a boost in self confidence." The Pleiadean noted with a set of raised eyebrows.

"You speak truth words." Ambrose pushed himself back up and over to the door to once again stab the blade into the crack of the door.

We reached Ambrose and the Pleiadean bent to take a grip on the bottom of the blade. Between the two of them, they were able to pry the door open wide enough to grip their fingers around the edge and pull. I squeezed in between the two of them and got my own grip, helping pull. The door squealed open a good five inches, wide enough for me to squeeze through but not enough for them.

One more hard yank gained another couple of inches.

"Try it." The Pleiadean jerked his chin at the opening, leaning back against the jagged wall and catching his breath.

"You first." Unsurprising, Ambrose argued. That was one thing that I had always loved about Ambrose, how giving and unselfish he was.

"You are bigger. If you can't fit then there is no point in me going." The Pleiadean denied, his intelligence on the mark.

"Fine." Ambrose rolled his eyes. I couldn't help but watch the way his muscles bunched and flexed as he pulled himself up and began to squeeze through the opening, arms and headfirst. "Fuck." He snarled, his body jerking when his thick pecs got stuck and he tried to muscle himself through.

Kneeling down, I grabbed one of his feet and shoved upwards.

"Motherfucker." He cried out in surprise, shifting back and forth with my pushing.

The Pleiadean crouched down beside me and caught Ambrose's other foot and helped me push. One hard shove and Ambrose groaned in pain right before his pecs finally scraped through. We kept pushing until he fell through to the other side with a loud thump.

"Owe." He whined, rising to his feet and rubbing his pecs. "I scraped my nipples."

I winced in commiseration and protectively covered my own nipples with my palms while the other man shook his head.

"Next." I bent to catch the Pleiadean's foot.

He frowned down at me only for Ambrose to reach his arms through the crack at him. "Come on, man."

With a hassled sigh, the man pulled himself up to the crack and, with Ambrose's help maneuvered his shackled arms and head through. I shoved as Ambrose pulled and the man slid through a hell of a lot easier than Ambrose did.

Ambrose reached through for me next. His hard hands caught my arms and easily pulled me up and through to the other side.

"Come on." Ambrose directed, guiding us down the shadowed hall and up a cross section of the slanted craft.

CHAPTER 4

LUX

W e were forced to climb up on our hands and feet which was not easy for the shackled man. Both Ambrose and I helped with a number of well placed shoves to his ass. I had to admit, the Pleiadean had one hell of a hard ass. Delightfully muscular and tight.

"I hope you too are enjoying yourselves." The Pleiadean noted almost derisively. He was apparently not as much of a fan of our help as we were.

"At least you've got a good butt." Ambrose stated.

"It is a good butt." I agreed with Ambrose's assessment, taking my turn to push said butt.

"Uh, thank you." The Pleiadean chuckled softly.

"Don't take it to heart. It's a good butt, not a great butt like mine." Ambrose shot me a playful grin.

I couldn't help but return that grin as he took his turn to shove.

"Someone here is almost over-confident." The Pleiadean laughed.

"It got us through, didn't it." Ambrose noted with one last shove that pushed the man to the t-section of hall that crossed the other direction.

"It did." The Pleiadean agreed, reaching down to help me up the last foot.

Once we were all stabilized, we made our way to the other door where Ambrose used the dismembered Lizard finger to open the door. I cried out and covered my eyes when blazing sun burned my retinas. We all darted back and took a moment to get used to the eye piercing sunshine.

The guys helped brace me as I crawled up the diagonal floor and out the door to the wickedly curved side of the saucer.

Ambrose and I helped the Pleiadean climb out before Ambrose muscled himself out.

Finally free of the ship, we took a moment to take in our surroundings.

"Come on!" Ambrose groaned in agony when he saw the same thing I did.

Sand.

Waves and waves of simmering sand.

"Please, please, please, tell me that we didn't crash in the middle of the fucking Sahara." I begged desperately, slowly turning and turning to see more of the same.

Scorching hot sand dunes.

My eyes burned with angry, frustrated tears to the point that I really just wanted to curl into a ball and cry. My heart was screaming at the impossibility of the situation we found ourselves in.

"And I thought the Ranch was hot." Ambrose growled with irritation.

"I will need to see the stars before I can tell you exactly where we are. My question is...how screwed are we if it is the Sahara?" The Pleiadean asked, his narrowed eyes studying the area.

"That depends on how much food and water the ship has." Ambrose answered, his teeth chewing on his lower lip. "We are going to have to walk to the nearest base which could take days if not weeks depending on which part of the Sahara we are in, if it actually is the Sahara."

"Not enough." I shook my head, turning to eye him. "Do you have any idea how to survive out here?"

"A little bit." He held his thumb and forefinger up, the fingers pinched about an inch apart.

"I know a bit." The Pleiadean raised his shackled hands.

"Well, that's better than nothing." I sighed wearily. "Maybe if the three of us put our heads together we might actually be able to make it out of here."

"We need to stock up as much as we can with food and water. We cover as much of our bodies as we can, protecting ourselves from the elements. We need something to make a tent with just in case of dust storms. And we should only travel at night." Ambrose voiced his advice.

"Bugs and snakes can be forms of sustenance but we need to be careful of the wild dogs that roam out here." The Pleiadean helpfully described.

"Ok, let's raid whatever we can from the ship and wait for nightfall." I groaned, not looking forward to climbing back inside. As hot as it was outside, I had come to really hate this ship.

We climbed back inside the ship where it was cooler and out of the blazing sun. It was there that we made a raiding plan.

"I am Lux, by the way." I politely held my hand out to the Pleiadean.

"I know who you are. I also know who Ambrose is." The Pleiadean smiled in greeting, taking my hand and giving it a shake. I had to admit, the man had a beautiful smile. "I am Kalbeliyas."

Ambrose took the hand the man moved to him next and gave him an added nod.

"Now that we are all in the know. I am going to check the lower levels because I can move the fastest. You two check the rooms up here." Ambrose directed.

"I am going to guess that there is no chance of getting a call out to the Base." Kalbeliyas brought up something I didn't even think of as he leaned his head back into the wall behind him.

"Unless we find our coms, not a chance." Ambrose shook his head. "The ships electronics are mostly destroyed and the Lizards took our coms."

"Well then." Kalbeliyas gestured down the shadowed hall. "Let's go digging."

I found myself watching Ambrose walk down the hall and slide down the cross to the bottom hall while Kalbeliyas began opening doors. Giving myself a shake, I turned to help Kalbeliyas dig out whatever we thought we could use.

"Tell me something, Mr. Pleiadean who is supposed to stay neutral, what on earth made you decided to 'check' on us?" I asked him once we had what we found piled up at the exit.

There was a couple of water bottles that we filled and some sort of snack food items that Kalbeliyas assured me were human safe. We found a bunch of fabric from some of the bedrooms that we were thinking of using to make coverings for ourselves along with some sort of stiff material that he said was weatherproof. Apparently it stayed cool in the heat and warm in the cold.

Then there was the thicker bedding that I rolled up for us to sleep on and the three large bags that were being used to pack everything in. We even came across a sort of first aid kit that carried some pretty odd items that I had no clue as to what they could be used for. I did, however, make use of the items I recognized to clean the back of Kalbeliyas head. I was slightly surprised and fairly relieved to see that it was already mostly closed. It could be a Pleiadean trait but he healed wicked fast.

"That is something we will talk about once we are all back together again." The maddening man denied me with a shake of his head.

"So, it wasn't just a spur of the moment decision." I guessed, narrowing my eyes intently on him.

"No, it was not." He stated, his red eyes meeting mine, his gaze piercing and intense.

Feeling my heart begin to pound and my breathing stutter under that penetrating gaze, I darted my gaze away before I got trapped again. "Ok." I whispered, turning my eyes down the hall, anxiously waiting for Ambrose to reappear and disperse the tension. "Was it worth it?"

"Yes." He breathed back, his tone sending shivers through my body. "Very."

"I am glad you are here, too." I told him honestly. I was. As much as I had faith in Ambrose to get us through, it was a vast comfort to have Kalbeliyas with us.

"Good. Because despite everything, I wouldn't want to be anywhere else in the universe right in this moment." His voice stated softly.

"I don't know about that." I chuckled and shook his head. "Ambrose's idea of still being safe in bed is sounding pretty good right about now."

"Yeah." He chuckled right along with me. "A bed would be nice."

A loud grunt was followed by a number of loud, incoming scrapes. Numerous bags began sliding around the corner, obviously thrown up by Ambrose. Kalbeliyas and I walked over to grab the items and haul them over to the pile we had going.

Ambrose found some more fabric materials along with more snacks and water bottles. What none of us found was our coms.

"They probably tossed them as soon as they could." Kalbeliyas noted as soon as Ambrose joined us. "They were probably afraid that they had trackers that they weren't able to detect imbedded in them."

"They did." Ambrose stated informatively.

We repacked everything into the three large bags that we could shoulder and worked on getting our personal coverings created. Thankfully, Ambrose found a bunch more of the weatherproof fabric that we were able to utilize for our personal coverings instead of the blankets. By using the curved blade Ambrose held on to and some ingenuity we were able to make ponchos with hoods to cover ourselves with.

By the time we were done, the sun was starting to descend and twilight was falling.

I was already tired and not looking forward to walking all night.

Kalbeliyas tilted his head up to the sky the moment we climbed out of the ship. He slowly spun in a circle, examining the stars appearing. "Yeah, we are in the Sahara. I would say middle Egypt near the Libyan border."

"Then we need to head east towards the Egyptian Base at Abu Minqar. If we are near the Libyan border it's about 200 to 300 km." Ambrose's description had my heart dropping with dejection. That was going to be a very long walk.

"That way." Kalbeliyas pointed in the direction Ambrose described.

We followed his lead, stepping out into the soft sand and climbing up, and up, and up onto the nearest dune. A very high dune.

Walking on soft, pliable sand was not easy and I was breathless by the time we reached the top. Thankfully, I wasn't the only one.

"That way." Kalbeliyas gasped breathlessly, pointing the way and gesturing for me to take the lead.

"Motherfucker." Ambrose wheezed, taking a minute to catch his breath before moving forward.

CHAPTER 5

N *IGHT 1*
I hated sand.

I figured that out real quick the moment I attempted to walk on the slippery shit. My feet slid underneath me with every step I took, making just the act of walking three times harder than it should've been.

One step forward, half a slide back.

I followed the shackled man in front of me. The redheaded Pleiadean and youngest brother of the family of two boys and three, triplet girls. Kalbeliyas. I had no idea how the hell he got caught but I wasn't going to question his presence. Over my time in the Base, I have come to the realization that more often than not, things happen for a reason. Even the shitty, fucked up things.

"Talk." The man ordered in a low tone over his shoulder.

I wasn't stupid, I knew he was referring to the conversation Lux and I had right before the ship crashed. Speaking of Lux, my eyes automatically moved passed him to the woman who was far enough in front of us that she wouldn't hear our low voiced conversation.

"Seriously? How is this any of your business?" I scowled at his back.

"I am in this, stuck with the two of you. Seems like a good enough time to share." He shrugged, shooting a look at me over his shoulder.

"Fine. I fucked up, ok. I was Lux's best friend, she was mine. I knew how her sister, Stella, had hurt her over the years. She shared

41

everything with me, all of it. And I still did...it. One night I was hanging with some guys that I once considered friends. I ended up getting hammered and fucking her sister. Lux rightfully, and immediately, dropped our friendship. Afterwards, I felt fucking stupid, empty, worthless. I hurt the one person I cared for most. I didn't deserve her. So, I did as Lux asked and I left her alone. And I continued to fuck Stella whenever the woman tracked me down to get her fix because in my mind that was my punishment. I hated myself every time I did it but then I hated myself period. But I never, not once, stopped caring for Lux." I chewed on my lip as I explained.

"You love her." He noted, giving me a knowing look.

My heart stopped and I felt my body freeze for a moment, my eyes darting between him and her. "Why do you say that?"

"Because only a man who fucked up his chance with the woman he loves would continue to punish himself the way you did." He stated accurately, seeing right to the center of the matter.

"It doesn't matter what I feel." I snapped out, my eyes becoming angry. "She may forgive me but she was right. She doesn't need someone like me in her life. She's better off."

"That's not what I heard in that cockpit." The irritating man argued. "I heard her apologizing for being a bad friend."

"She wasn't the bad friend. I was." I denied with a sharp shake of my head.

"Could it be that you were both bad friends? You betrayed her and she betrayed you. You fucked her sister while you weren't in your right mind and she refused to allow herself to even entertain the possibility of forgiving you, someone she clearly cared very deeply for. The fact of the matter is that you both got fucked over by a jealous toxic woman who saw what her sister had and wanted it. She set out to break you two apart. And she succeeded. She won because both of you let her win." The damned man was a fucking sage.

"Well, aren't we just the insightful fucker." I growled, my fist clenching in preparation of punching the man in the back of the head. "You really don't have to pound that nail in, believe me, it's already fully hammered home."

Done with his shit, I shouldered passed him to walk in front of him so I didn't have to look at his ass.

"That is not what I meant." He snarled, catching my arm and swinging me back around. My angrily narrowed eyes met a set of blazing red ones. "We all make mistakes and if we are smart, we learn from them and move forward. You have learned from them, that nail of yours isn't just hammered home, it's fully imbedded and has been for so long it's practically a part of you. But you haven't moved forward. Because that nail makes it impossible."

"Why don't you fuck up so bad that you lose the one person you...care about then talk to me?" I demanded fiercely, pushing my face into his.

"Care? You can't even say it. You won't allow yourself to admit how much you 'care' for her." He hissed, his face pushing closer until we were a mere inch apart. "Because it would hurt so much more if she was to deny you again."

"When." I clipped out. "Not if. When."

"When what?" Lux's voice came from right behind me.

"Nothing." I yanked my arm free of Kalbeliyas' hold and turned around to brush passed her and continue walking.

"Uh, ok." Lux murmured at my back.

"We aren't done here." The maddening man followed me.

"Oh no, we are." I argued.

"Tell her." His hard voice ordered as he darted around me to stand in front of me. "Tell her."

"Stay out of it." I snarled, shoving him away from me. He yelped when my shove caused him to stumble backwards and trip over the edge of the dune we were walking on. His shackled hands reached out to grab me at the same time mine reached for him. Our hands connected but that didn't help as all he did was bring me with him. We ended up sliding and rolling down the dune in a twisted pile of limbs.

"Fuck." He groaned when we finally stopped rolling and he inadvertently landed on top of me.

"Owe." I whimpered before jerking when the shackled hands that somehow ended up caught between us moved, drawing right over my dick. I bit back my groan and bit down on my lip when my mindless dick immediately jolted to life, swelling into a throbbing hard erection. "Fuck."

"Sorry." He winced, his face inches from mine, right before his body froze solid. "Are you hard?"

"I have a very attractive man wiggling all over my body, his hands rubbing all over my groin. Of course, I am fucking hard." I growled, gripping his shoulders and rolling him off of me. Sitting up, I set my arms over my drawn up knees, attempting to count down my erection. As much as I had tried not to notice, I couldn't deny that Kalbeliyas was gorgeous, sexy.

The man sat up beside me, his fascinating red eyes assessing over me. "You are bi-sexual."

"Yup." I nodded slowly, staring down at my hanging hands.

"So am I." He shared with a grin, nudging my shoulder with his. "Your dick isn't the first I've had in my hands."

"Yeah?" I found myself chuckling, nudging him back playfully. "How does it compare?"

"Seriously?" His head fell back as he laughed.

"Seriously?" A familiar female voice had both of us looking up to see Lux hooded form standing over us, her arms crossed, her face not impressed. "What the hell was that?"

"I slipped." Kalbeliyas shrugged, pushing himself up to his feet.

"I tried to catch him." I stood up, brushing the sand off of myself.

"Men." Lux rolled her eyes and turned to climb back up the dune.

"Fuck." I groaned with the realization that I once again had to climb back up that shit.

"Heard." Kalbeliyas studied the dune as he held his fist up.

I knocked my knuckles against his and we began to climb.

"This doesn't mean I am giving up." He huffed out his warning.

"I literally just pushed you down the dune." I stated in disbelief at how stubborn the man was.

"And presented me with a pretty impressive handful of dick." He grinned maniacally.

"Wait, you touched his dick?" Lux exclaimed as she spun around and slid down the three feet she had on us.

My eyes widened and my face went bright red. "Not purposefully." Kalbeliyas stammered, his face just as red as mine was.

Lux was silent for a long dragging moment as her dark eyes darted between us.

"She knows, right?" Kalbeliyas whispered to me.

"That he's bi. Yes." Lux nodded slowly, her dark eyes filled with confusion. "I just, never saw him show attraction to another male before."

"I am sorry." I winced, biting my bottom lip. I wasn't a fan of her seeing my attraction to someone else, especially after what happened with Stella. But on the other hand, Kalbeliyas was the first person besides Lux that I had been truly attracted to in years.

"I, uh, no, don't be. I am, uh, happy...." She stammered, trying to figure out the words she wanted to say.

"For fuck sakes." Kalbeliyas groaned, crawling passed her. "You two really need to work your shit out."

"Our shit was fine until you stuck your nose in it." I yelled after him, gesturing to Lux to follow him.

"No, it really wasn't." Kalbeliyas disagreed, his voice sharp.

"What did I miss here?" Lux asked, shooting me a worried look.

"Nothing. Ok, something." I glared right back at Kalbeliyas when he glared at me. "Why don't we concentrate on getting some miles between us and that ship and talk about this when we have to stop in the morning?"

"Very well." Kalbeliyas' glare took on a determined bent.

"Look, we are in this together. I deserve to know what is going on." Lux very accurately pointed out.

"And you will." I assured her.

She gave a frustrated sigh and kept climbing, surprisingly taking me for my word.

CHAPTER 6

AMBROSE

I was pretty sure that we had indeed made some sort of headway by the time the sun rose and got too hot for us to continue walking. Unfortunately, it was hard to definitively tell when all I could see was never ending waves of dunes.

We found a spot on the side of one of the dunes to set our low strung tent up. It was just high enough that we were able to sit up inside, long and wide enough for the three of us to lay down comfortably. We used metal poles and rope we stole from the ship to set it up along with fabric and bedding to protect us from the ground and set up beds.

The first thing I did was strip off my hooded poncho before pulling my boots and socks off my sore feet. Kalbeliyas was already barefoot as he hadn't been wearing shoes to begin with. Something that I just noticed now.

"Where are your shoes?" I demanded, concern flooding me and my hands darting over to grab one of his feet to check it over.

"I don't need shoes." Kalbeliyas shrugged negligently, watching as I made sure his feet were ok. Surprisingly, they looked good, smooth and well formed with his nails unexpectedly well cared for.

"Are you sure? Because if you need, I am sure we can fashion you something." Lux began to dig in the bags.

"I am good." Kalbeliyas reassured her, sliding the feet I released into a cross legged position.

Lux dug out some water and food which we all took part in. I didn't know about the others but I was fucking exhausted.

"Talk." Lux ordered, rubbing her own bare feet.

"You first." I demanded, jerking my chin towards her. "Finish what you were saying when we were crashing."

She looked slightly stunned, her eyes moving between the two of us before she gave a hassled sigh and an eye roll. "Ok, fine. As I was saying, I am sorry. Once I was away from the Base and...everything that had been colored by her, I was able to actually think. And I realized that I was a shitty friend. You never promised me anything but friendship and I threw it all away because you did something I...didn't like. That wasn't a friend. Friends are supposed to support one another even if they disagree with the other's actions. I knew that you regretted it. I saw it on your face, and I still left you to it."

I didn't know what to say to that other than, "You warned me."

"I did." She nodded slowly, her face filled with pained regret. My heart twisted at that look yet skipped wildly at the thought that we might just be able to work our way through to the other side of this. "But the fact of the matter is that I left you when you needed me the most. I left you, to her. And I honestly hate that thought. I left my best friend in the hands of a monster."

"Tell her what happened that night." Kalbeliyas jerked his head towards Lux.

"No." I vehemently denied. "She doesn't need that shit in her head."

"What she needs, what you both need, is to have some fucking honesty between the two of you." Kalbeliyas growled fiercely at me.

"I, uh, I would like to know." Lux whispered softly, her dark brown eyes staring intently into mine. "I know it will hurt, but I need to know what happened to you that night."

My eyes searched hers, trying to see inside of her. Haunted need. That's what I saw. "I need you to be sure."

"I am." She nodded slowly.

I hated this. I hated that I was right about to hurt her all over again.

I mimicked her nod and looked down at the bedding I was sitting on, my mind filling with images from that night. I anxiously chewed on my bottom lip, hating those memories, despising myself and my ultimate stupidity.

"It was supposed to be a guys' night." My voice was a quiet rasp as I began to speak. "We were drinking, playing poker in one of the other guys' suites. James. I was already fairly drunk when Stella arrived. The guys decided since they now had a woman in the mix that we should play strip poker. The more people got naked the more...things started happening. Stella was kissing and touching the other guys. At first I refused her."

I was forced to pause for a moment, taking a couple of steadying breaths in before being able to continue. "But the more I drank and watched them play with her naked body the more aroused I got. The guys kept egging me on, telling me how good she felt, how good she tasted. All of them had already fucked her at one point or another, so it got pretty graphic. Before I truly realized what I was doing I had her in my lap. I was kissing her, touching her naked body while they watched and continued with the comments. By that time, I was no longer thinking straight at all. All I knew was that I was hard as hell and aching and I had a readily available woman right before me."

I paused again in, rubbing my hands harshly over my face, pinching the sides together over my lips and silently praying for the strength to get through this. "At least I wasn't stupid enough to fuck her right in front of them like they wanted. I took her back to her suite to do that. I fucked her, over and over again, until the early morning hours. When we finally stopped, she got dressed and smirked, crowing about how she knew I couldn't resist her. She laughed as she walked out. That was the moment that I realized how much I fucked up. I showered, changed my bedding, and went to track you down. I wanted to tell you before you heard it from anyone else but it was too late. You already knew. And you hated me. You looked so fucking devastated that when you told me that you didn't want to associate with me anymore I found myself giving in. I refused to cause you anymore pain. Later that night, Stella showed up at my door and I told her that I fucking hated her. She stripped her clothes off as she shrugged and said that I didn't need to like her to fuck her. And she was right. That was the day that I found out that hate fucking was a thing."

"I never went to her. She always tracked me down and the moment I saw her that anger rose right up." I sighed sadly. "After each time I felt the same. Disgusting and weak and pathetic."

"Would you have done the same if you knew back then that you were in love with Lux?" Kalbeliyas asked causing both Lux and I to snap our heads towards him. Me in fury, her in shock.

"What?" She exclaimed sharply, her wide eyes snapping towards me. "You never said..."

"Because I didn't know that's what it was. Not until I lost you." My snapping statement cut her off. Her eyes flashed with hurt right before they dropped away, her body silently curling into itself. I really wanted to pull her into my chest and hold her tight, I wanted to make everything better, but I didn't know how. All I knew was that I felt raw, ripped open, bleeding all over. And I once again hurt Lux. I couldn't fucking win.

"Finish it, Ambrose. Would you have?" Kalbeliyas maddeningly pushed causing my knuckles to itch. I really wanted to punch him. Hard.

"Fuck no! The moment her sister arrived I would've been out of there. By that point I wasn't thinking of Lux and our friendship like I should've been, I was thinking about the fact that I was single and unattached." I yelled at him. "But then, I probably wouldn't have been there in the first place. I would've been with Lux."

"Was the sex at least good?" He asked curiously. I clenched my jaw tightly and sucked in a deep, calming breath.

"Honestly, I don't remember." I hissed softly, my eyes narrowed on his. "I think I blocked it out."

Laughter burst out of his chest at that. "You hate fucked a woman for years and you don't even remember the actual fucking part?"

"Nope." I shook my head, risking a glance Lux's way to see her hands cupping over her mouth, her down bent eyes shining. I couldn't tell if she was laughing or crying. "I don't even really remember any of our time together. Just the beginning of that night up until the moment we left and the feelings it left inside of me."

"I really am sorry." Lux's hands dropped and her beautiful eyes rising to meet mine, carrying a look of deep sadness.

"So am I." I whispered, my voice husky.

"Maybe, uh, maybe we can start over." She whispered back, her eyes taking on a slight look of hope.

"You want to start over, as friends?" I asked her with a set of raised eyebrows.

"Yes, no, maybe, I don't know. I just know that we both fucked up and hurt one another. And I don't know about you, but I still care about you. I was never able to stop. And I, uh, I miss you." She nervously stumbled over her words as they steadily got lower until I was forced to strain just to hear. Her dark eyes were carrying a shine that looked eerily like hope.

"I miss you too." I found my lips moving, speaking the words that my heart was screaming. "So fucking much."

"Then maybe we can start over and, uh, see where this takes us." She brought up, her eyes darting over me before dropping back down.

"A clean slate?" I asked, needing to know where she stood on the past.

"No." Kalbeliyas disagreed with a slow shake of his head. "That's not possible. It happened and it traumatized you both. You can't just deny that trauma because it will never heal that way. And you both definitely have some healing to do."

"Ok, how about we simply make a deal to never use it against one another." Her eyes came up to meet his before turning to mine. "Because I really do forgive you."

"I forgive you too." I agreed, reaching my hand out to her, palm up.

She gave me a small smile and slid her delicate hand into mine. I felt my body shiver under her touch. A touch that I hadn't felt in so long. A touch that I had missed so fucking much. A touch that I had prayed for, everyday for years.

Before I could stop myself, I pulled her hand up to my trembling lips and pressed a kiss to the back of it. That kiss turned into a full blown smile when her fingers slid through my hair the way she always used to do. Then they tightened down and my head was yanked up. "Dick?" She asked in a demanding voice.

"He's hot." I stated honestly, causing the devilish redhead to burst into laughter.

Her eyes narrowed and turned to him. "Yeah." He chuckled out and nodded his head.

"So, what does this mean?" She asked, releasing my hair to point between the two of us. "Wait, don't Pleiadean's have soulmates, connections as they call it? He's your connection isn't he?"

My eyes widened with realization as I turned to the man sitting beside me. My heart was beating so hard and so fast that it echoed in my ears.

"No." Kalbeliyas shook his head in denial. I would love to say my heartbeat returned to normal but it didn't. Instead, it felt like something stabbed me in my heart. "You both are."

CHAPTER 7

KALBELIYAS

"I, uh, what?" Lux stammered as Ambrose stared at me in shock. I was just as stunned as they were, well, I had been when I first saw their pictures and realized what I was seeing. Dark eyes. That's what my sister Asp told me. And both of them had dark eyes. Lux's were dark brown while Ambrose's were dark blue. They were so similar that unless one was right in their faces you wouldn't be able to tell the difference.

I was in the Security tent with my sister Ela, one of Asp's triplets, and her connection, Grayson, when the call came in about the Drako ship and the kidnapping of two Base residents. Their files were pulled up one of the computers and I inadvertently saw them. First the beautiful, delicate Lux. Then the masculine mass that made up Ambrose. Both of them such opposites yet carrying the same, haunted look.

I quickly read the reports on them and connected the dots before swirling into energy and tracking them down. It didn't take long as I am an expert tracker. Unfortunately, despite how careful I was, it wasn't careful enough and I missed something. The only defense I had was that I was worried for my connections and due to that I may not have had my mind focused where it should have been.

One of the damned Lizards got the jump on me. I still wasn't sure how as I had dropped into energy behind one of the Lizards walking down a hall and taken maybe two steps towards it before my head suddenly exploded and darkness fell.

I woke up shackled, my abilities contained, and under the delicate hands of one of the most beautiful women I had ever seen. The feel her warm hands moving over my cold body shivered through me and had my heart trying to pound right out of my chest. Lux efficiently checked me over and helped me sit up. She stayed calm through everything and took the time to care for me. She stayed strong and supportive and was surprisingly intuitive.

When I was finally able to focus on something beyond the woman of my dreams I saw the huge blond man kicking some major Lizard ass. The Lizard in question was throwing himself and thusly the man on his back around as Ambrose violently strangled and stabbed the Lizard.

It was fierce and frankly impressive. Sexy. That strength was made even more sexy by the keen intelligence and emotional depth he showed.

The moment I felt their energies I was hooked, obsessed. I could also feel the tension between them, the unresolved pain. So, yeah, I may have been a little pushy about it, but the sooner we got it all out in the open, the sooner they could start healing and moving forward.

"Both of you are my connections." I reiterated.

"I told you he was hot." Ambrose breathed through slack lips.

"I wasn't disagreeing. I was just worried that you would..." Lux started only for me to cut her off. "Want me instead of you."

"Well, yes." She blushed adorably and tucked both sides of her sweaty, tangled hair behind her ears.

"And now?" Ambrose asked, his lips tilting up in corner. "Now that you know that it isn't a you or him situation?"

"Just like that? You are just going to go with my claim?" I frowned at him.

"Hush. She gets to go first." He held his hand up to me before pointing at her.

"Second. You already went." I told him, grinning at the glare he slid me.

"You aren't helping." He hissed at me.

"I am hot, I don't need to help." My comment had Lux laughing and Ambrose shaking his head in amusement.

"Lux?" Ambrose turned his gaze back to Lux.

"Well, he is hot." Lux giggled mischievously.

"Woman." Ambrose threatened, his hand rising. "I think it's been too long since you were punished."

"No!" Lux exclaimed, still giggling while holding her hands up in surrender.

"Punishment?" I asked curiously.

"Tickling." He grinned at me.

"Oh." I returned his grin with one of my own.

"Ok, ok, fine. You are hot too." She finally gave him what he wanted. "I have always thought you were hot."

"I never thought you were hot." He told her, his grin softening into an adorably bashful smile. "I thought you were the most beautiful woman I had ever seen. I always have."

"Now that we have all decided that we find one another attractive, I think we should get some sleep before we have to wake up and walk our asses over dunes. So many fucking dunes." I advised, cringing at the thought of all of those dunes.

"Oh my God, so many." Lux vehemently agreed, collapsing onto the bedding beside Ambrose and wiggling around until she was comfortable.

"Uh, no." Ambrose's hands hit the ground, his muscles tensing and flexing in a very fascinating way as he twisted his body over Lux and nudged her into the middle.

I helped by grabbing the waistband of her pants and pulling her over.

"I can sleep on the end." She claimed.

"Nope." Ambrose denied her before I could. "Not with the chance of wild dogs dragging your delectable ass out. Kal and I are heavier, it will be harder for them."

I jerked slightly at the sound of the shortened version of my name on his lips. I really, really liked that.

I laid back and rested my shackled hands on my stomach. I grunted when Lux squeaked because Ambrose laid down and shoved her into me to gain more space. I raised my arms up and tucked my hands under my head, giving the woman a little more room.

"We are going to smell so good when we finally get out of here." Lux noted, eyeing my arm pit.

"I already have sand everywhere. Like everywhere." Ambrose whined, making an uncomfortable face and wiggling his hips around. He was laying on his side, facing us, with his arm cocked under his head.

"I hear that." I grunted, feeling said sand in a number of uncomfortable places on my own body.

Exhausted after the long assed, emotional and physical day we all had, I quickly found myself drifting off within the thankfully warm but not hot tent.

CHAPTER 8

LUX

NIGHT 2
 I woke up to see that the tent was darker than before. Sitting up from the between the two very hard bodies that surrounded me, I carefully parted the opening to see that the sun was starting its descent and the side of the dune we were on was now in shade.

"Wake up, boys. I am leaving the tent." I dug what I needed out of the bag and checked my socks and shoes for any interlopers. Then I pulled them on right along with my hooded poncho. The outerwear surprising kept me warm last night when the desert air dropped to below zero. Crawling out of the tent, I looked around for the perfect spot.

"Wait for me." Kal called after me.

"This lady requires privacy." I called back, finding a spot and making use of it. Using some of the paper we grabbed from the ship, I cleaned myself before kicking sand over top of it.

"Switch." Ambrose called when he heard me approaching.

Instead of answering, I simply crawled back into the tent and waited for the two men who crawled out to finish.

"Fuck. I need some real food, protein." Ambrose growled as he returned.

"Done?" I asked.

"Yeah. Let's get packed up and get moving." Kal called.

I crawled out and began to help the men break down our tent and pack our stuff up. We shouldered our bags and followed Kal's direction down the dune and up the next one.

The evening fell quickly and the stars came out, lighting up the sky and guiding our way over the icy dunes. We ended up passing a water bottle back and forth, trying to make it last as long as possible. We also stopped for a break and some food about two hours in.

I sat down on the dune and looked up at the stars, eating the bar of unappetizing Lizard food while really wishing for a hairbrush.

"Do you miss it?" I ask the redhead beside me, my eyes trained on the sky above.

"Miss what?" He asked, making a disgusted face as he chewed the bar, his sharp jaw moving in a way that had my palms itching to feel over it.

"Your home?" I swallowed the suddenly very dry mouthful of bar and questioned, turning to look at him.

"You mean my planet? Weirdly, no. I became a juror as soon as I was done school. The job requires a lot of travel, so it was never really home." He explained, his eyes carrying a far off look as they turned from me to the sky above. "This place, it feels more like home than anywhere I have been."

"Where is it?" Ambrose asked from Kal's other side, jerking his chin up to the sky.

"On the other side of the galaxy, that way." Kal stated, pointing to a specific area the starlit sky.

"Is it nice?" I asked curiously, wanting to know more about where he came from.

"It is...different. I like it here better. This place, it has a certain energy." Kal touched his chest as his brow furrowed.

"I forgot that you can feel energy. Can you feel mine?" Ambrose asked.

"Weirdly enough, I can." Kal chuckled as he shook the shackles. "I can feel both of you."

"And?" I asked, nudging him with my shoulder.

"It's hard to explain. Lux, you feel like the Earth herself, like life. It's probably why you got so bogged down while you were at the Base, trapped within rock and stone, away from the earth's energy." Kal described for us. "When you got to the Ranch and out among nature you were finally able to clear your head. As for Ambrose, he's like an underground river. Strong and deep, carving out caverns and tunnels before bursting free of the ground to give sustenance."

"I like that." Ambrose stated softly, his eyes lowered to the hang of his hands, his lower lip set between his gnawing teeth.

"Me too." I looked around Kal to smile at Ambrose. "He nailed you."

Ambrose's eyes slid up and over to meet mine and a grateful smile crossed his face. That smile slowly extended into a mischievous grin.

"No!" I exclaimed right as he said it.

"Not yet, he hasn't." Kal burst into laughter at Ambrose's words.

"I knew it." I groaned, my head hanging. "I knew right after I said it."

"Yeah, you walked right into that one." Ambrose laughed.

"Did I mention the inner shit disturber he's hiding?" Kal grinned.

"He hides it well." I shared with my own smirk. "Most people don't even know he has a sense of humor."

"And I plan to keep it that way." Ambrose warned with a set of narrowed eyes.

"I know how to keep a secret." Kal put his hands up in surrender.

"Nooo." I gasped sarcastically, pressing my hand to my chest. The Pleiadeans were the ultimate secret keepers. In fact, they were so secretive that they were considered to be mythical beings throughout the whole of the universe.

"No kidding." Ambrose laughed, shooting me a wink. I had missed this playful side of Ambrose.

"For real." Kal gave us a set of dramatically wide, assuring eyes as he nodded quickly.

"Fucking hell." Ambrose laughed even harder, bending over as he started to wheeze.

"Nice." I laughed, nudging a laughing Kal as we watched Ambrose lose his shit.

Ambrose's laughter eventually slowed and we once again started walking.

Another couple of hours passed before I was suddenly shoved into Ambrose's back hard enough to push both him and me down.

"Burrow into the sand. Hands and legs in the poncho. Quickly." Kal directed from beside us. I shifted off of Ambrose and pulled my arms and legs into the Poncho as I wiggled my body into the sand until I was completely covered, everything except a tiny space for my eyes to look out. Beside me, the two men were doing the same.

"Freeze." Kal hissed.

I froze just as a handful of Drako ships appeared over the dunes, flying low and slow as their lights searched over the dunes. That was when I knew that they had found the downed ship and were now looking for us.

My breathing stopped, holding as one of the piercing lights drew over us. My mind jolted back to the last time I saw those lights and the excruciating pain of being torn right down to my smallest cells in order to be transferred. It was so painful that I had lost consciousness, only waking once I was locked in that horrifying cell.

One light slowly moved on, only to be replaced by a second. They were really being meticulous. That light soon moved on and I waited, frozen with terror. The ships moved out of my field of view but I still waited. I continued to wait even after the hum of their ships died down.

It wasn't until Kal sat up with a wave of sand that I finally allowed my lungs to start drawing air in. My body was shaking, my eyes stinging as I pushed myself up out of the sand and began to brush myself off.

Hard arms surrounding me had me jolting violently before calming. I found myself shifting around to bury myself in the safety of those beloved arms while circling Ambrose with my own arms. My hands clutched at his back, my arms holding him just as tightly as he was holding me. Ambrose was trembling just as hard as I was.

Kal, however, bent over his upraised knees, his distant eyes looking exhausted.

I wanted to smile when both Ambrose and I reached out at the same time to pull him into our hug, but I didn't. I couldn't with the fear still chilling my blood.

Kal kind of just fell into me, the arm I freed from around Ambrose circling Kal's bent head. Ambrose moved his arms beyond me and around Kal's shoulders.

"Fuck." Kal whispered hoarsely, his body stiff against mine.

Tipping my head back to meet Ambrose's, I saw the same knowledge in them that I had in my own. Kal was having a really hard time being left without the use of his abilities. It had to be frustrating, maddening, downright terrifying to lose something that was so intrinsically a part of him. And being trapped in the middle of the Sahara while being hunted by Drako's was not helping the matter.

"We will get through. We are smart and strong. We know where we are going thanks to you. We just have to get there." I whispered down to Kal.

"We will." His voice came out muffled, stubborn.

"We will." Ambrose agreed.

We sat there for another couple of minutes, comforting each other before we felt steady enough to move, walk.

When night turned into day and got too hot to continue walking, we set up our tent once again along the side of a dune, only this time we made sure to hide it with mounds of sand. We crawled inside the warm tent and collapsed on our bedding.

I fell asleep and dreamed of endless sand.

Forever walking.

CHAPTER 9

AMBROSE

N*IGHT 3*
      I woke up to the tent shaking violently and a deafening roar filling my ears.

"Fuck." I hissed, rolling to my back to examine the dark tent covering us. It was extremely dark and shadowed, filled with swirling dust.

"What's happening?" Lux cried as she jerked awake and immediately began to cough.

"Sandstorm." I groaned, reaching up to rub my palms against my eyes. I pulled my shirt up to cover my mouth and nose, breathing shallowly in order to avoid inhaling to much dust.

"Fuck." I heard Kal repeat.

I felt Lux shift forward until her ass was pressing into my hip. Looking over, I smiled when I saw that she had buried her face into Kal's shirt. His amused red eyes met mine over his own piece of lifted shirt that one of her small hands was holding over his mouth and nose.

The storm lasted a good hour before it finally stopped. Leaning up on an elbow, I carefully felt over the sun lightened top of the tent to feel that the ends were covered with sand while the center was still free. With a sigh, I laid back down and attempted to get a little bit more sleep before we would have to start moving again.

When I woke up next the light was dimmer, time to get going. I slowly sat up, my motion jarring my lungs and sending me into a spasm of harsh coughing.

"Here." Lux whispered hoarsely, handing me a bottle of water and pounding on my back.

I attempted to get a hold of myself long enough that I could get a drink. Unfortunately, it didn't happen. I was coughing so hard that I ended up bent over, struggling to breathe.

A set of hard, shackled arms drew over my head, the fists pressing deep into my pecs as a hard, ridge covered chest pressed into my back.

"Breathe with me." Kal whispered in my ear, his chest moving, slow and rhythmic, against my back.

With him bracing my torso, I tried to concentrate on breathing with him. Shallow at first before slowly deepening until I was finally able to draw air in my lungs. Dusty air.

"Out." Kal abruptly ordered, drawing his arms back.

He crawled across the dust covered bedding to the entrance, threw the sand covered flap open and pushed his way out. Lux was right behind me as I followed his lead and got my ass out of the tent.

Once I was outside, away from the dust and breathing fresh air, I felt my lungs ease momentarily. Then I was right back to coughing, this time bringing up copious amounts of sand filled phlegm. Kal dropped behind me, his arms circling me, his fists pressing into my chest and holding me to his chest. My strained and sore lungs eventually cleared and I honestly felt like crap.

Collapsing back against Kal, I allowed myself to take a moment to just relax and breathe.

"We should've gotten up and shaken all of the dust and sand out before going back to sleep." Lux coughed, not half as bad as I was but still enough to bring up her own phlegm.

"Yeah." Kal nodded, doing his own set of coughing.

My hands caught his arms and pulled him harder into my back, giving something for him to brace against. It took a bit before everyone was breathing clear. That was right about when my eyes caught on something weaving through the sand further down the dune.

My eyes widened in disbelief and I threw Kal's arms over my head. I ignored his cry of surprise at my abrupt actions as I moved as fast as I could. I caught the curved blade I had strapped to my thigh and yanked it free at the same time I ran down the incline in a hopping slide. I took aim and threw the blade. It flashed through the twilight, landing with a small splatter, putting an abrupt stop to the weaving.

I almost wanted to cry with relief when I reached the blade and pulled it free. My other hand caught the body of the snake I had killed and raised it high.

"Yes!" I bellowed out over the dunes, celebrating the fact that we now had more food. Protein.

Lux and Kal cheered right along with me.

Returning to the tent, I quickly cleaned the snake while Kal got a fire going using some sort of weird device he found in the ship and some cream like substance from the first aide kit that he slathered on a piece of fabric. The magical cream somehow made the fabric burn astonishingly slow, giving me time to fully cook the snake.

While I was cooking the other two shook everything out and packed up. Lux helpfully brought me my hooded poncho and pack, sitting down beside me and laying her head on my shoulder as we eagerly watched the meat sizzle.

"You know, I don't even care what it tastes like, I am just excited for something other than those stupid bars." She told me, her dark eyes lit with anticipation.

Tipping my head down to her, I smiled in complete agreement.

"Considering that we don't actually have very many of those bars left, it's good Ambrose found the snake." Kal voiced his own agreement, sitting down at Lux's other side.

"How many?" Lux asked with a set of worried eyes.

"Five." Kal winced as he spoke.

"Well, that fucking sucks. I have a feeling that we still have a hell of lot more walking to do." Lux sighed wearily.

"We are currently clocking one to one and half kilometers per hour which means we are travelling anywhere from fifteen to twenty kilometers a night. At this rate it will take us almost two weeks to reach Abu Minqar." I shared with them the distance I was guessing we were covering.

"We are going to run out of water long before than." Lux's face took on a concerned look, her hopeless eyes moving over the dunes.

"We need to keep our eyes out for wet spots in the sand. Usually that means water is close to the surface. If we can find one we should be able to dig down to that water." Kal described informatively. "But beyond that, let's pray that we come across an oasis."

We all nodded in agreement and watched the meat finish cooking. Once it was done we ate, packed up the leftovers, and began our evening walk.

We walked. And walked. And walked.

By the time the night turned into day and we got our tent erected, I was exhausted and my feet were killing me. I winced as I pulled my boots and socks off. My feet were looking raw and red from the sand that was constantly working its way inside my boots. Looking over, I saw that Lux's feet were just as bad.

"Here." Kal dug out the first aide kit and pulled out a container of cream that he handed to Lux.

She eyed him for a moment before twisting open the container and fingering out a dollop that she rubbed into her sore looking feet.

"Oh my God. That is so good." She moaned, her pleasure filled voice hitting me right in the dick. I winced and drew up my knee in order to mask how hard the sound of her pleasure had made me before stealing the cream from her.

The cream tingled and soothed in way that almost had me moaning right along with her. "I am in love." I found myself whispering, holding the container up to my face so I could examine it.

"It's very helpful at soothing sore skin and muscles. It also has some antibacterial properties, so it's also good for open wounds." Kal described with an amused grin.

"I don't know about you, but I am thinking Kal's shoeless thing has its merits." Lux eyed Kal's bare feet.

"Not for you, flower." Kal denied her with a shake of his head. "It gets cold at night. I am used to walking over all types of grounds, including ice cold sand, you are not."

"I see your point." Lux sighed in disappointment.

We dug out some food and water before settling down into sleep. That day was quiet and once the throbbing in my pants finally abated I actually got a decent couple of hours of sleep.

NIGHT 4

The next night was more walking. Mindlessly trudging over dune after dune.

Dawn started breaking when Kal suddenly slid down the dune we were walking on.

"Kal!" Lux called after him only for him to simply wave over his shoulder in return.

Lux's confused eyes met mine and I gave her a shrug. I had no idea what he was doing but I wasn't about to let him do it alone.

"Ambrose!" She exclaimed in frustration when I followed him down the dune.

Reaching the bottom, I knelt down in the icy, coarse sand right beside Kal to see him using one of the poles to dig into what looked like damp ground. I immediately pulled out another pole and began to help him dig. Lux slid to a stop beside us and exclaimed happily. The ground got wetter, the sand heavier, right before life giving water began to seep up. My eyes feasted on that fluid just as my mouth began to water when the scent hit my nose.

"Yes, yes, yes." Lux gasped with excitement, digging her own hands in to help widen and deepen the hole. Kal immediately began to start filling up some of the water bottles. It was at that point that I was really glad we had as many as we had.

We each immediately filtered and purified three of those bottles which we took keen advantage of. The vaguely dusty taste of the water didn't detract from the way the cool fluid felt in my throat. I honestly didn't realize how thirsty I was until that very moment. And by the way my fellow travellers were gulping back their own water I could tell that they felt the same.

"We are camping here today." I determined, looking over the slightly flat area that was set between three dunes. The sun had fully risen while we were digging and was now starting its way across the sky, already heating up our golden surroundings.

We thankfully got the tent set up and our beds ready before it could get blazing hot. After refilling the bottles for the second time, and almost as one, we all started stripping. Well, Kal and I did while Lux ducked behind the tent.

I ignored the sun beating down on me while I pulled off my shirt and pants before wrapping an extra sheet around my hips and pushed my underwear off. All of it was coated in dust and sand. Including me. My jeans were now a blueish beige right along with my blue t-shirt.

As much as I tried not to stare I couldn't seem stop my eyes from drawing over the bare chest that Kal revealed. All lean, sharp muscles, built for speed, covered with effervescent skin. Hard pecs tipped with pale pink nipples. The sheet wrapped around his waist accented his abdominal muscles. Eight highly defined ridges that were surrounded by scaling obliques and a sharp Adonis belt. All of it was deliciously palm itching. The man really was mouthwatering.

When I was finally able to force my eyes off of him, I couldn't help but notice his flaring red eyes drawing heatedly over my chest.

I smiled and shook my head, glad I wasn't the only one feeling it, before kneeling down and using the water bottles to try and wash the sand from my clothes. It was not easy. Kal silently snarled as he struggled to work on his own clothes.

Both of us looked over and froze when a sheet covered Lux appeared. She looked like a goddess with the long sheet tied around the luscious swell of her breasts and hanging down the length of her body. That devious sheet playfully parted around the smooth length of her legs as she moved. My feasting eyes really wanted to know what was under that sheet. My arm immediately dropped to my lap in order to hold down the throbbing muscle that successfully stole all of the blood from my brain.

It was then that my mouth dropped open in astonishment. The woman proceeded to shake the hell out of her clothes, sending sand flying off. Forcing my eyes from the erotic way her breasts jiggled and rolled with her movements, I dropped them down to the clothes that I did not shake off before soaking. My dumbfounded gaze found Kal's to see his lit with disbelief and disappointment.

Yeah, we fucked up.

It took us twice as long to wash our clothes off as it took Lux to wash her clothes.

Once they were finally done, we hung them up on a line we set up before returning to the water hole. Time for a sponge bath.

I used some ripped up fabric to wash the sand from my body. It did nothing about the smell but at least I no longer had sand imbedded in the crack off my ass and the crease of my balls.

Clean, somewhat. Refreshed, definitely. We all ate, drank more water, and filtered water into the rest of the bottles that we immediately packed away.

By the time we crawled into the tent we had been out in the sun for a couple of hours and Kal and I were looking a little pink. Kal more so than me as my naturally tanned skin held up better under the sun than his pale effervescent coloration.

I watched as he dug out the cream we used on our feet and began to rub it over his pink skin. My hand was once again forced to covering my rising erection at the sight of the cream glistening over his flesh before sinking in. My fingers twitched, hungry to take over for him so that I could run my hands over his body.

I couldn't say I was disappointed when Lux was the one to cream up her hands and swipe it over the muscles of his back. Seeing her delicate hands stroking over him like that had my dick pulsing in an almost violent fashion. I had honestly never been so aroused seeing something so innocent before.

My mesmerized gaze blinked into focus when Lux moved away to put the cream back in the first aid kit while Kal flopped back onto the bedding with his leg closest to us cocked up. I had a feeling that he was hiding his own erection.

"That feels so much better." Lux groaned with a mixture of exhaustion and satisfaction, collapsing on the bedding between the two of us. "No more sand."

"I can tell you, I am really not fond of how sand seems to settle in the most uncomfortable spots." Kal growled, hooking his shackled hands under his head, his leg lowering.

"I hate sand." I whined, laying on my stomach with my head on my crossed arms.

"I miss the color green." Lux breathed, shifting around until she was able to rest her head on my bicep and lay her legs over Kal's. I shivered when the sheet covering him ended up being disturbed enough that I got an eye fill of his pink tinged, muscular leg, bared all the way up to the indent of his hip.

"Flower girl." I chuckled, my eyes blinking closed, too tired to even think about checking out that leg even further.

Not that I didn't want to. A lot.

CHAPTER 10

KALBELIYAS

N*IGHT 5*
  I woke with one smooth leg tangled with mine and another cocked up to rest along my hips. Morning wood was definitely a thing this morning. The tent my dick was erecting in the sheet was pulsing along a bare feminine thigh.

My eyes moved from the top of the tent we were sleeping under and over the sleeping woman whose own sheet had risen up her deliciously curved thighs. Her head was still resting on Ambrose's shoulder, her hand laying curled on his back. I had to say, I loved the way she seemed to like connecting with both of us at the same time.

I winced as I moved my shackled hands, the metal grating over my raw flesh and thankfully detracting from the desperate staccato that was beating in my cock. Over the last couple of days, the shackles were really starting to do a number on my wrists. Unfortunately, the man who I didn't notice was awake noticed me examining my wrists and he immediately began moving. Ambrose gently guided Lux's head off of him and levered up to dig in the bag.

"They are fine." I reassured the worried looking man, my eyes slightly mesmerized by his bulging muscles flexing.

"Bullshit." He denied, pulling out the cream and a couple strips of cloth.

"Seriously." I sat up, continuing my denial.

"Shut it and give me." He motioned sharply for my wrists.

I rolled my eyes and handed over my wrists, my skin sensitizing under the calloused touch of his fingers. He gently rubbed the cream into my wrists before maneuvering the cloth between the metal and my flesh. Once he had it protecting my skin, he tied the material off.

"There, that should help." He determined, giving me a satisfied smile. The man really liked to take care of people.

Not able to resist that smile, my hand snapped out to catch the back of his head and pull him into me. He froze when I pressed our lips together, his body tensing tight. Thankfully, by the time I spread his lips with mine, he came unfroze, relaxing into the kiss.

My breath sucked in and my pounding heart sent rivers of burning blood through my body and down to my cock. My tongue met with his, stroking, rasping, tasting. He tasted really good. Dick twitching good.

Our lips sucked and slid over one another, deepening. His hard hands caught at my biceps, squeezing down before stroking up to grip the nape of my neck and delve into my hair. I couldn't seem to get enough of him, I didn't know if I ever would.

By the time we drew apart I was breathless with arousal and his dark blue eyes were blown with desire.

"We shouldn't have done that." His whispered words stabbed right into my heart and had my aching dick crying. "Sand isn't conducive to fucking and you currently have me so hard I can't even think straight."

My disappointment was immediately joined by amusement and I found myself chuckling. While I was disappointed that I wouldn't be able to take it further, I was in complete agreement with Ambrose about the time and place. And this wasn't it.

"I feel like I should be jealous but that was oddly sweet and arousing." Lux's voice had both of us jumping apart like guilty teenagers. We all burst into laughter when we realized how we had acted.

"That is good to know." Ambrose smiled, his face red with embarrassment, his hands covering his crotch. "Because I have a feeling it's going to happen again."

"Oh, yeah." My vehement agreement had them both laughing.

"Well, I don't know about you guys, but I have to go." Lux dug in the bag before crawling out the tent door.

Ambrose and I gave her the time she needed. Time we also needed as peeing with an erection was not fun.

When she returned, we crawled out and I found a place to do my business. Finished, we helped ourselves to more water and the last of the leftover snake. We gave ourselves another quick wash and refilled the water bottles one last time. I shook my clothes out, examining them for new biting friends. Cringing, I pulled the stiff material on, finding the most comfortable settle I could.

Ready and packed we started walking with the sun setting at our backs. The burning sand quickly cooled under my feet as we travelled.

That night we were forced to burrow into the sand and hide twice due to searching Drako ships. Instead of giving up like I thought they would, they seemed to be upping their search. Unfortunately, I knew why they were doing it. They were looking for me.

"It's not just you." Ambrose denied when I shared that with them after we unburied ourselves for the second time and resumed walking. Thankfully, we were all mentally handling the appearance of the searching Drako ships a lot better than we did the first time. "Yeah, you may be a Pleiadean but I am the head of the Bay. They really like getting their hands on the heads. Luke, Zara, Marko, Malachi, Amber. The Drako's made attempts for all of them. They even somewhat succeeded with Malachi. The fact of the matter is that even if you weren't here, they would still be hunting for us."

"I kind of feel left out." Lux playfully pouted, trying to ease the tension.

"I am sorry." I stated, spinning around from my lead.

Doing what I had been wanting to do for days now, I cupped her face and bent to press my lips to hers. A gasping cry slid from her mouth and straight into mine as my tongue licked inside. My heart kicked up and desire flared. Her tongue twitched before slowly coming up to meet mine. Long slow swipes brought her mesmerizing taste over my humming tastebuds.

Slowly drawing away, I winked down into her stunned eyes and flushed face. Spinning back around, I continued my lead, my hand subtly readjusting the swollen muscle poking at the zip of my pants.

"I get it, Lux. It's good, but you need to start walking." Ambrose's amused voice guided.

"He kissed me." Lux whispered breathlessly.

"He did." Ambrose chuckled.

"Was it this good for you?" She kept whispering, her voice filled with disbelief.

"Probably." Ambrose's statement caused my twitching grin to fully release itself.

"I have to say, you two are fantastically confidence boosting." I told them as I attempted to add an arrogant strut to my sliding stride over the sand.

My muscles were finally getting used to this new way of walking and no longer ached so much at the end of the night. I also noticed that I was losing weight, but then by the way Ambrose's jeans hung off his hips he was also losing weight.

That weight loss didn't seem to do anything except enhance his heavy muscles. Yesterday morning when I looked up to see him wearing nothing but that damned sheet, my mouth went dry. My eyes absolutely feasted on the sight of all of his large, well defined muscles. Thick and wide. Bulging and flexing. The man was gorgeous.

My palms had itched to feel the skin stretched over the sharp ridges that made up his torso. Eight ridged abdominals, a fascinating V leading into his pants, heavy pecs, the scales of his obliques. So many muscles just calling to be investigated. And if anything, I loved a good investigation.

"Yup." Ambrose laughed.

I noticed that Ambrose's playful side was coming out more and more everyday, his attitude relaxing despite our circumstances. Lux was the same, the stress of being hunted and trapped in the desert not getting to them. That definitely helped me keep my own attitude up and I found myself opening up and relaxing around them.

"Ok, new topic." Lux began and I automatically knew what was coming.

They both seemed to be taking turns asking me about my travels and the worlds I had been to. Thankfully, they had yet to mention my loss of ability and how hard they both knew it had to be for me. Instead, they both simply accepted me as I was, ability-less, and relished in my knowledge.

"Tell me about the most off the wall, weirdly colored world you have ever been to." Lux coaxed.

I had to think about that one for a moment before smiling. "It was a small planet with a purple sun. Which made the sky look purple. So many different shades of purple. The plants were shades of yellow and the ground was blue and black. The water, like the sky was various shades of purple. It was almost mind bending."

"That would be disconcerting." Ambrose agreed. "What about the life forms?"

"The intelligent species were similar to humans in intellect but they lived a lot closer to nature. They were kind of small, spotted yellow and black with long limbs and short torsos." I described to them. "There were also these highly intelligent, dragon like beings that were weirdly friendly carnivores."

"It must be amazing to see stuff like that and learn all about different worlds." Lux's voice was wishful.

"It gets old." I warned her. "For years I was forced to stay hidden and neutral. I watched so many different beings fighting, killing, breeding, loving. Just living their lives to the fullest. I didn't really have a home because I was travelling so much. My job, while one of the most important and heralded, right behind being a Judge, was not conducive to any type of relationship."

"So, have you ever...?" Ambrose drew out his question and left it hanging.

"I tried but they never lasted. We would get a couple of days together before I would have to leave for work. Sometimes I would be gone for a couple of weeks. Sometimes it would be months. Either way, they decided that it was too hard to wait for me." I shrugged, those memories no longer as frustrating and hurtful as they once were.

"That kind of sucks." Lux stated sadly.

"Yeah, it did. I was never able to get a relationship passed the initial flush, so I am going to warn you that I may not be the best at this." I shared with a wince.

"Man, look who you are talking to." Ambrose gave a self derisive chuckle.

"I had one boyfriend." Lux spoke up. "We dated for about a month before I walked in on him fucking Stella. He didn't even look sorry. We obviously broke up and he immediately started telling everyone at school that he was dating Stella. When she found out, she laughed at him and said just because they fucked didn't mean they were together. Instead of being mad at her, he took his anger out on me. Somehow it was always my fault. He was only one of many males who took their anger issues pertaining to my sister out on me.

That's one of the reason's why I walked away and kept myself from Ambrose for so long. I was afraid that he would treat me like they did."

"I know, flower." Ambrose sighed sadly. "But I need you to know that I never hated you, I never blamed you. My anger was never directed at you. In all of that you were the innocent one."

"I see that, now." Lux reassured him. "You are so much of a better man. You are one of the best people I have ever met. And that hasn't changed. Although, I will point out that Kal is right up there with you."

"He's so much better than me." Ambrose scoffed. "He's the one who forced us to talk and work through it."

"Don't paint me as the hero. I did that for purely altruistic reasons. I didn't want my connections at odds with each other." I stated firmly.

"See, Ambrose, you both are beautifully flawed. Just because I think you are the best men I have ever met doesn't mean I think either one of you is perfect. I don't want or need perfect. Because I am not perfect and there is no way I could live up to that." Lux claimed.

"I don't know about that. I have seen your ass." Ambrose noted.

"Right there. That is pure perfection." I completely agreed.

"Yeah, you think?" Lux asked skeptically. My head tilted back when I heard strange movements coming from her to see her twisted around and holding her poncho out of the way so that she could examine her own ass.

"Oh, yeah." Ambrose pulled his dark eyes from her ass to meet mine. He gave me a knowing grin and an acknowledging nod.

"Huh, I never really noticed before." Lux re-covered herself and turned her eyes forward.

"That's ok, we noticed for you." I laughed

"I am so not going to bring up what I noticed." Lux laughed right along with me.

"Oh, now I am curious." Ambrose exclaimed curiously.

"Well, the devil man here..." She began.

"Devil man?" I exclaimed in surprise.

"You are all devilish with those red eyes and hair. It's not a bad thing. It does, however, give you this extra little something that is really very attractive." Lux shared before continuing. "If you put it together with the rest that is all of you, woah. Especially those legs. I have to say, I have never been attracted to a man's legs before but yours are pure yum."

"And Ambrose?" I really wanted her opinion on him.

"He's like this wicked smart cave man, big and delicious. One who you kind of hope is right about to carry you away and do naughty things to you. For him, it's all about his arms." She praised.

"I completely get that." I grinned, completely agreeing with her assessment.

"Mind you, both of you also have nice asses as well. Kal's is tight and muscly while Ambrose has some serious bubble-age. Both of them are eye catching in the best ways." She shared.

"So, we have come to a concession. We all have nice asses." Ambrose joked.

"Fuck, yeah." I cheered.

Once twilight hit, we all started looking for something to add to our diminishing food stores as we finished the snake earlier. We unfortunately found nothing and were forced to make do with our last bars.

With the sun heating up, we got the tent set up and crashed.

CHAPTER 11

LUX

NIGHT 6
    We woke up and got going, tired and hungry but determined to continue onwards.

The first half of the night passed in a blur of sand and footsteps. It was in the middle of the night when my eyes caught on a set of desert monitors racing over the dunes, chasing something that looked frankly alien like.

"There." I exclaimed, frantically pointing out the lizards.

Both men immediately shot into action with me on their heels. We stumbled down the dune and raced after the lizards. The closer we got the more I saw of the creature they were chasing. An admittedly large camel spider. I had a moment of pause at the sight of that disconcerting creature but my hunger quickly overrode any fear.

"Fuck." Kal yelped when he inadvertently tripped and crashed into Ambrose's back, knocking Ambrose to his hands and knees. Ambrose, his eyes locked in on the lizards, was already pushing up and somehow throwing Kal right back onto his feet.

The stubborn man was so set that when I tripped and skidded down on my stomach all he did was jump over me. But then so did Kal.

Spitting out a face full of sand, I pushed myself to my feet and ran after them, descending quickly on the lizards. I was going so fast that I slid right into Ambrose's side and bounced off to go in a different direction and try to block the lizards' retreat. Kal darted to the other side, tripping over the sand.

The fuckers were quick. But not as quick as the blade that Ambrose had hidden on his person. A flash of steel landed expertly, killing the first lizard. Ambrose, still moving, slid onto the sand beside the dead lizard, sending sand waving out, mixing with another flash. The blade landed true for a second time, taking down the fleeing lizard and leaving the camel spider to run off un-accosted.

"Fuck yes." Kal cheered.

I jumped up and down with happiness, bouncing into a rising Ambrose and gripping his arms to take him with me in my excitement. His fist pumped up into the air as his other arm circled my waist and spun me around. My head tipped back just in time for his fist to drop down and grip the back of my neck and his lips to find mine.

My whole body froze in astonishment. My heart pounded so hard that I could hear it in my ears.

Ambrose was kissing me. It was just as intense as when Kal did it, but in a whole different way. I had honestly been waiting years for Ambrose to kiss me and now that he was it almost felt like a miracle.

When I felt his lips expertly spread mine my trembling body jerked into action. My hands cupped his beard covered face as my tongue met his. His lips were hard, hungry, his tongue swiping and twining with mine. He tasted good, just as good as a Kal, but once again different.

I was breathless and slightly dizzy by the time Ambrose released my spinning body into Kal's waiting arms. Kal's shackles looped over me and he hugged my desire laden body tight as he too spun me around.

My excitement returned as I remembered why we were celebrating.

We had food.

We quickly wrapped up the lizards and climbed our asses all the way back up the dune. We walked for another couple of hours until the sun starting peeping at the horizon. That was when we stopped and set up our camp.

Ambrose cleaned and cooked the lizards. Stripping off his stained and sweaty shirt under the heat of the sun, he took extra time to smoke the bulk of them into jerky. While Ambrose was doing that a shirtless Kal and I got the tent and bedding set up before going to lend Ambrose a hand.

Once the meat was prepared we ate and drank before making sure everything was packed away and well hidden.

I sighed, tired but full, as I climbed into the tent and curled into my spot. "I got kisses." I slurred out happily as my eyes closed.

"You sure did, flower." Ambrose's voice whispered as his arm slid around my waist.

I blinked tiredly when I felt myself shifted until I was laying along Kal's chest with Ambrose spooning me.

"I like this." I mumbled, my body sliding into the comforting dark of sleep.

NIGHT 7

The next morning, I woke up to a man pressing kisses along my neck. I shivered and hummed, my nipples beading under the erotic sensation of those damp sucks. My hand came up to cover the side of Kal's red beard covered face. I apparently switched positions in the day and was now laying along Ambrose's chest with Kal spooning me.

The shackled arms that had somehow found their way around me in the night tightened as his body shifted over my shoulder so he could find more of my neck. His head rose as my head turned to him.

Bright red eyes met mine and I felt my heart jump. I could feel myself already falling for this beautiful man. It seemed so unreal that I had somehow ended up connected to two very strong willed men. Caring men who had a frankly astounding depth of character. I honestly loved everything about this man and was indeed very attracted to him.

"Good morning." He whispered, his lips tipping up into a soft smile.

"Good morning." I whispered back, my fingers investigating over his face, his skin cool to the touch. His skin was always cool. I drew my fingers over his bearded chin and jaw, circling up over his cheekbone and forehead caress down the length of his nose to his plush lips.

That smile widened under my fingers and his eyes took on a warmer tone of red.

"Devil man." I smiled, leaning up to press a gentle kiss to those smiling lips.

He chuckled and returned the kiss with a quick lick and a soft suck. When he drew back, he pressed his forehead to mine for a long moment, his eyes fluttering closed. "I feel like I have waited forever to feel this. And now I have been gifted doubly."

The feel of the chest under my hand shifting drew our eyes over to see Ambrose stretching, his eyes cracking open. "Good morning." He smiled before frowning and reaching up to frantically scratch at his fuzzy chin. "How the hell does Luke do this? It's itchy as hell."

"I feel like I am going crazy." Kal vehemently agreed, scratching at his own chin.

"I don't have that problem." I bragged. When I was a teenager, my sister dragged me with her to get laser hair surgery. I was a little upset about how pushy she had been at the time but now I was grateful for it as I never needed to shave. Anything.

"Oh, believe me, I noticed." Ambrose waggled his eyebrows as he drew his heated eyes down my body.

"Nice and smooth." Kal hummed in my ear, the sound of his voice had my vagina clenching and leaking.

"Ok. Time to get going." I laughed, rolling over to press a quick, wet kiss to Ambrose's chapped lips. While I was busy, Kal crawled out of the tent to take care of his morning business.

Drawing back with a slight frown, I drew my fingers over the splits that were forming over the width of Ambrose's lips. While he wasn't chewing on his lips half as much as he usual did the dry desert air was making them worse than ever.

"Ouch." I whispered softly, feeling bad for his poor lips.

"They are ok." His lips moved against my fingers.

"Hmm." I hummed and sat up to dig through the bag. Along with other things I needed, I dug out the container of ointment. Helping myself to a dab, I rubbed it over his lips, smoothing the cream into that tender flesh.

Underneath that dryness, he really had a nice pair of wide lips.

"There." I smiled happily, closing the container and tucking it away.

"Thank you." He hummed, sitting up and cupping the side of my head with his strong hands and their long, talented fingers. My heart swelled with the love I felt for him, love that had been bruised but not irrevocably broken. After everything we went through, I honestly didn't think anything could destroy my love for him.

"Anytime." I assured him, staring into his deep, dark blue eyes, my hands gripping around his wrists.

"Done." Kal claimed, jarring us out of the moment and crawling back into the tent.

I traded out with him and took care of my needs only to return to the tent and give Ambrose his time outside.

While Ambrose took care of his business, Kal and I began to shake out the bedding and pack it away. The tent was next. Before we started off, we took a moment to eat and drink.

Then came the walking. I didn't know about the men, but I was getting really tired of walking. I even started having nightmares about walking.

That and sand.

What I wouldn't give to dig my hands into moist, cool dirt. That was one thing I really missed about the Base, the plants. And while I had been enjoying the outdoors of the Ranch, loving it, I had spent more time in the Base Garden, planting and growing my babies, watching them flourish and bloom under my care.

I had a special touch when it came to plant life. They loved it when I sang to them and cared for them. Because of that, Herman, the elderly head of the Garden, quite often used me for the more important growths or ones that were having difficulty growing. And it's probably one of the main reasons the botanists jumped on their chance to have me as their assistant.

This talent, unfortunately, was useless out in the middle of a dry, sand covered desert and honestly, I was starting to feel slightly anxious not having anything green around me.

It was just after midnight when something hit my nose.

Water.

I could smell water.

My abrupt stop had both Ambrose and Kal walking right into my back. Ambrose's hands automatically caught my shoulders when I stumbled forward a step due to the pressure of their bodies butting into mine.

I took deep, probing breathes in as my eyes searched over the moonlit shadows of the dunes around us.

"Fuck, do you smell that?" Ambrose breathed, his nostrils flaring as he scented the air.

"Water." Kal agreed, his own eyes searching. "There." He pointed out a number of spikes rising up from the desert a number of dunes away.

"Let's go." Ambrose commanded a little too late as I had already started racing forward.

My mind was centered around the thought of water, and trees. Green life. I scrambled along the dunes before once again skidding to a stop and staring down at the oasis in front of me. I gasped, my hands covering my quivering mouth, tears of relief popping into my eyes.

"Holy fuck." Kal breathed at the same time Ambrose cried, "Thank God."

All three of us skidded down the dune and over to the palm tree surrounded oasis. The glistening pond of clear water was around the size of a large swimming pool. That and it miraculously had a small tent camp set up within the tall palm trees and scrubby brush.

The camp was a complete mess. It looked as if someone had attacked whoever was once staying there. Old blood splatter sprayed over the ground and trees around the area confirmed that theory.

Despite the clear fight that had taken place, three of the seven tents were still up and in somewhat decent condition. There was also a fire pit set up in the middle of the camp along with a bunch of supplies that were strewn about.

Then Kal came across something truly miraculous.

A shower.

Someone had run a pump system from the oasis to a shower head that was attached to a tree behind one of the tents. There was even soap and shampoo.

Soap!

"Can we stay for a day or two?" I asked, feeling the life of the plants humming around me. "You know, give ourselves some renewal time."

"I think that's a good idea." Ambrose grinned gleefully at the possibility of having a day with no dune walking. "Although, I am thinking that if we are going to stay here, we should hide our tent a little bit away from the oasis. Just in case." Ambrose stated, looking over the area.

"I agree." Kal nodded slowly.

"Let's get set up and maybe catch a sleep so that we can check things out in the light." Ambrose turned to examine the area for the best spot to set up.

"I cannot wait for a shower." I hopped excitedly.

"You, my flower, can go first when we wake up." Kal chuckled, nudging me with his shoulder.

We got the tent set up and got our sleep, waking up when the sun started to rise. The first thing we did, besides the men stripping their shirts off and torturing me with sweat glistened muscles, was to dig through the supplies. We found so much. Clothes, shoes, dishware, cookware, bedding. We even found water skins. Then there was the tools, hammers, axes, even a small set of bolt cutters that Ambrose immediately tried on the metallic attachment that held Kal's shackles together.

"Fucking hell." Ambrose snarled as his muscles strained around the grips. His whole body popped with muscles and veins, his neck and face turning red. I couldn't lie, seeing him straining like this was dead sexy and had my vagina pulsing with desire. He sucked a breath in and relaxed long enough to readjust his grip before once again bearing down. "Give, you motherfucker!"

Reaching between them, I covered Ambrose's hands with mine and added my strength to his. When it still didn't work, Kal shifted my hands away to take my place. I set my hands on his and we all bore down at once. The hard metal finally gave with a loud snap and the shackle attachment was finally detached. While that didn't solve the ability confinement issue, it did give his arms maneuverability and the ability to shake his bunched shirt off his wrists.

"Yes." Kal groaned as he stretched his arms out, finally somewhat free, while Ambrose and I smiled happily.

I laughed when Kal reached around both of us and pulled us into a hug. "This feels so fucking good."

"Now I just need the right tools to rip the lock on those fucking things open and find the damned release switch." Ambrose chuckled as we drew back.

"You can do that?" Kal's brow furrowed as his face took on a mixture of disbelief and hope.

"I work on engines and am very familiar with electrical components and boards. Plus, I was the one who designed the new rifles and weapons systems for the Base. I think I can handle your shackles. I just need the proper tools to do it." Ambrose stated, firm in his knowledge.

"That was you?" I crowed proudly. "I heard about those weapons and how badass they are. A mixture of human and Nordic tech that has the ability to track the lightning fast movements of the extraterrestrial spaceships."

"Yeah." Ambrose adorably blushed and ducked his head.

"I honestly couldn't be more aroused." Kal shared with a set of desire bright eyes.

Ambrose laughed as he pushed on Kal's shoulder. "Fucker."

"Well, yeah." Kal gestured to his lap with a sly grin.

"Let's get those clothes washed and hung. Then we will have something else to wear." I pointed at the pile I made.

We filled a wooden tub full of water and used some of the soap to wash the clothes down. It took a couple rounds of rinse water before we had them fully clean and rinsed and ready to be hung to dry.

After that, I skipped off to the shower with my sheet in tow.

CHAPTER 12

AMBROSE

While Lux showered, Kal and I organized the items into what we could use and actually carry and what was to be discarded.

A hissing whistle had me turning from the pile I was crouched beside to see him expertly flipping a shining scimitar over his hand. I watched him test the weapon, swinging and thrusting it, his body moving with it in an elegant dance.

I couldn't tear my eyes from the graceful flex and twist of his body.

"Can you do that fully naked?" I winced at the words that came out of my mouth while he froze in position. His wide eyes came to mine just as I dropped my forehead into my palm, my head slowly shaking back and forth. "I cannot believe I just said that."

"I will be honest." The scimitar stabbed into the sand beside me as he crouched down. "I am willing to do a lot of things naked, but swinging a sharp weapon around isn't very high on that list. I am pretty sure you can guess why."

"Yeah." I chuckled, risking an embarrassed look up to see his eyes glowing with amusement and desire.

"Although, it's awesome that you want to see me naked." He crowed, rising to his full height, dancing around as he sang. "You want to see me naked. You want to see me naked."

That turned into both of us dancing around chanting the word naked.

"Uh?" Lux's voice had us skipping to a stop and turning to see the wet, sheet covered woman.

I could smell her all the way from here, the soft, flowering scent tickling deliciously at my nostrils.

"Fuck you smell good." I groaned, walking over to sniff over her.

"You too can smell good." She laughed, patting my chest before walking over to the wash tub and dropping her dirty clothes in.

"Me first." Kal raced off for his own sheet and the shower.

I chuckled and headed over to the pond, examining the surface and wondering if there might be some fish down there.

I was turning to go dig for something I might be able to use to fish with when my eyes caught on the figure stripping down. Smooth skin was revealed, inch by inch.

My mouth watered and my dick filled so fast I almost stumbled. I sucked my bottom lip in, my eyes drawing over that body to find the one thing I had yet to see. A thick, pale, bluish dick tipped with a pale pink cap. It was hanging limply over the rounded cushion of his balls. He had a good dick, big but not too big. And I really wanted it in my mouth. I wanted to feel it over my palette. I wanted taste it.

Kal stepped forward and flipped on the shower. Water started streaming over him in glistening rivers, washing the sand and dust away. His muscles rolled and flexed with his movements as water was followed by soap suds. His sinewy hands glided over his skin as he washed and my hands immediately wanted to shove his aside and take over. I wanted to feel all over that wet skin, caress over all of the sharp dips and ridges.

I wanted to work the soap over his dick and balls, just like he was currently doing. I wanted to wash his tight ass, clean it for my use. I wanted to sink my teeth into the hard muscles of his ass cheeks.

Forcing my gaze away from him, I ignored the desperate throbbing of my dick and walked back to the camp to dig through the items.

"Can I help?" Lux asked as she finished hanging up her newly cleaned clothes.

"I want to see if I can catch any fish." I told her, pulling out a small roll of thin wire.

"That's smart. What are you thinking?" She eyed the roll of wire.

"I need a pole that I can tie a length of this to. I think I might even be able to fashion some sort of hook by twisting some of it together." I explained to her as I began to measure out the wire. She wandered off and returned with a couple of sticks.

"I want to try." She said as she helped me form the hooks and tie the measures of wire to the sticks.

"Clean." Kal called, walking over to us still dripping with his sheet tied around his waist.

I immediately stood and headed to the shower, eager to finally be clean. Stripping out of my disgusting clothes, I kicked them aside and turned the shower on. Cool water flowed over my sun heated body, rinsing away the sand and grime.

I sighed and used the shampoo that I found there to wash my hair. I cringed as I ended up having to do it three times before I successfully scrapped all of the sand off of my scalp. Moving on, I used my soap filled hand to scrub my body down, carefully getting every single spot. Twice. Once I finally felt clean, I turned the water off and used my hands to scrape the water from my face and hair.

My eyes opened as I turned to catch up my sheet and froze at the sight of the red haired man leaning against a nearby tree. Kal had his arms crossed, his bright red eyes trained on me.

"Tit for tat." He claimed arrogantly as he turned and strolled away.

I found myself laughing while I tied the sheet around my waist and skipped after him.

"I don't care, I smell good." I told him, dropping my arm over his shoulder.

"So do I." He bragged, waggling his eyebrows at me.

"How many times?" I asked him curiously. "I only caught the first."

"Same as you. Three times for my hair and twice for my body." He described.

"Four times for my hair and three times for my body." Lux shared as we approached. "Although, I did mine peeper free."

"He started it." Kal pointed his thumb my way.

"I was examining the pond for fish. It's not my fault that there was naked man washing himself fifteen feet away." I shrugged carelessly.

"Men." Lux rolled her eyes at us.

I chuckled and walked over to cup her face. Tipping her lips up to mine, I took advantage of that position by feeding myself her taste. She hummed softly, her delicate hands pressing into my pecs and sending shivers of fire through me. Her lips and tongue moved against mine, softer than my own hard possession of her.

I slowly pulled away with one last nip and carried my dirty clothes over to the wash bin in order to scrub them down. Once they were cleaned and rinsed I hung them up beside the others.

The three of us walked over to the pond and sat down on the blanket that Lux thoughtfully brought. I smiled when Kal pulled Lux down to sit in the spread of his legs. She leaned back into his chest as they both caste their lines.

I caste my own line and waited. After about five minutes of nothing, I pulled the line out and examined the hook. It needed something to draw the fish in. A pop of color. Rising, I went to examine the fabric that we had available and cut some strips off one of the colorful blankets.

Tying that to the hooks, I caste out into the water and once again waited. It took a while but eventually I did get a bite. Muscling the wire in as fast as I could, I slowly reeled the fish in. It was a good size and perfect for our next meal.

Kal was the next one to reel a fish in, displaying it proudly. "I can't believe I actually caught a fish." He exclaimed excitedly.

"You did good." Lux praised him as I gripped his shoulder. "Good job, man."

Seeing him happy just to catch a fish hit something inside of me, telling me that despite spending his life watching others, his personal experience was low. That was when I decided to give him as many experiences as I could.

"Now all you have to do is clean it." I chuckled, helping him unhook the slippery fish and tossing it into the cask full of water we had set there just for that reason.

"I have seen people do that." He smiled at me, recasting his line.

"And now you get to get your own hands dirty." I told him.

His eyes took on a slightly worried look.

"Don't worry about it, man. I will be right there to help." I assured him.

"Thank you." He turned to look at me, his eyes warm and grateful.

"Not a problem." I turned back to our fishing.

We caught four more fish before calling it a day and I guided him through cleaning the fish.

Kal started the fire and Lux found a seat on the ground as I set up a smoking system for five of the fish. Once the fire was burning, Kal wormed his way between Lux's legs and leaned back to lay his head on her chest. She giggled and slid her arms around his shoulders.

I got the last fish set up on a spit over the fire. When I was done, I cuddled up to Lux's back and slid my arms around her, gripping one hand on her hip and the other on Kal's arm. I rested my chin on her bare shoulder while Kal reached up to lace his fingers with mine. I felt something ease inside of me at the feel of us all connected.

I breathed Lux's scent in, running my nose over her neck and causing her to giggle. "I cannot tell you how many times I wanted to do this."

"Probably about as many times as I wanted you to do it." She smiled, resting the side of her head against mine.

"This was a really good idea." Kal hummed softly. "I feel almost peaceful. Like I don't have to be anywhere, studying anything, not that I could even if I wanted to. Just laying here, under the sun, shaded by trees and tents, with the two of you. I can honestly say I wouldn't want to be anywhere else."

"Me neither." Lux smiled, playing one of her hands through his hair.

"Yeah." I nodded slowly. Kal was right, despite the danger surrounding us and the extreme circumstances we found ourselves in, I couldn't imagine being anywhere else.

Once the fish was done, we ate our lunch and doused the fire, cleaning up as much of our presence as we could before crawling into our hidden tent for a nap.

I wasn't sure how long I had slept for but it was still light out when I woke up with a hard hand pressing over my mouth. My eyes popped opened to a set of red eyes staring at me, filled with warning. Kal lifted his finger up to his lips in the universal sign for silence before removing his hand from my mouth.

My perked ears picked up the sound of hissing words and heavy feet thumping around outside. I also caught the low sound of a humming spaceship. Silently sitting up, I carefully picked up the curved blade I took to resting against my pack and parted the entrance flap just enough that I could gain a very limited view outside.

About five Lizards were wandering around the oasis and tent village making me thankful that we had removed just about any sign of our continuing presence. The dried clothes and food were packed away, our footprints smoothed out, the fire smothered.

I was also slightly surprised that it was just Lizards with no Grays or Insectoids.

Turning my head slightly, I saw that Kal had a pale face Lux safely tucked in his arms and his eyes narrowed on the tent entrance. I held up five fingers and mouthed 'Lizards'. He gave me a sharp nod in understanding.

Returning to the tent entrance, I watched the Lizards toss stuff around as they investigated everything they could. A couple of them even wandered concerningly close to our hidden tent but thankfully never found us.

It took them a good half an hour before they were satisfied enough to group up and return to their ships. The two ships lifted up and began to slowly move on, searching over the dunes at that familiar slow rate.

"Gone." I breathed, feeling myself relax at how close of a call we had.

"Thank God." Lux seemed to just deflate against Kal's chest, her face turning into one of his pecs while his hand protectively covered the side of her head.

"That was close." Kal stated, his eyes hard in a way I never saw them before.

"Almost too close." I agreed, my body still vibrating with adrenalin.

Setting my blade back in its spot, I collapsed back onto my bed and rested my forearm over my eyes.

"Ok?" Kal asked softly.

"Yeah." I mumbled, waiting for my heart to slow. "Why?"

"Because you are currently showing off." He noted.

"What?" I frowned over at him.

Lux's eyes peeked from her cuddle against Kal's chest and immediately widened. "Oh, my."

Following her gaze, I tilted my head down to see that my sheet had parted right over my lap in way that no longer left anything to the imagination. "I got it so I am going to flaunt it." I stated, giving my hips a little shimmy that rolled the heavy length of my dick back and forth along my thighs.

"For fuck sakes." Kal snorted on a laugh as Lux blushed beat red and giggled.

Reaching down, I flipped the sheet back over myself and shifted into a more comfortable position, my eyes closing.

I hummed softly and cocked my arm under my head when I suddenly had a woman sprawled over my chest. That hum turned into a grunt when I found two different legs cocking up over my outstretch one.

I cracked an eye to see Kal curled along Lux's back, his arm extending over her waist and resting on my abdomen. My other hand moved to link my fingers with his in a light grip. With that, I once again fell asleep.

CHAPTER 13

KALBELIYAS

NIGHT 8
   I woke up when the tent started to darken into night. Deciding that it was time to get up, I peeked out of the tent to make sure everything was clear before crawling out.

I was returning to the tent when Ambrose came crawling out. He yawned and scratched his chest as he walked by me to take care of his own needs.

While he was doing that, I made sure to check over the clothes for crawling things, giving them a good shake before pulling on a pair loose, linen pants with a drawstring waist. Along with it was a long linen shirt with long sleeves and a neck that opened down the center of my chest. The pants were dark while the shirt was lighter.

Once Ambrose returned and started on his own dress, I made use of the deodorant and the toothbrush and toothpaste we found. It honestly felt miraculous to have something so simple as a toothbrush.

Ambrose joined me, dressed almost the exact same only with boots on his feet. Although, it had to be noted that both the shirt and the pants were a lot more strained due to his thick muscles. That and the part that ran down his chest was spread a lot more, giving off a very delicious glimpse of those heavy pecs of his.

He also made use of the toothbrush he claimed and the shared deodorant.

That was right about when Lux came crawling out and everything repeated for the third time. She ended up dressed in something similar only her pants were fluffier and her shirt was longer, hitting her around her knees. I couldn't help but admire how gorgeous she was and by the look in Ambrose's eyes, I wasn't the only one.

Wandering over to the edge of the pond, I stared up at the stars. Once so close yet now so far away and somehow still just as beautiful. It hammered in the true fragility of mortality.

While I was just as mortal as humans were, it was easy to forget that fact. The powerful abilities of our race and the job we had been gifted with tended to make mortality seem like an illusion. To us it was normal, to others it could be fairly mind blowing and awe inducing. And now, without my abilities, I finally understood the reality of mortality, how fragile life truly was.

And to be honest, it felt oddly inspiring. It made me want to be more than just my abilities, more of an individual.

Ambrose and Lux helped with that. They looked beyond my Pleiadean heritage to see the man underneath the ability and they appreciated that man. They showed that appreciation everyday with so many little things and the best part was that they didn't even really think about it when they were doing it, they just did it.

And I loved that about them.

My body shivered at the heat of Ambrose's chest pressing into my back, his arm circling my collarbone, holding me back into him. My hand automatically came up to grip down on his arm, deepening that connection.

He didn't say anything, he simply looked up at the stars with me.

Reaching out, I caught the arm of the woman standing beside us and pulled her in front of me, sliding my arm around her waist.

"I do have to say, the stars are so beautiful out here, almost magical." Lux noted, rubbing her hand over my arm.

"It's a reminder of what we are fighting for, to regain the ability to see sights like this without fear. This fight isn't just about survival but recovering everything we lost, the earth, the oceans, the stars." Ambrose's chest rumbled against my back.

"It's like they say, you never really know what you have until you lose it." Lux hummed.

"True." Ambrose nodded slowly, his body tensing slightly. "But then when you finally succeed in getting it back, you appreciate it so much more."

"You really do." Lux tilted her head back and smiled at Ambrose, the look in her eyes silent portraying her appreciation of him.

He chuckled and shook his head at. "That's my line."

"We should probably get our asses covered just in case another ship comes by." Ambrose sighed.

"Another minute." I tightened my grip around them.

Both of them settled, relaxing into me. My eyes moved from the stars to the shadowed oasis and the darkened dunes around us. A sight that I had seen before in so many ways on so many different planets, but one that I was now seeing with all new eyes. One that I was experiencing for myself and sharing with the two people who were quickly becoming the most important people in the universe to me.

After another minute we broke apart and walked back to the tent to dig out our hooded ponchos and pulling them on. Safely covered, we decided to check out the rest of the oasis, walking around the pond to see if we missed anything.

"So, we know about my sister and Ambrose didn't have any siblings, but you do." Lux hinted as we walked.

"Ok. I have an older brother, Pacifier, he's a Judge. My triplet younger sisters were jurors with me. Aspis has precognition and is now connected to Scope, she's blue in color. Elapidae can astral project and is now connected to Grayson. She's indigo. Echis is orange and is connected to Diad, she's a telekinetic. We all have the ability to turn into energy." I shared with the group.

"You all seem very close." Ambrose noted what he had seen among my siblings.

"We are." I nodded in confirmation. "Our mother died in childbirth with the triplets leaving us with our dad who was a Judge. Our uncle watched over us when dad was away, which was a lot. Unfortunately, our uncle was kind of clueless and a lot of the triplets' care fell to Pacifier and me. Then Pacifier started to take the training to become a Judge. His reasoning was that he wanted to take dad's place and give dad a chance to actually spend time with his kids. The training was pretty severe but nothing like the weeks of testing Pacifier had to go through. He was twelve when he was accepted as a Judge. The youngest ever. Too young."

"He came home changed. Cold and emotionless. The triplets and I did everything we could to bring him back and show him our love but we didn't have much time before he had to start leaving for work. Dad was able to retire and the triplets and I had him for a couple years until he died. I was around sixteen at the time and was left raising the triplets. I graduated from school and became a juror. The triplets followed in my footsteps, their reasoning the same as mine. We could be closer and spend more time with Pacifier if we were working under him. And we did. A little bit anyways." I paused in my speaking.

"That's really very bittersweet." Lux sighed sadly, reaching over to take my hand in hers.

"What do you mean?" I frowned in confusion.

"You lost your mother when you were probably too young to remember much of her." Ambrose very accurately pointed out.

"Your father was never around so you probably never really considered him as a reliable parental figure." Lux continued where he left off.

"Then the one person you did rely on, your brother, left you far too soon. Yes, it was to give you the chance to have your father the way you should have all along but by then you would already been old enough for his loss to really effect you." Ambrose winced on my behalf.

"After your brother practically gave up everything for you and your sisters, leaving you all confused and alone in the process, the very reason he did it, your father, died." Lux rubbed my hand between two of hers in a comforting gesture.

"You lost so much but you still persevered. You did everything that you could to keep what was left of your family together. You obviously love your sisters and would do anything for them and would clearly do the same for your brother if he would let you." Ambrose stated. "And now that they have found their connections and are moving on...?"

"Yeah, I can't lie. That one kind of...it is a very lonely feeling." I winced, the thoughts that I assumed I had successfully buried rising up once again.

Watching each and every one of them find their connections and building new families, leaving me behind, it hurt all at the same time it made my heart glow with joy. I was truly happy for them but I was also really lonely.

"So, kind of a topic change, but if we are really doing this we should probably talk about certain things so that we are all on the same page." Lux brought up, pulling my thoughts from the loneliness I once felt to the ones who were currently with me, filling my heart and mind with them.

Needless to say, I wasn't lonely anymore.

"True." Ambrose pointed at her as I frowned in confusion. "Kids? Wedding? Housing?"

"What?" I questioned, dumbfounded.

Lux smiled up at me as she answered. "Yes, kids. Two if possible, no sex preference. I don't really need a wedding but it's not a firm no.

As for housing, I kind of like the open skies of the Ranch and being surrounded by nature instead of stone."

"She has a connection to plants." Ambrose explained at my continued confusion. "You should see her working with them, it's honestly pretty amazing how they react to her.

"Really?" I smiled proudly down at the woman who just kept amazing me, bringing her knuckles up so that I could press a kiss to them.

"It's a talent." She blushed as she tried to shrug away her embarrassment. "Now you."

"Ok." I nodded and thought about it. "If I am understanding this, I do want kids. I would like three, hopefully at least one boy and one girl. I would love to have a wedding. They are a tradition that I would like to take part in as it will give me a chance to celebrate my connections to the two of you. And I don't give a damned where I live because my home is wherever you two are."

"Fuck, how the hell do I follow that?" Ambrose groaned, chewing on his bottom lip. "I want kids. I would be good with one but I am not against having more. I don't care what kinds. I want a wedding. The Ranch sounds good to me, although, the transfer could take some time and I would probably still have to go back and forth in order to help out in the Bay."

"How soon do we want to try for kids?" I asked curiously.

"I don't care." They both stated at the same time, chuckling at each other in the aftermath.

"Then we don't need to worry about birth control." I nodded slowly.

"Since there is two of you and only one of me, are you both wanting one that is biologically yours?" Lux brought up.

"I honestly didn't even think about it." Ambrose frowned. "I just assumed that any children you bore for us would be mine despite their biological influences."

"I assumed the same." I nudged his shoulder in agreement.

"Ok, good." She nodded slowly. "Because if we are going to do this we can't think of his or his. We have to think ours."

"Already there, Lux." Ambrose grinned proudly.

We returned to the tent camp and started to reorganize our packs before taking a nap until the sun started to rise.

CHAPTER 14

LUX

NIGHT 9

With nothing really left to do, we caught another couple of fish and got them smoking as we all kind of relaxed on the beach close to the camp. The blanket underneath us provided a nice buffer against the burning heat of the sand.

I opted to wear my underwear and my bra while the guys both stripped right down to their underwear. Tight boxer briefs dark in colour. Both accenting glorious asses and fascinating crotch bulges that after a couple of minutes I was successfully able to ignore in favor of soaking up some sun. I was careful not spend too long on each side as the sun was very hot and I didn't want to burn.

I couldn't help but notice how Ambrose browned up nicely due to his skin tone. Kal, who also had a starter tan from spending the odd time here and there out in the sun also began to brown right up. It seemed weird to see his pale, effervescent skin so dark. It made his eyes blend in at the same time it made them seem even more devilish. It also made the metallic lines and designs on his face pop and practically glow.

Laughter burst from my chest when Ambrose suddenly sat up and pulled the band of Kal's underwear out to display the top of his pale white ass.

"That is awesome." Ambrose laughed.

Kal elbowed up and turned to look down into the lifted band. "Right?"

Ambrose let the band snap back into place and turned to me, his hand running over my back. "I kind of wish we had some suntan lotion so I had an excuse to massage my hands all over you."

"You don't need an excuse." I told him, shifting my back under his hand. "I am all for a massage."

He chuckled softly and shifted around until he was able to use those strong hands to massage my back. I moaned softly at how good it felt. Rough and calloused. Talented fingers worked over muscles I didn't realize were tense, loosening them until I felt like a gooey puddle on the blanket.

His hands moved to my lower back before finding my ankles and calves and working upwards. My legs shifted into a more comfortable position as my humming body began to hum even more. Those deliciously calloused hands moved up my legs and, in reaction, my pussy began to pulse, slicken. My nipples pebbled and my arousal rose right along with his hands, now on my upper thighs.

I moaned when his wicked hands found my ass, first over the panties, then sliding under to massage over the swell of my ass cheeks. This pushed my underwear up and pulled them tight against my aroused pussy and the crack of my ass.

Another set of fingers caught the length of my hair and moved it off my back and over my shoulder, leaving the nape of my neck bare for the lips that followed. I shivered and arched, those lips licking and sucking over my nape and shoulder.

"This is not a massage." I stated, my voice husky with desire.

"I never said it was." Kal whispered in my ear, his teeth nipping at my earlobe.

"Ambrose did." I murmured.

"I am still massaging." Ambrose noted shifting around until he was straddling my lower legs, his hands working my ass cheeks, rotating while rubbing his thumbs along the crack.

Every gripping caress drew more and more liquid from my center. His movements delightfully shifting the tightened band of my underwear along my pussy. The fabric worked into the split of my sex to drag over the swollen bud of my clit. I whimpered, my legs spreading just the slightest bit more.

Kal's lips moved over my back, his spread fingers caressing up and down the length. It took me a minute to realize that nothing was stopping the length of those long strokes, not even my bra strap. That hand firmly glided to my side and moved up, the tips of his fingers grazing over the pushed out curve of my breast.

"This isn't fair." I whimpered under the onslaught of sensations they were drawing from me. "There is two of you and only one of me."

"Twice the pleasure, flower." Kal's breath blew over the wet mark his mouth left on my skin.

Kal's fingers glided backdown to grip down on my side just under my breast. Ambrose's hands kept massaging, driving my pussy crazy right before they tightened down to grip my ass cheeks harder.

A soft sucking sound had me pushing up onto my elbows and shifting my upper body around to see Kal and Ambrose kissing. Kal had one hand buried in Ambrose's hair, pulling his head back for his lips. Hard, bearded jaws moved as their lips twisted and rubbed against each other. My pussy clenched tightly when I caught a flash of tongue.

An aroused noise slid from Ambrose's chest and his hips rolled forward until the hard length tenting the top of his underwear thrust along the crack of my ass. The tight underwear tightened even more around the rounded tip as the material became moist and clinging. His chest flexed, his abdomen rippled as he drew the long length of his dick back and forth. His breathing thickened, becoming quicker with the arousal that I could see beating in the veins of his neck.

My hips began to roll back, grinding his cock even harder along my ass.

"Fuck." Ambrose groaned, his mouth pulling away from Kal's to look down at my ass.

Kal's chuckle cut off and his hips jerked when Ambrose lifted one of his hands from my ass. I couldn't see exactly what Ambrose was doing as Kal's kneeling form was facing away from me and right in my field of view.

I did, however have a nice view of Kal's muscular ass flexing right along with Ambrose's arm. Really wanting to see, I caught my loosened bra against my chest and slithered out from underneath Ambrose.

His hand released my ass and moved to grip the fat column throbbing in his underwear. Dark blue eyes were blown wide with pleasure and centered down on what his hand was doing. His face was flushed, his nostrils flaring.

Kal's hand tightened on Ambrose's hair, pulling his head back to meet Kal's eyes. With Ambrose's head tilting back like that, it extended his neck deliciously. Kneeling up, I leaned over to feast on that neck, my free hand moving over hard, heaving pecs and tight nipples. My mouth sucked and licked over his salty skin, feeling the pounding of his heartbeat pulsing against my tongue.

Ambrose's arm slid around my waist, his hand once again gripping down on the cheek of my ass. Not able to resist, my finger's played over his nipple as I turned my head to see his hand fisting Kal's naked dick.

Long and pale, carrying a bluish tinge due to the blue veins that glowed from underneath the stretched skin. The pale pink head was round and moist, fatter than the admittedly thick length itself. There was a number of intriguing veins that popped up right around the root, snaking outwards in a star shape.

Ambrose's tight fist pulled Kal's cock out in a harsh looking fashion before pushing back down the hard length, milking that erotic muscle. Kal's hips rolled right along with Ambrose's pulls, his lips parted, his face flushed with desire.

Now that I saw Kal's dick, I really wanted to see Ambrose's. In that effort, I released Ambrose's nipple and glided my hand down the ridges that made up his torso and pulled his underwear down. His dick slapped out, bouncing off his abdomen and drawing Kal's arousal bright eyes down.

Hard and throbbing. His dick was a long, smooth length of thick flesh, darker than Kal's with the pointed head flushed a dark red. Seeing that erotic jut of male genitalia had my female genitalia contracting emptily. My hand somehow found it's way around that muscle and began to feel over it, stroking the hard yet giving flesh up and down. Ambrose's breath hissed in and his hips began to roll with my pulls.

"Work the head, flower." Kal advised in a husky voice.

Glancing up into his bright red eyes, I gave him a playful smiled and began to roll my palm over the head of Ambrose's dick with every up stroke. Ambrose groaned softly, his hips shivering.

"Bad man." He growled, his hand gripping down just under the head of Kal's cock, his thumb rubbing over the head before pressing into the hole in the tip.

"Fucking hell." Kal snarled, his head falling back in pleasure. "And you call me the bad man."

"I don't know why you guys are always so fascinated with breasts when you have these things to play with." I noted, my hand playing over Ambrose's heated dick. Precum slid from the tip, making the friction between our skin a smooth glide.

Ambrose's head tipped down and his hand curved up, pulling away one of the cups of my bra to look down at the breast he revealed. "Because that right there is fucking glorious."

"Oh yeah." Kal vehemently agreed.

"It's nowhere near as interesting," I denied.

"We are going to have agree to disagree." Ambrose rasped as his head ducked down to take my lips with his at the same time his hand gripped down around my breast. His fingers played over my sensitive nipple and his tongue twined with mine.

Pleasure flooded from my sensitive nipple down to pool in my vagina, pushing my desire even higher. I whimpered into Ambrose's mouth, my hand jerking the cock it was fisting even harder.

I gasped when I was suddenly shifted back to the blanket and my legs were spread. Ambrose's head dipped down and sucked my nipple into the rapturous heat of his mouth. His lips pulled and his tongue stroked while I felt fingers pulling my underwear off. My legs were spread around a set of hard shoulders and a strong tongue licked right up the split of my pussy.

I cried out and arched into the rapture of those torturous mouths. Heat blazed through me setting my whole body on fire. Pure, scalding pleasure.

Kal's tongue found my throbbing clit, circling and rubbing over it, sending more and more pleasure flaring through me. I never realized that anything could feel so good. My hands reached out and desperately gripped down on whatever they found. Soft hair, hard muscles.

Ambrose popped off my swollen nipple and kissed over my chest to draw deeply on my other nipple.

Kal's wickedly pleasurable tongue found my entrance and thrust right inside. My pussy spread around that thick organ as it licked over the sensitive muscles there. His tongue thrust in and out before moving back up to suck my clit inside his mouth. His tongue stroked over my trapped clit, pushing my rapture higher and higher until my legs were shaking and I was right on the cutting edge, hanging off of it. Right up until Ambrose dragged the sharp edge of his teeth over the highly sensitive nerves that made up my nipple.

I tipped right over and flew into skies of pure ecstasy. My breathing stopped as my pussy pulsed against Kal's tongue. Fireworks lit in my eyes and my body arched and twisted against the hands and mouths surrounding me.

My orgasm abated and my breath sucked in, returning functions to my brain. My body was still vibrating with the aftermath when my eyes found the two men who were now kissing. Their bodies were straining against one another, their hands fisting pulsing cock's, rubbing the leaking tips together.

Ambrose groaned loudly as Kal hissed. Both men tensed, their bodies shuddering and trembling, their cocks flexing as white cream sprayed from the swollen tips. I hummed softly, my hands moving over my highly sensitive body as that delicious looking sperm splattered over hard muscles and tight fists.

They were so beautiful in their joint pleasure that I couldn't tear my eyes away from them.

Ambrose drew back with one last kiss, his ass collapsing back on his knees as Kal's ass hit the blanket. Both men were breathing hard, their faces and bodies carrying a satisfied and relaxed look.

Sitting up, I hugged my arms around my cocked up legs, my body feeling just as relaxed as theirs.

"I think I have something new to dream about besides sand and walking." Ambrose stated, his hands rubbing the sperm covering him into his skin.

"Yeah." Kal breathed in agreement. "I don't think I have ever come that hard and I didn't even get inside anyone."

"Your tongue did." I smiled as I pointed out.

"That doesn't count. My tongue gives orgasms, it doesn't receive orgasms." Kal chuckled.

"Well, it definitely is talented." I informed him with a satisfied smile.

"Thank you." He bowed his head to me.

"No, thank you." I told him. "Between your tongue and Ambrose's hands, I had no chance."

"You didn't even get the good stuff." Ambrose held his hand up and wiggled his middle finger up and down. "My fingers are used to doing fine work."

My pussy gave a pulse at the thought of what that teasing fingertip could do.

"I can attest to that." Kal grinned at Ambrose.

"Well, I don't know about you guys but I need a shower." Rising from the blanket, I walked over to the shower.

I just got it turned on when I was surrounded by two very helpful men. We played and laughed as we washed each other down. Once we were clean, we redressed and ate, cleaning up and getting as much packed away as we could before grabbing a nap.

We were heading out as soon as the sun set. As much as I was loving the break, I knew that we still needed to get out of here.

CHAPTER 15

AMBROSE

NIGHT 10
I woke up feeling like a new man. Something about having a positive sexual interaction ending with a mind blowing orgasm that I didn't want to kill myself over did wonders for my mental health.

Tightening my arms around the woman whose delicious ass was pressing into my rock hard cock, I tilted her head to mine so that I could kiss her awake. She hummed, her lips moving with mine, her hand rising to cover the side of my face.

"Good morning, flower." I smiled warmly down at her, my heart feeling so full right in that moment.

"Good morning, Ambrose." She smiled back, her dark eyes warm and happy. "As much as I am loving this wake up, I need to use the bathroom."

"Go." I jerked my head to the entrance and watched as she crawled over and peeked out before leaving the tent all together.

Kal stretched, his eyes peeking open and landing on me. He grinned and rolled right into my ready hands. I gripped the nape of his neck as we kissed, deep and wet. By the time we finally drew apart, Lux was returning.

She yelped when Kal yanked her inside and right into his waiting lips. I chuckled and crawled out to take care of my business and get ready to go.

Kal eventually joined me outside, calling to Lux when he finished. Once she was ready, we finished packing everything up, shouldered our packs, and started walking.

It was around midnight when a yipping in the distance had my heart squeezing with fear. Kal's head snapped in the direction of the sounds, his eyes narrowing.

"Fuck." I hissed, frantically pushing a frozen Lux forward. "Run."

Lux darted a look towards the sounds as she started running, bypassing Kal who was drawing the scimitar he claimed. As we raced over the sand, I handed the curved blade I stole from the Drako ship over to Lux and pulled out the metallic rope. Both Kal and I stayed right on the heels of the woman in front of us, our eyes trained back towards the yipping that was now getting louder, closer.

"Move that ass, Lux!" Kal yelled when dark shadows appeared over the dunes.

"I am running as fast as I can. Fucking sand." She screamed back, her eyes wild with fear, the curved blade clutched in her hand.

"There is no fucking way we can outrun them." I snarled, counting the shadows and coming up with a pack of thirteen. "All we are doing is needlessly using up energy we could use to fight."

"Fuck." Kal exclaimed, sliding to a stop and turning to the shadows that were darting over the dunes at a surprising speed and coming straight for us.

I skidded to a stop right beside him, my body preparing for the fight.

"They are going to surround us." Kal described, shifting around to cover our six. "Come at us from all sides."

Lux jumped when the metallic rope in my hand snapped out, extending into a whip and slashing over the first dog to launch itself at us.

The whip slashed over the wild dog's face causing it to yelp in pain and scramble back. It was quickly replaced by another dog while a group of them circle around only to meet Kal's scimitar.

I snarled and slashed as the dogs darted in to attack only to meet the crack of my whip. While the whip was good for long distance fighting, it was kind of useless when they got too close. That's when the blade in my boot came in handy as I kicked out, sending one of the dogs flying back into a group of others.

I tried to keep track of how many I took down, but it was hard considering that the tough fuckers kept shifting, moving. That and they just wouldn't stay the fuck down.

At first they were darting forward one or two at a time, but then they seemed to change up their strategy and I suddenly had five of them snapping at me.

I snarled in fury and pain when one of the bastards made it passed the cracking whip and locked its jaws around my calf. It shook its head, violently ripping and tearing at my leg before attempting to yank me right off my feet.

I somehow kept the whip snapping at the same time my other fist punched down into the dog's head. I got one punch in when another one of the fuckers snapped at my arm. With a stumbling twist and a kick, I sent the creature flying in a spray of blood. Bringing my foot back and up, I stomped right down on the spine of the dog still latched on my leg. It's back broke with a disturbing crack enabling me to kick it off my leg with a sharp, tearing burn.

Kicking the limp dog away, I turned to throw off another dog that got a hold of my poncho. With a snap of the whip, I had the rest skittering away and regrouping.

They paced back and forth in front of me, growling and snarling, eyeing me hungrily. My whip snapped out, catching the fuckers before they even had a chance to dart away. They scattered before darting back in to meet my boot.

I sent another flying just as a flash of a blade took out another. The last dog darted passed me only to come flying back in another spray of blood.

"Fuck." Lux breathed heavily as she shook the blood off the curved blade I lent her.

Kal glared around the circle of dead wild dogs, expertly flicking the blood off the blade of his scimitar.

"Yeah." I agreed, reverting the whip back into the metallic rope it originally came as.

I hissed out in pain when I shifted to tuck the rope away and the bite marks in my leg flared up.

"You are hurt." Lux's gasp had Kal's head snapping to me and assessing over me to fall on the bloody circle of sand surrounding my boot.

"One of the fuckers got me." I shrugged, pulling the poncho aside so I could examine the damage. The pant leg was torn all to shit and covered in blood. Before I could do it myself, Kal crouched down and ripped the pant leg even more so he could see the wound better.

"Holy fuck, Ambrose." Lux exclaimed in horror, her hand coming up to cover her mouth.

My calf looked just as bad as my pant leg did, punctured and torn all to shit. The dog definitely did a good job. Mind you, the bastard kept yanking at my leg, hanging on no matter my movements which would explain the long ripping tears.

"This is bad." Kal stated calmly, rising to his feet. "Let's move up the dune further and find a place to get this cleaned and wrapped."

"Sounds good." I nodded, reaching out to take the curved blade from Lux's lax fingers and tucking it away.

My teeth clenched with the pain as I started to limp forward only for Kal to pull my arm over his shoulder and help me walk. Lux kept darting worried looks back at me as she led the way. We walked a couple dunes further before Kal determined that it was far enough away from the massacre.

"Sit." He ordered as he let my arm go.

With a sigh, I sat back in the ice cold sand, thankful to have the poncho to sit on. Lux dug out the first aid kit as Kal sliced my pant leg off at the knee and pulled my boot and sock off. Kal washed my leg with soap and water before digging in the kit.

I winced when he pulled out a bottle of some kind of liquid and read the label before cracking it open and pouring it on my leg. Burning pain sliced through me, so excruciating that it stole my breath. My hands gripped down on the leg that felt like it was melting off, the violently shaking leg, as my jaw clenched so tight that I feared for my teeth. A groan of pain uncontrollably broke from my chest and my body bowed over.

"I forgot how much it burns." Kal's regret filled voice echoed in my ears as hands gripped my shoulders and covered my back.

"What is it?" Lux's concerned voice asked.

"It's a type of disinfecting antibiotic that basically kills any and all germs. It burns like a motherfucker because it actually enters the blood stream." Kal described.

"No fucking kidding." I grated out, finally able to speak now that the pain was slowly starting to diminish.

My eyes opened to see Kal using some sort of glue to close the wounds and slathering cream on it and wrapping it up in a sterile cloth.

"That was worse than the bite itself." I hissed at him.

"At least we won't have to cut your leg off due to infection." He gave me a hinting look.

"I am sure I will feel a hell of a lot more grateful when the feeling of my leg melting off stops." I mentioned through my clenched teeth.

"I get that." Kal winced in commiseration, reaching out to grip my shoulder.

He and Lux packed everything away as I changed out my bloody sock for a clean one and pulled my boot back on.

I carefully stood and winced in pain. It was going to be a long night.

When Kal stepped over to help me walk, I shook my head at him and started to limp forward. I ignored the concerned looks that Lux and Kal shot me as they followed. Once I became used to the pain, it became easier and I was able to move faster. We kept going until the sun started kissing the horizon.

That was when we stopped and set up the camp. After we ate, Kal insisted on examining my leg. It was swollen and bruised as hell but the glue held and it thankfully didn't look infected. Kal cleaned it and put more cream on before wrapping it up again.

"Are you ok?" Lux asked, soothing her hand over my forehead and through my hair.

"Yeah. Just tired." I told her, cupping her face and drawing her lips to mine.

I kissed her slow and deep, relieved that neither her nor Kal had been hurt. If I had choice when it came to that, it would always be me.

"Are you sure?" She pressed, her lips moving against mine, her eyes examining mine.

"Very. Kal did a good job doctoring me up and his bedside manner is vastly better than Luke's." Luke Graden was one of the heads of Medical, a doctor with a very distinctive attitude that had a tendency to rub certain people the wrong way.

"Ok." She nodded in agreement and moved back so Kal could crawl over.

"Luke is definitely an acquired taste." Kal added his own agreement. "I am sorry that there was no painkillers. I don't like seeing you in pain."

"It's ok. I am just grateful that we had you. Neither Lux nor I would've known what any of that crap in that first aid kit was for. Thank you." I met him for a soft kiss.

"This was definitely worth the wait." He smiled warmly. "Try to get some sleep."

I nodded and shifted back to lay on the bedding, my arm cocking up under my head and giving the woman who laid herself on my chest more room. Kal spooned himself to Lux, his hand reaching over her to link with the one I laid on my belly.

I would love to say that I slept, and I did. Only it was in fits and starts, broken up by throbbing pain. Thankfully, my waking moments didn't disturb my sleeping partners.

NIGHT 11

When twilight rolled around, I felt more drained than I did when I first laid down but I still forced myself up and moving. We ate and packed and started walking.

And walking.

I frequently felt my exhausted mind drifting off only for stabbing pain to bring it right back to the present. The sky and sand seemed to extend in a vast endless sea of dark shadows and twinkling stars.

The time passed with one limping step after another. Limp, step, limp, step. Even the slide of the sand under my feet was never ending.

CHAPTER 16

KALBELIYAS

Ambrose was completely out of it, his eyes staring blindly over the surroundings, his raw looking lip caught in his teeth. Exhaustion and pain clearly getting to him. He didn't even react when my hands caught his shoulders to guide him to a stop so I could examine him.

"Ambrose." I called, watching his glazed eyes blink a couple times before settling on mine.

"Kal." He murmured, his forehead furrowing.

"We need to stop early." Lux noted, feeling over Ambrose's pale face. "He's not fevering but he's completely exhausted."

"I am fine." He snarled stubbornly, his hand coming up to catch Lux's wrist, bringing it down and linking their fingers together.

"A couple dunes more, then we will stop." I told her, ignoring Ambrose's claim.

"I am fine." He reiterated.

"You lead the way, I will guide him." I gestured for Lux to take the lead.

Ambrose kept hold of her hand as he lurched after her. As lost and in pain as he seemed, he was still keeping a good pace.

I used my hands on his shoulders to guide him over the dunes and down to the spot we were planning on camping at. We sat Ambrose down and got the tent set up along the dune, hidden among mounds of sand. We got the bedding rolled out and sat down with Ambrose to eat. He ate slowly, his eyes blinking tiredly.

I helped him into the tent and took off his shoes, socks, and hooded poncho then I checked over his leg to see that it was really swollen. Once I got him settled on his back, I used one of the packs to brace his foot up in order to help with the swelling. He was sleeping within seconds and I turned to pull a worried Lux back into my arms.

"He will be ok." I reassured her. "He just needs sleep."

"He's in so much pain." Lux sniffled softly, tears sliding down her face.

"He is, but he's strong." I pointed out, using my thumbs to rub her tears away. "He will heal."

Lux and I cuddled together as we slept. Well, she slept. I woke up every time that Ambrose did which was constantly throughout the rest of the night, his face twisted in pain, his body shifting to get more comfortable. Every time I was forced to resituate his leg on the pack. Fortunately, by the time the sun started to rise, his pain seemed to have settled. He was finally able to achieve a deep, restful sleep. And so was I.

NIGHT 12

By the time we woke up the next evening, Ambrose looked a hell of a lot better. His leg looked almost normal and his face once again had color. His eyes were clear and focused.

"Sorry." He winced when his eyes met mine.

"Don't apologize." I denied him, shifting a sleeping Lux off of me to the bedding and sitting up. "It honestly could've happened to any of us."

"I am glad it was me." He murmured softly.

"Ambrose." I shook my head slowly. "I get that, I do, because I am fucking furious that it was you and not me. I hate seeing you in pain."

Ambrose chuckled and carefully pushed himself up to a sitting position. My head tilted when he pulled the blanket off and examined his leg. It looked a lot better today, the bruising now a fading yellow, the swelling completely gone. He was healing quickly due to the Ranch's healing influence.

He shot me a smile and shifted around to crawl out of the tent. I followed him. We took care of our business and switched out with Lux. I smiled when we were packing things up and Ambrose took a moment to pull Lux into his arms. She ran her hands over his face and chest as she whispered up at him.

There was soft look of love in his eyes as he stared down at her, his fingers brushing her hair back, his palm cupping her face. I frowned as my heart skipped a beat before raging forth in a rapid staccato. I studied those eyes, seeing the clear love they carried in those dark blue depths, and I realized that I had seen that look in his eyes before. Centered on her, centered on me. So many times.

I knew that he retained some sort of love for her from their past relationship but now that love was very clearly deeper, stronger. And he also felt it for me.

My eyes dropped away as my own love for the two of them jumped up to strangle my throat.

I loved them.

Forcing my mind away from that jarring realization, I returned to packing. Now was not the time.

Once we were packed up, we started walking.

We made good time that night and the next and we finally made it far enough east that the dunes started to stretch out with lengths of hard ground spaced between them. This made it easier yet more difficult as we were forced to climb up and over the high dunes before reaching the solid ground on the other side.

Although the climbing took time, we were able to make that time up by basically sliding down the other sides to the bottom.

"This is kind of fun." Lux giggled as she pushed herself up to her feet.

"I kind of wish we had a sled." Ambrose laughed as he took the hand I held out to him and allowed me to pull him up to his feet.

Once the sun started coming up, we found a spot along the bottom of a dune surrounded by rocks. It was still hidden in the sand, providing us with a soft spot to sleep on.

"Do you think the Drakos finally gave up?" Lux asked as we settled down to sleep.

"I don't know. We are getting close to the Abu Minqar Base so maybe or maybe they are still searching for us further out." Ambrose shrugged. "However, I don't think we should drop our guard until we are home."

"Agreed." I nodded slowly.

"That doesn't make me feel better." Lux sighed wearily.

"It wasn't meant to." Ambrose shook his head.

We fell asleep only to wake up and walk some more.

It wasn't until the next night that we came onto an abandoned town that was set close to a flat topped hill. Ambrose directed us in the direction of that hill only to pause at the edge of the town.

"Now what?" I frowned at him as we found places to sit on the broken stoop of a run down house.

"Now we wait." Ambrose shrugged nonchalantly. "If they don't have us in their sights yet they will as soon as it gets light out. Once they see that we are human they will send out a team to question us."

He was right.

I rested back into the cracked wall behind me and stretched my feet out. I couldn't help but smile when Lux leaned into Ambrose's side. He slid his arm around her and pulled her back with him as he too relaxed into the wall behind us. We talked quietly as the moon and stars slowly moved across the dark sky above.

As soon as the sun started peeking above the horizon a number of desert Camo covered individuals appeared out of the dilapidated buildings around us, their weapons trained right on us.

Lux automatically put her hands up as Ambrose stood to meet them.

"Ambrose Sokolov. Rocky Mountain Base. Head of the Bay. Security, Mike Echo Charlie Hotel 1." Ambrose stated in a firm, calm tone.

One of the camo masked individuals touched their ear and a muffled voice repeated Ambrose's words before once again focusing completely on us.

No one moved, no one said anything for long dragging moments before the masked person touched their ear once again. The individual listened for a couple seconds before slicing a sharp hand out.

The group silently disappeared back into the buildings with the main one giving us a nod before they too disappeared.

"That's it?" Lux breathed in disbelief.

"They are still there." Ambrose shook his head. "They will stay until our ride arrives."

"Our ride?" I frowned at him.

"They would've had to contact the Base in order to get confirmation on my identity. As soon as the Base found out we were still alive they would immediately have Wings in the air, coming to get us." Ambrose explained.

"That was quick." I sighed, slightly shocked at the suddenness of it all.

I groaned, my head dropping when a purplish black energy cloud suddenly descended out of the sky and circled around me. Pacifier. He checked me over before settling on my back. His energy pulsed with disappointment and anger.

The disappointment disappeared when I held my shackled wrists up and gave them a hard shake. The cloud shifted down my arms to surround the shackles, examining them before taking on an even angrier feel.

It took about twenty minutes before a sudden flash of light slammed to stop right above our heads. The Andromadan ship slowly hummed to the ground. The door opened and the ramp lowered. Ambrose gave the hidden Egyptian team a grateful wave as we picked up our packs and walked up the ramp and into the ship.

We walked into the large cockpit to see Wings seated in the pilot's seat that was set to the back of the room behind a small metallic table. There was another seat to the side of the room in front of another small metallic table. Two more seats were set in front of the view screen and a long metallic table.

Scope, a blind sniper who was also connected to my sister, Asp, was sitting in one of those chairs, his hand pressed to the table. He had dark red hair and hazel eyes with naturally tanned skin. While his face was clear the rest of his body was covered in freckles. Both men were soldiers who worked under Malachi's command on the first team.

Along one side sat a semi circle of six seats meant for passengers. That was where we headed as soon as we found spots to stow our packs.

The moment we were seated and the energy straps were activated, Wings lifted up and we were flying back to the Base.

"What took you so long?" Wings asked conversationally. Wings was an interesting looking man with white blond hair and dark brown eyes.

"Walking over miles and miles of fucking sand dunes takes a bit." Ambrose told him.

"Seriously?" Scope asked, his voice filled with disbelief.

"Over 250 kilometers." Ambrose sighed tiredly.

"And I thought our vacation to the Peruvian jungle was bad." Wings winced.

"Yeah." Ambrose breathed.

"Is there a reason your friendly Pleiadean couldn't help with any of that?" Wings asked curiously, eyeing me.

"I also would like to know that answer." Pacifier asked from beside me, his hooded head turned my way.

I knew what that hood covered. A shaggy length of purplish black hair, purple eyes lined with black, and effervescent skin covered with both the facial Pleiadean metallic marks right along with black scars that covered the length of his body. I also knew that those black marks were his Judge marks, lines of mineral that helped him conduct the massive amounts of energy that the universe held.

"The shackles. They were made to contain Pleiadean abilities. I am guessing it was designed from the blueprints of the large containments that the Drako got their hands on." I explained, once again holding my wrists up.

My brother's black tipped fingers caught my wrist and brought it over to him so he could examine the shackle.

"I thought we destroyed all of those blueprints." Scope scowled.

"We did." I confirmed. "There is no way Ech missed anything. The shackles were most likely created before the blueprints were destroyed and could viably be the only ones."

"How did they get them on you?" Scope questioned.

"I was a little distracted and one of the bastards got the jump on me. I don't even know how he did it as he knocked my ass out. I woke up shackled and locked in a cage." I cringed at that memory.

"You are never distracted." Pac pointed out softly.

"I was that day. I had my connections to worry about." I shared with him.

His hood came up and he examined the man and woman sitting next to me.

My mouth tightened when that hood turned to me. "You are going to have to wait until the shackles are off. They are grounding all of my abilities."

With a small jolt of power, the shackle in his hand fell open. I rolled my eyes and handed over the other shackle that also immediately opened under the onslaught of Pac's power.

As soon as the shackles were off, I rubbed at my torn, raw wrists at the same time I tilted my head back and opened my third eye for his delving touch. His black fingertip touched down and the memories of the last few weeks flashed through my mind as he studied them.

Pac drew his finger back, releasing me from his hold. "I like them." He stated as he swirled into energy.

"Like you have a choice." I yelled after him as he flashed away.

"I like him too." Lux laughed.

"For fuck sakes." I groaned causing Ambrose and Scope to join in on Lux's laughter.

CHAPTER 17

KALBELIYAS

We reached the Base and were immediately ushered through the smoothly squared off rock halls straight to Medical.

This particular part of the Base was carved into two large areas that were connected by a wide hallway. The front area had a half wall that blocked the entryway from the rest and housed a number of waiting chairs. There was a large circular nursing station in the middle of the room with eight exam rooms, four that ran along each side. There was some bathrooms, a staff room, and some supply rooms that were set into the back wall where the hall leading to the back section was placed.

The back area boasted another large circular nursing station. Surgery rooms, testing rooms, and the DNA lab ran along the side walls there. Along the back wall were more supply rooms and the doctors' offices.

We were met by Dr. Carter Claws, one of Pac's connections, Asp and Ech, Malachi DeMarques who was the human head of the Base and the leader of the first team, and Lysander who was the Nordic head of Base.

The wolfish Carter with his brown hair, scruff covered face, yellow eyes circled with black was the one who checked us over while the others waited. The man also carried numerous scars that now held a thin line of the same black mineral that quilted Pac. This was due to an unfortunate need for blood after he and Skylar were viciously attacked by a Fallen. That need was efficiently and dangerously taken care of by Pacifier.

Carter quickly proclaimed us malnourished but healthy and released us from his care with orders to drink lots of fluid and eat something fattening.

The moment I stepped out of the exam room I had two armfuls of worried girls. All of my sisters looked exactly the same, even boasting the exact same Pleiadian metallic design formation that marked their faces. Effervescent skin and feline shaped eyes were joined by high cheekbones and wide mouths. The biggest difference between them was their coloration. As for the two currently present, Asp had blue eyes and hair while Ech had orange hair and eyes.

Both of my sisters assessed me with narrowed eyes before Ech's eyes landed on Lux.

Ech started hopping happily and darted forward to hug my woman. "Pac told us that you are connected to Kal. I am so excited that we are now sisters."

Lux giggled softly and hugged the woman back.

While Lux and I were busy with my sisters, Ambrose was talking with Malachi and Lysander, probably debriefing.

Lysander had his long curtain of shining blond hair braided down his back, his striped white and blue eyes centered on Ambrose. The brown haired, brown eyed, and bearded Malachi frowned slightly before his eyes lit up and his hand fell to Ambrose's shoulder. Something about the seeing the man touch Ambrose in such a familiar way had me moving over to them. I didn't like that at all.

Malachi looked surprised when I brushed his hand away at the same time that I pulled Ambrose out of the man's reach and pushed him towards Lux. Our intelligent woman immediately caught Ambrose's hand and arm, holding him to her.

"Uh, sorry." Malachi spoke, confused at my possessive movements but understanding that he might have overstepped in some way.

My mind knew that I was overreacting but my heart was fully on board.

"Kal?" Ech appeared at my side, her eyes questioning as they drew over Ambrose and Lux.

"Mine." I growled possessively as I backed away from the men watching me cautiously.

"Kal." Ambrose's voice called as his hand came up to grip my shoulder in a reassuring grip.

"Mine." I reiterated firmly, making sure that the men understood that I was not fond of people who weren't family touching my connections.

"I got you, man." Malachi held his hands up in surrender.

"Good." I nodded slowly and turned back to see Ambrose studying me with a mixture of confusion and warmth.

Gripped the nape of his neck, I pulled his mouth into mine. My kiss was hard and deep, marking my territory.

When I let him go, my eyes turned down to Lux, silently telling her the same thing. She was mine.

"Ok, Kal." She nodded slowly, accepting my claim.

"Now that you have been checked over and debriefed, why don't you go get some rest?" Lysander stated, drawing our attention to him.

"Good idea." Ambrose agreed, guiding both Lux and I to the door and out of Medical.

"Kal, wait." Ech called after us, darting around Lux and Ambrose to catch my arm and pull me aside.

I frowned down at my sister as Ambrose and Lux backed off to give us some space.

"What are you doing? Do you know who that is?" Ech whispered in a soft yet frantic voice, her eyes darting over Ambrose.

"Yes." I confirmed, my brow furrowing in confusion.

"How can...? What are you doing with him? He's the one who hurt Diad!" She hissed angrily.

"No, he's not." I slowly shook my head as my eyebrows rose in disbelief.

"He's the one Stella was cheating on Diad with." Her quiet voice clipped out.

"Actually, sister dearest, Ambrose came first so if we are going to turn that shit around to blame someone else than the one who really deserves that blame, Stella, it would be Diad who was the one Stella was cheating with. But then those two weren't the only ones that bitch was using and abusing. If my memory serves me correctly, there was a number of others." I hissed down into Ech's stunned face. "And to blame someone, anyone, for being sexually abused is pure bullshit."

"Sexual abuse?" Ech's face paled.

"What would you call it, Ech?" I asked her, furious. "What would you call being taken advantage of like that when you aren't in your right mind? You may want to blame Ambrose for Diad's pain, but that man, one of my connections, is completely blameless. And if you still don't believe me, ask the woman who loves him, Stella's own sister." With that I left her, spinning around and rejoining my connections to walk down the hall.

We stayed quiet until we reached Ambrose's suite. He used his palm on the security pad to unlock the door and we walked into the bachelor suite. A made bed was set in the middle of the back wall. Built in cupboards and shelves ran along one wall with a TV and some gaming systems set in front of a couch that was facing it. Behind the couch and against the other wall was a small kitchenette and a round table and three chairs.

"I know what that was about." Ambrose spoke up as he shut the door behind us.

"That was about bullshit." I snarled angrily.

I didn't know if I was more furious or more hurt that she did that. My own sister. I stood by her, stayed with her, took care of her, supported her every decision. Fuck, I even accepted her choice of the man who initially denied her for another woman. And all she had to give me in return was highly erroneous assumptions when it came to my connection.

"That was about a woman worried about the mentality of the man she loves. A man who almost lost his sanity. And I didn't help with that." Ambrose stated, gesturing to the door.

"No fucking way are you taking that on." Lux snapped, ripping her hooded poncho off and throwing it across the room.

"I knew that she was seeing him. I could've told him what she was doing but I didn't." Ambrose defended.

"I knew she was sleeping with both of you along with a bunch of others. And I didn't say anything. Why? Because it wasn't any of my fucking business." Lux stated, crossing her arms and narrowing her eyes on him. "Plus, do you really think that he would've believed you if you told him? Because the ones I told, my ex boyfriend for one, didn't believe me. They all needed proof. They needed to see it with their own damned eyes."

"She's right." I snapped out. "Stella had that man was so tied up that he denied his own fucking conversance. He practically threw away his own family. Both him and Ech should be thanking you for opening his eyes to that woman."

"That right there, Ambrose." Lux pointed at me.

Ambrose nodded slowly, his eyes still carrying that haunted look that I hated.

"Hey." I reached up to grip the sides of his face and turn it towards mine. My mouth opened to speak when the door dinging had my head snapping to the annoying thing.

"For fuck sakes." I snarled, stomping over and ripping the door open.

"Nope, nope, nope." Diad came storming in with an anxious Ech on his heels.

"Seriously?" I snarled, slamming the door shut behind the two.

"I never blamed you." Diad dove right in, pointing at Ambrose. "Not once. In fact, I felt fucking bad for you. I know you hated her and that she had you trapped. For years. And I should've come to you and talked to you. But I couldn't find it within myself..."

"Stop." Ambrose held his hands up in surrender as he backed up. "Please, just stop. She fucked us both over. Neither one of us blames the other. It's time to let that shit go and to stop letting it fuck us up."

Diad froze as his eyes examined Ambrose's eyes. "I am sorry. And I know that it was only because I caught her with you that I couldn't ignore the red flags she was giving me any longer. And for that I am extremely grateful."

"I told you." Lux claimed, jabbing her finger at Ambrose and drawing a smile from him.

"I am sorry too." Ech stepped forward, her eyes shining, her face filled with regret. "I was so worried about Diad being hurt that I was completely blind to everyone else's pain in that situation and I should've been more understanding."

"It's ok." Ambrose nodded at her, his face taking on a look of relief.

I felt my own tension dissipate when the haunted look left his eyes. "Now that we have that covered, get out."

"Kal." Ech hissed at my rudeness.

"Ech, I love you but I just spent weeks walking across a desert with limited food and water. I am starving and exhausted and in sore need of a shower. So...get out." I started to herd the two surprised family members to the door.

"I wasn't going to say anything." Ech crinkled her nose at me.

"That's very nice of you." I opened the door and ushered them through. "Goodnight."

"Goodnight." Diad called as I slammed the door behind them.

I stripped out of my clothes as I made a beeline straight to the bathroom. Lux blushed when I walked naked passed her while Ambrose let out a sharp whistle.

Flipping on the shower, I started scrubbing myself down. I was frankly amazed at the amount of sand I ended up washing down the drain. I left the shower running and stepped out, holding the door open for the naked woman waiting. Lux grinned and eyed me as she stepped inside. I chuckled and dried myself off, pursing my lips and making kissing sounds at the naked man who was leaning against the doorframe.

Both of us turned to watch our woman wash her sexy little body down. Suds ran down her smooth, wet skin in delightful rivers.

"How the fuck did we get so lucky?" I mumbled, mesmerized.

"I have no clue." Ambrose breathed. "But I am going to take that luck and run. There is no way I am ever letting her go again."

"I am in complete agreement of that." I held my cocked up hand out to him. He blindly gripped my hand in his own, sealing the deal. "Now, go wash that cock because the moment I wake up I want it in my mouth."

Leaving him with that, I sauntered out.

CHAPTER 18

AMBROSE

T he maddening man was going to drive me insane. And he apparently had one hell of a possessive bent.

I traded places with a wet, slippery woman, unfortunately too exhausted to do anything about that. Kal was right, that would have to wait until I had more energy. I washed what felt like buckets of sand from my body and dried off. I chuckled when I walked out of the bathroom to see that both Kal and Lux had helped themselves to my underwear with Lux adding one of my shirts to her attire.

Pulling another set of underwear up my damp thighs, I settled them around my hips as I walked over to the cupboard and dug out some snacks. After being gone for so long, I was pretty sure that any food in my fridge had gone bad.

Surprisingly, when I risked a peek it was empty. Thankfully someone must have come in while I was gone.

Kal and Lux opened the snacks, carrying them over to the coffee table. We cuddled together on the couch and watched a quick half an hour comedy as we gorged ourselves on crap.

"It's nice to be back but after spending so long in the desert, alone, it almost feels like there is too many people." Lux mentioned from her sideways lean into the side of my body relaxed under one of the arms I tucked around her. Kal had his arm wrapped around the legs she cocked up and over his lap.

"It will take a bit to get back to normal." I told her.

"I honestly just want to sleep." Kal's jaw cracked as he yawned.

"Let's do it." I caught up the woman leaning against me, carried her over to the bed and flopping back onto it with her falling beside me.

"Later. Too tired." Kal collapsed on his stomach beside us.

I was out within seconds.

When I woke up it was indeed to Kal's mouth on my cock. My very hard, raging with pleasure, cock. And my very sensitive balls.

My hips were moving, driving my throbbing length through the heated suction of his mouth and right down the mind blowing tight tube of his esophagus.

The man really knew what he was doing. My hand found the back of his head, twisting into the red strands my fingers found there.

"Fuck, Kal." I moaned softly, fire tingling up and down limbs.

His red eyes tilted up to meet mine, bright with desire. His cheeks were concaved around the erotically glistening muscle he was bobbing up and down, his tanned face flushed. His fingers squeezed and rolled my testicles, pushing my rising pleasure even higher.

I could feel it building and building with ever draw, every wicked stroke of his tongue. With a snarl, I pushed him back and gripped my edging root tightly, just barely holding my orgasm back.

"That wasn't nice." Kal growled softly.

"Neither is this." I warned as my body snapped into action.

Before he could even cry out, I had him pinned under me on the bed. Stomach down.

My eyes caught on the confused woman who was now sitting up, blinking sleepily at us.

Leaning down, I hissed into his ear as I kicked his legs apart. "As good as that mouth of yours is, it is not where I plan on coming."

"Fuck." Kal groaned as I pushed my hard dick along the crack of the ass I was planning on possessing.

"Lux, flower, grab the bottle in the nightstand for me." I ordered the woman who was now flushed and wide eyed.

"Are you going to fuck him?" She asked as she did as I asked, her eyes gleaming with anticipation.

"Oh yeah." I hissed, releasing the hip I was holding down so I could hold my hand out for her to squirt some lube into.

The first palmful was coated over my dick, the second was rubbed into the tight little asshole I found between those muscular cheeks. He groaned, his hips jerked, when I pushed my fingers into his ass, working the lube deep inside of him, preparing him for the length of my dick. The delightfully strong muscles of his ass twitched and squeezed around my thrusting digits.

His voice wheezed out when the tips of my fingers found his prostate and began to rub over it. "I warned you."

"Fuck." He emoted, his tone high pitched, his hips shuddering almost violently.

"Just wait until I show you what I can do with my cock." I stated as I finger fucked his ass and played with his prostate.

His groans were coming regularly as his ass worked back against me. His hand slid out to link with Lux's who was now kneeling beside us. He breathed out in a rush when I pulled my fingers free of the delicious hold of his ass only to replace them with the tip of my cock.

Kal cried out, his hand white knuckled on Lux's, when I broke through the ring of muscles at his entrance and pushed my dick through those gloriously tight folds. He tightened around me before releasing, his bowls hot and mind blowing. The pleasurable friction of my entrance was only compounded when I hit root deep, my balls pressing into his, and drew right back out.

My dick stroked deep as I slowly worked his muscles open. Gripping his arms, I pulled him up and back until he was sitting on my lap. My arms circled his chest, one gripping his heaving pec, the other finding the pulsing extension of his cock.

His red eyes were practically glowing, wild with pleasure. He grunted, his body jolting along mine when I began to fuck up into his ass with hard pounds. I grinned when I felt my cock draw over the swollen nodule of his prostate with every stoke.

"He looks delicious, doesn't he, Lux?" My voice rasped along his ear as my hand jerked his cock.

"He does." She licked her lips, her hungry eyes devouring him.

"Why don't you have a taste, my flower?" I coaxed, watching her eyes light up with desire. She shifted over to kneel in front of us, her hands gliding over his heaving chest.

Kal's head fell back to my shoulder when she found his nipples. First her fingers played then her lips got in on the action.

"Oh, that looks real nice." I crooned in his ear, my teeth nipping at the tender lobe.

"Fuck...you." He grated out breathlessly.

"Maybe tomorrow." I sucked his lobe in, biting down on it before releasing it and moving down to the tensed stretch of his neck. "Today is my turn."

Lux, my beautiful woman, moved my hand from his dick and took over milking him. Her eyes centered on the action. I felt my balls pulse at the feel of her eyes moving over them. Something about having her watch us was really getting to me.

"Any minute now she's going to take that big dick of yours into her mouth. She's going to stroke those sensitive glands with her tongue as she sucks the come right out of you." I rasped, feeling his ass clench around me in reaction to my words.

Kal cried out, his body arching, when she did indeed duck down and guide his very flushed crown between her lips. The wet sound of licking and sucking joined the slapping of my hips and balls.

Kal's eyes rolled back in his head and his body went bow tight, shuddering in my arms. His ass contracted tightly before milking at my dick, coming. Lux moaned softly, her lids lowered in pleasure as she sucked his pleasure out and swallowed the sperm his flexing dick was releasing.

I kept fucking him through his pleasure, quickening my strokes. His orgasm slowed and his body relaxed, his unfocused eyes staring up at the ceiling. My hand glided up to grip his jaw and turn his face to mine. My lips found his, feeding on his taste.

"Ambrose." He stuttered out against my lips.

"This ass is mine." I stated, thrusting even harder, railing his ass, my ass.

My balls began to draw up, my orgasm boiling within.

"Yes." He groaned, his body once again tensing with the beginnings of another orgasm.

"Are you going to come again?" I asked, licking at his pleasure tightened lips. "Come all over my cock? Paint Lux's wicked little tongue with your orgasm? Is she as good of a little cocksucker as you are?"

"Fuck, yes." He stammered. "So fucking good."

"Gonna need to feel that, Kal." I slammed my dick deep and gave it a hard ground right over his prostate. "Now."

That did it, threw him right over the edge and taking me with him. Pleasure gripped me tight and threw me high. My eyes blanked and my breathing stalled. Our bodies shuddered and strained against one another, his ass massaging around my dick, milking the burn of my sperm right up and out of my testicles. That scalding output of rapture spurted deep into the bowels I was buried in. Mind destroying shot after shot. Pure ecstasy.

My orgasm abated and Lux helped me lower Kal's limp body to the bed. He groaned, his boneless body shivering with after shocks. Withdrawing my well used dick from the glorious hold of his bowels, I soothed my hands over his sweat slicked back and leaned down to press kisses over his nape.

"Never before." He slurred.

"You never had me before." I whispered, reaching out to take the soapy cloth Lux handed me and used it to clean him and me up.

"I don't know if I will survive having you again." He moaned softly, his arms finally moving and pushing himself up on his elbows.

"You will." I chuckled, shifting over to drag a surprised Lux under me. "Now, since I did such a good job, I am going to treat myself by eating some pussy."

Lux arched and cried out when I spread her legs and licked over her pussy. I moaned at the taste that filled my mouth, my lips sucking at her delightfully swollen clit.

"Fuck, you taste good." I growled. "I am going to have to eat this pussy every day."

"Ambrose." Lux cried out with the pleasure I was driving through her.

I licked her, slurping up her juices as I drew even more from her. My tongue worked her clit, rolling and flicking over the throbbing bud. Needing to taste her right from the source, I pushed my tongue inside of her, licking along her tunnel, fucking her with my stiffened organ. Her hips rolled with my movements, shivering within my hold.

I could tell this wouldn't take long, my eyes moving up from the spread of her legs to see Kal playing with one of her breasts. His hands were plumping that breast, his fingers pinching and rolling her aroused nipple. Her body was arching with sinuous movements, her lips parted around the cries that were falling from her chest. Her body was glistening, her face flushed.

She was so fucking gorgeous in her pleasure.

Sliding my tongue free of the tight grip her pussy had on it, I returned to her clit. My tongue rubbed over it with firm strokes, relishing in the feel of that bundle of nerves running over it. It didn't take long before I felt her bursting, her clit pulsing under my manipulations, her pussy flooding my mouth with her come.

Her legs shook with her orgasm as her hips twisted in my hold, grinding my mouth even harder against her.

I kept licking, driving her pleasure to completion.

"Holy fuck." She breathed, her body finally relaxing under me. I licked my lips of her taste as I knelt up and looked down at her soft, slickened pussy. Swollen and pink.

"Fuck that was good." I hummed.

"Yeah, it was." Lux agreed with a shaky nod.

"She really is a delicious little snack." Kal agreed from his satisfied sprawl at her side.

"You are a pretty good little snack as well." She smiled over at him.

"Little?" His head rose and he scowled at her.

"I mean big snack. Huge. Like, mind boggling huge." She exclaimed, wide eyed and clearly trying to cover her screw up.

I couldn't help but laugh, causing them both to join in.

"It's ok, Lux. I understand what you were trying to say." Kal rolled over to kiss her. "I am big."

"Brat." She giggled into his mouth.

Sitting up to check the time, I threw my legs over the side of the bed in preparation to get up. It was around four in the morning. We had slept for a good sixteen hours which made sense with how tired we had been. Something about walking for miles with very little food and getting limited sleep.

Stretching, I walked into the bathroom in order to shower, shave, and get going. I needed to check the Bay, meet with Malachi and Lysander about my replacement, start getting together a list of supplies I would need out at the Ranch. Malachi was even talking about setting up an airfield out there with a couple of Nordic ships that Lysander was planning on bringing in. While Nordic ships did come in and out with deliveries, they never stayed. That was something that the Nordics never offered to share with us before.

Due to the Drako mothership that tried to take out the Base that was now changing. The fucking thing almost succeeded because we only had three ships available to defend ourselves with. Then there was the fact that the Andromadans actually gave Wings a specially designed craft.

The Nordics were now open to sharing their ships with the caveat that those ships were flown by their own pilots. Lysander was thinking that having the Nordic ships stored at the Ranch and the Andromadan crafts here at the Base would help secure both areas.

Thusly, my transfer request was actually good timing.

Clean and shaved, I got dressed and turned to look at the man lounging on the bed.

"I have an important meeting today with Lysander and Malachi." I shared with him as I walked to the kitchen to make some coffee. "But it sounds like the transfer is going to be easier than I thought. Although, that doesn't diminish the amount of work I am going to have to put in to get everything I need moved out there and set up."

"Sounds good. I need to meet with Pac and collect my stuff. I am also going to need to get my research packed up and ready to go." Kal mentioned as he rose from the bed and joined me in the kitchen.

"Research?" I frowned at him.

"I am helping River, Callden, and Madron with translating the temple that we found in the Antarctic Pyramid." He explained.

"You know, I always kind of had thing for the professor type. If you slap on some glasses I am pretty sure you wouldn't be able to keep me off of you." I eyed him, picturing him wearing a dark brown vested suit and a set of black framed glasses. "Yeah, that'll get me there."

"You are a thirsty bastard." Kal laughed at the heated look in my eyes.

"Like you don't have fantasies." I rolled my eyes at him.

"I can't lie. You with a set of coveralls tied around your waist, bare chested, sweaty and smeared with grease is definitely something I wouldn't mind seeing." He grinned at me.

"I think I might be able to pull that off for you." I returned his grin.

"I have one." Lux mentioned as she stepped out of the steaming bathroom.

"Oh?" Kal turned to her, his eyes curious.

"I always kind of wanted to watch someone getting tattooed." She shared, walking over to dig in my cupboards.

She pulled out a set of drawstring sweatpants and a hoody, both of which she pulled on commando style. I inwardly smirked at the thought of knowing that she was going to spend the day completely naked under my clothes.

"Fuck, now that's really not nice." Kal hissed, his desire bright eyes intent on her.

"Heard." I held my knuckles up for him to tap. "I honestly thought about getting some ink just never got around to it."

"I guess we need to find an artist now don't we." Lux gave me a mischievous smile.

"I know how to tattoo." Kal stated, crossing his arms.

"Uh, what?" I turned to him in surprise.

"Yeah. It's actually something that is done in various ways on a lot of worlds including my home world. Although, it's not very commonly utilized by the Pleiadeans so much anymore. I ended up getting interested in it during my investigations and taught myself in my downtime. I practiced with various mediums and in the different traditions, including some of the human traditions." Kal explained. "All I need to do is track down the equipment and ink I need and you need to tell me what you want so that I can draw it out."

"I want a mechanical clock in the middle of my chest with rivers of grease extending out, over my torso and around my arms." I described, using my hands to show him.

"I gotcha." He smiled and nodded, turning to Lux. "Ambrose has meetings today and I have to pack and get my shit together."

"I think I will go check on the Garden and pick up my new coms and some other things I could use out at the ranch." Lux shared her plans with us.

"Awesome. I will come find you when I am done." Kal cupped her face and pressed a kiss to her lips before disappearing right in front of my eyes.

"Oh." Lux's face took on a surprised look. "I completely forgot that he can do that."

"So did I." I laughed, pulling her in for a kiss of my own. "I need to get going, I will message you later."

"Ok." She smiled up at me, her fingers playing over my newly shaven chin.

With one last kiss, I caught up the travel mug of coffee I made and left.

CHAPTER 19

LUX

After Ambrose left I grabbed something to eat and wandered down to the Garden. It was still dark, too early for the working day to start. That didn't stop me from wandering into the huge cavern with its 100 foot high ceilings.

I traversed the dirt paths that wound through the wood sided dirt plots, using the low light provided by the bioluminescent area. I stepped up into one of the plots that looked a little sad and began to weed as I sang to the plants.

They really liked it when I sang to them. They all perked up and turned to me. I felt a sense of peace settle over me at the feel their life thrumming through the damp loam my fingers were working through. This is what I missed.

I was still working when the various growth lights flipped on and the misting systems kicked in.

"How was the desert?" Herman, the head of the Garden asked from the path beside the plot I was working in.

"Barren." I gave him a happy smile as I sifted my fingers through the cool dirt. "And hot. A lot of walking."

"I bet." He gave a deep belly chuckle. "It's nice to see you here. Missed you, girl."

"I missed you too." I smiled at the greying, husky man that was almost like a beloved uncle. "But I should let you know that I am only here until Ambrose gets his transfer figured out."

"Ambrose, huh? So, the two of you finally pulled your thumbs out of your asses?" He smiled happily.

"You could say that." I nodded slowly.

"Good. About damned time. If you have time before you leave, the poppies in the back east section could use some attention." He threw a thumb in that direction as he ambled away.

I finished with the plot I was working in and decided to go do my running before coming back and tending to the poppies.

My first stop was to Operations where I picked up my new coms. Operations was a highly secure room that had lines of computer covered desks running along one wall and a huge, round conference table that was set to the other side. The room also boasted a well worn, comfortable looking couch.

Coms up. I messaged Ambrose to let him know I was hooked back into the system.

Heard, flower. He messaged back.

Going shopping. Any requests? I typed out as I made my way to the Store area in order to restock on some of the items I was running low on.

Shit, yeah, but I need to do up a list so don't worry about it. He returned.

I am going there now. Just send me the list. I shook my head at my coms.

Give me a couple minutes.

I entered the extensive Store cavern and grabbed a cart. I had just started through the aisles when something occurred to me.

Should I put in a request for a bigger tent since we are going to be sharing? I asked.

Already taken care of, flower. Grayson has security already moving your stuff because they have our new tent set up. Not to brag or anything but it has a California king sized bed. His tone was definitely bragging.

Stop bragging and get on that list. I ordered playfully.

Within seconds I had the list and began to add his stuff to the cart along with the odd thing here and there that I thought he or Kal would like.

Once I was inventoried out, I carried everything back to Ambrose's suite and paused to stare at the locked door and the security panel. I didn't think this one through when I left this morning. With a wince, I decided to try it. I was honestly surprised when my palm print worked and the door unlocked for me.

Ambrose must've had them put me on as a suite resident. Dropping the arm straining cloth bags onto the couch, I began to go through them, separating the stuff and packing it away in the cupboards. I wasn't sure exactly when we would be officially moving and I didn't want to leave the stuff out to clutter the suite.

I gasped and jumped in surprise when someone suddenly appeared in the suite with me. It took me a second to recognize Kal who was carrying two duffle bags of stuff.

"I don't have much." He noted as he dropped the bags on the now empty couch.

CHAPTER 20

KALBELIYAS

I swirled into energy and made my way over to my brother's suite where I was currently rooming. A four bedroom that he was living in with his connections, Carter and Skylar.

I dropped to physical in my room and gathered up some clean clothes to take with me into the bathroom. After I showered and shaved off the two week old beard I had going, I returned to my room and began to pack my stuff up.

"What is the plan here?" Pac asked from the doorjamb he was leaning against.

He was dressed in a set of dark grey slacks and a vest with a purple dress shirt. His black and purple hair was still damp from the shower. Purple eyes surrounded by black were centered right on me.

"I am pretty sure you already know that." I shot him a knowing look.

"You are moving to the Ranch." He nodded slowly, his brow furrowing.

"Lux has a connection with plants. Being out there among them is good for her." I reminded him.

"I am not disagreeing with that." He stated, his eyes watching me pack.

"Is there an issue?" I frowned at how weird he was acting as I straightened from the bag.

"No, no." He shook his head. "I knew that you would find your connection, connections, eventually. I just didn't know it would come with a move."

"Ela is out there so it's not like I am going to be alone." I tried to reassure him.

"I know." He stated softly. "It seems like we were just starting to connect, as brothers."

"I am going to miss you too, Pac, and I am sure we will visit each other all the time." I told him honestly. And I would miss him. I always did.

"I don't know if I ever told you how proud I am of you." I paused at his words, my heart giving a strange jerk.

"Proud?" I questioned, confused.

"You took care of them when I wasn't there. When I was in training and testing and dad was still working. And then again when dad died and I was working. Hell, you still take care of them." He detailed in a way I really didn't need. I blinked down at the bag, pushing away the burning sensation that rose in my eyes.

"I was their big brother." I stated firmly.

"So was I." Pac informed me.

"And you were mine. You were the one who taught me how to be a big brother. You may not have been there for everything but you made sure that they had you in me." I returned back to my packing.

"No, Kal, that was all you." He said in a soft voice. "I may have shown you the way but you were the one who actually walked it."

"You gave up everything for us." I vehemently denied, shoving the next pile into my bag and turning back to the cupboard to grab more.

"That doesn't diminish what you gave up." He maddeningly pushed.

"I didn't give up anything, Pac. I did what I wanted." I argued, grabbing an armful out of the cupboard.

"Kal." Pac caught my arms and stopped me, his eyes staring into mine. "I am trying to tell you how much I appreciate everything you have done for me, for them."

"I get that, Pac." I sighed, my eyes dropping from his. "But I really didn't do much."

"See, the thing is, I may have taught you to be a big brother, but in the end, I didn't end up being that person. Not to any of you. I became a Judge. That's who I was. That's all I was. I wasn't a brother, I wasn't a friend, I wasn't even a man. Instead, I left all of that to you. Because I knew that you were what they needed. Not me. You were there for them every step of the way, for their entire lives. You protected them, you taught them, you supported them, you took care of them. You loved them." He was really working on breaking me.

"Stop, Pac, just, please, stop. I don't want this. Fuck, I don't even need this." I shook my head and pulled free of his hands. "I chose my path and I walked it. And I don't regret one minute of it. As for your appreciation...I never wanted that."

"You wanted a brother." Pac nodded in understanding.

"Yeah, I did. But that wasn't part of my path. And while you are here, now, and you have been trying which has been frankly awesome, you are still walking your own path. And that's a good thing. We all have our own paths to travel." I reassured him, tucking my armload into my bag.

"We do." He agreed, his voice sounding sad.

"We are always going to be brothers, Pac. That will never change. But I have come to realize that it will never be like it was when we were little boys with two parents and no worries. The reality is that you now have a family that you love and I am in the process of building my own family. We will always be there for each other but we won't ever be best friends. We won't see each other everyday, we won't talk the deep talks because that's not who we are now. You will do your job and I will figure out who I am in this world." I felt those tears edging as I gave him the cold, hard reality.

The last weeks I spent with him and his new family had been great and I did indeed get to spend more time with my brother but our interactions still seemed to have a certain line that had inadvertently been drawn between us. We didn't do deep and tended to keep things fun and surface.

Seeing him with his connections and how close and open they were with each other helped me truly understand that while I missed having my big brother, that relationship we once had was completely gone.

"I am sorry." He whispered.

"Don't be. I am not." I turned to grip his shoulder. "That day, the day you returned home a Judge. That was the day I knew that I had lost my brother and there was good chance that I would never get him back. That day, I cried for what both of us lost. That was the day I came to terms with everything and decided to move on, move forward. There was no point in dwelling on any of it, it's not like I could change it. But, I still had them and they needed me."

Pac was silent for a long time, his head bowed to the floor while I continued to pack. "You are right. And that is fucking heartbreaking. I did everything I could to save my family, to give them what I thought they needed, and in the end all I did was leave them with more pain. You know, I remember those times. So clearly sometimes. That little red haired, red eyed boy who would follow me everywhere. I remember how much I loved him. That love is gone now. Changed into something that seems so far away. It's like you are always there, but just out of reach. And I don't know how to cross that distance."

"As much as I want to, I can't fix that for you, Pac." I crossed my arms and turned back to him. "But, as you said, I am always here."

Pac nodded slowly, his eyes coming up to meet mime. "So am I. I know I haven't been the most open person when it comes to personal things but I am working on that. If you ever want to talk, I have ears that are ready to listen."

"Thank you, Pac." I went to turn back and finish packing only to find his hands once again catching me, pulling me into his arms for a hug.

My arms automatically hugged him back. As I said, he would always be my brother despite the emotional distance between us. When he drew back, his hands gripped the side of my head and his forehead pressed into mine. My hands came up to grip his head, holding us together.

"I do love you." His eyes stared into mine as he whispered.

"I love you too." I returned with a smile.

After a few moments, we released each other and he stepped back. "I know the details of what happened but I don't know how it effected you."

"The desert?" I questioned.

"More like being stuck without your abilities in the desert." He detailed, his eyes taking on a slightly concerned look.

"Honestly, having such a vital piece of myself removed was not easy. But it would've been a lot worse if I didn't have them." I shared him. "They kept my mind off that loss and kept it centered on my physical attributes and the knowledge I carried. It made me see things with new eyes and appreciate who I was as a person, a man, and not just a mythical, all powerful Pleiadean."

"I have to say, it's weird seeing a Pleiadean as tanned as you are. It looks good on you." Pac noted, his head tilting to the side as he studied me.

"Yeah? Ela is getting quite the tan out at the Ranch." I mentioned.

"She's darker than Asp and Ech but not half as dark as you." Pac refuted.

"It's funny, we mostly walked at night and didn't actually spend that much time out in the sun. A couple hours here and there." I described for him.

"It was enough." He noted, pulling the bottom of my shirt up to reveal my tanned abdomen.

"Get." I playful slapped his hand away.

"Woah, with that tan I am guessing that your ass is bright white." Carter pointed out from the doorway.

"I am not commenting on that." I pointed at my brother-in-law.

Carter grinned as he ran his eyes over my form. "Did you eat yet?"

"No." I shook my head. "We ate before we went to bed."

"You need to eat." He pointed at me before disappearing from the door. I rolled my eyes at the sound of him moving around in the kitchen.

"I didn't lose that much weight." I frowned down at myself.

"You lost enough that even I was concerned when I saw you come out of the bathroom this morning. I didn't see it yesterday because of the clothing you were wearing." Pac stated, stepping forward to catch my healed wrists and the scars left behind. "I am also not a fan of seeing my brother carrying shackle scars."

"They aren't so bad." I shrugged, kind of liking the proof of my connections with Lux and Ambrose. To me, that is what they were, a physical reminder of the time we spent together, just us. "Nothing like the scars you carry." I pointed a finger at one of the black marks.

Pac frowned at me, his black tipped fingers moving over my shackle scars. "I still don't like them. I spent weeks searching for you and I couldn't find you. We didn't know if you were abducted by the Drako's and being tortured within an inch of your life or if you were already dead. The girls were losing their minds with worry. Hell, I was worried."

"I am sorry you went through that." I cringed on his behalf, reaching out to cover his hand.

"I cannot tell you how relieved I was to get the news that you were ok. Alive." Pac frowned.

"I get what this is now." I couldn't help but chuckle as I gestured my pointed finger between the two of us. "You aren't getting rid of me that easily."

"Yeah, yeah." Pac rolled his eyes at me. "Can I help it if I have developed some issues pertaining to the loss of my brother?"

"Nope." I shook my head, knowing how that felt. "If it makes you feel better, I give you permission to stalk me all you need to."

"Don't promise anything you aren't willing to follow through with, because I might just take you up on it." Pac chuckled softly.

"I have no issues with that. I never have. But don't whine to me if you get an eye full of something you never wanted to see." I warned him.

"I will keep that in mind." Pac outright laughed.

"Get your asses out here, breakfast is ready." Carter called from the kitchen.

Catching up my bags, I walked out into the main area of the suite to see Skylar had woken up. Skylar had dark, almost black eyes which looked out from a very pale face. Her long, dark hair boasted streaks of white that extended from her temples.

My sister-in-law was dancing around the kitchen as she sang. "I told you so. I told you so. I to-old you so-o-o!"

That was the day that I realized my sister-in-law was truly talented at so many things.

Dancing was not one of them.

CHAPTER 21

AMBROSE

My first stop was to Operations in order to get set up with my new coms before messaging Malachi and Lysander about our meeting.

Even though it was still early, they were eager to get going on this so we all met at Lysander's office. Malachi and I took the seats in front of Lysander's heavy, wooden desk while he sat in the office chair behind it.

"Ok, the ships will take about a week and a half to get here. Five in total. The pilots are combat trained and highly recommended. They have been fully debriefed by both the Nordic Ministry and the Andromadan Alliance on the current situation here on Earth. The commander of the group will be working almost side by side with Grayson. Their security clearance will be the similar to his barring certain highly sensitive intelligence. As for maintaining their ships and whatever other transports that are housed out there, that will be under your control. Callden and I both agreed to have you trained in the maintenance of both Nordic and Andromadan crafts instead of bringing someone in for that. You and Harper will be the only ones given clearance on this as you were the one given permission to use Nordic tech to develop the new weapons." Lysander explained what he had already put into place.

"I am going to need more autonomy when it comes to the ships than I was given with the weapons." I informed them. "Especially since it will be just Harper and I. I cannot take time out to seek permission for every little thing I do pertaining to those ships."

"We understand that. And since Andromada seems to trust you with their flight tech, we are willing to do the same. Although, we would like to be kept up to date on any changes you make or anything you decide to develop from the tech." Lysander stated.

"I honestly wouldn't dream of developing anything from yours or the Andromadans tech without your permission. That is a disrespect I refuse to even indulge. As for the changes, if I see an area for advancement when it comes to maintaining those ships, I will simply make those changes, just as I do with the transports here. And as I do here, I will make extensive reports and instructions on what I have changed and how I changed it." I reassured the man.

"I have seen what you have done to make the transports even better and I am honestly impressed which is why we are giving you the clearance you need to do that. As for the respect you are showing us, I appreciate that." Lysander bowed his head towards me.

"Your training is being set up out at the Ranch so that Harper can also take part in it." Malachi described from the seat beside me. "Bane and Grayson have already built another mechanical tent that will also double as the hanger for the crafts. Maintenance supplies for the ships in question are being brought in and set up as we speak. As for anything else you might need, the first team is already out there raiding garages for a list that Harper helpfully generated for them. This will be your baby and you will be fully in charge when it comes to the maintenance of these ships. Your title has been changed along with your new clearance. Code, Alpha Sierra Charlie Mike 1. You are now the Head of Alliance Space Craft Mechanics."

"This is not just a Base title but one that is also being recognized by the Alliance. It is their hope to eventually make a hub here on Earth and are setting you up to be the one who runs it." Lysander smiled happily.

"Let me get this straight." I held up a finger. "They are planning on having me run what is essentially an extraterrestrial truck stop with full garage capabilities."

"Well, yes." Malachi laughed as Lysander looked confused. "A truck stop is a place set along well used highways that offers a bunch of amenities to the travellers who use it. They were created to give long haul drivers somewhere to stop if needed."

"Exactly." Lysander nodded at me.

"Very well." I nodded slowly. "However, I do have some rules of my own if that is going to be the case. As I am sure so does Malachi. And one of those rules is going to be that this will be a fully backed Alliance run hub. Highly secure. I am not willing to invite bullshit we aren't advanced enough to handle and I am definitely not willing to have a repeat of the Drako's current occupation happen with other races."

"That is completely understandable and you will indeed have that backing. You are going to be taking care of Alliance ships and people and the security made available to you will reflect that." Lysander reassured me.

"Good. I am going to need contacts for inventory purposes." I told them.

"You will be provided those contacts as soon as the ships and the inventory coming in with them arrive." Lysander nodded in agreement.

"You are also going to have to adjust Wings' clearance. You know damned well he's going to be sticking his nose in all of this and rightly so. The man has some frankly brilliant ideas." I described what I knew of the first team member. Wings was an expert. He could drive and fly just about anything and was brilliant when it came to pinpointing ways of making transports better. Unfortunately, he wasn't so brilliant when it came to implementing those changes and quite often needed a mechanics help. Usual that person is either me or Harper. Well, me now that Harper had moved to the Ranch.

"I will look into that." Malachi nodded.

"I can't speak for the Andromadans but I don't see a problem with it. As long as he does it under your watch." Lysander shrugged.

"That's already a rule. He's not allowed to play unless Harper or I are there to help." I assured him.

"Good." Lysander nodded.

"I am guessing Kalbeliyas is going with you." Malachi brought up.

"Yeah. You are going to have to have his 'identification' updated to reflect his 'transfer'." I air quoted. The Base had been forced to create false identities for the family in order to hide their true heritage from the rest of the world. This was done because the Pleiadeans had only given permission to that the official residents of the Rocky Mountain Base to know who they were. It was a secret none of us dared let out for fear of the very heavy consequences. The Pleiadeans were considered a myth for a reason. They were world enders, star destroyers. Anything that was deemed detrimental to the health of the universe was removed. Killed, destroyed, or even wiped clean. That could include the memories of those they came across.

"Should I be adding a last name change to that?" Malachi grinned mischievously.

"Yes." I nodded, making a split second decision. "You can do the same with Lux. Sokolov for both."

"Will do." Malachi nodded, already typing in his coms.

"I need to get my replacement set up." I gave them a set of raised eyebrows.

"We wanted to get your opinion on that as you will still be working very close with him." Malachi lifted his head from his coms.

"Nate." I didn't even have to think about that. "He's been my second for a while now."

"He's fairly young isn't he?" Lysander noted, bringing up a holographic image of the young man's file. Nate was only 22 years old.

"True, but he grew up working in a garage. I have worked with him since the day he got here five years ago. He's almost just as versatile as I am and he's got a good head on his shoulders." I shared my opinion with them.

"Is he ready for a command post?" Lysander delved.

"Tell me, who has been running the Bay while I have been gone?" I questioned, already knowing the answer.

"Nate." Malachi chuckled, nodding in understanding.

"I am heading there next to check on him and make sure he's ok handling things. And I am willing to travel back and forth if needed." I told them. "But I would like to get out to the Ranch as soon as possible. I want to make sure everything is getting set up in a way that is going to work for me."

"I assumed as much which is why I have Wings booked to fly you out tomorrow." Malachi nodded. "And thank you for being so accommodating with everything."

"I am pretty sure that you are the ones being accommodating." I shook my head in denial.

"Actually, this is something that we have been playing around with for awhile. We were just waiting for the perfect person to come along and offer themselves up." Lysander gave me a sly grin.

"I was always here." I held my arms out.

"Yes, but you were also doing your thing in the Bay and dealing with other shit. So, while we did think you were the perfect person, we didn't want to upset your life more than it already was." Malachi shot me a knowing look.

"I would've welcomed it." I sighed, chewing on my lip.

"At the time, we didn't see any of what was happening. We just saw you in some sort of relationship. We didn't realize that it was what it was." Malachi sighed, rubbing a hand over his face.

"It wasn't anyone's business." I shook my head at them.

"True." Malachi nodded slowly.

"And now it's done." I told them, my voice firm. I was done going over and over that shit. I was ready to move on from that part of my life, move forward with the ones I loved. Yes, loved. I loved them and the moment we were settled I was going to tell them. I wanted to do something nice for them to show them how much they meant to me. "I am going to head to the Bay and get Nate set up."

"Sounds good. Let us know if you need anything else." Lysander rose as I did.

"I will." I nodded, heading for the door and the Bay.

"Welcome back, man." Nate grinned as he held his hand out to me. The tall, young man had come a long way from the boy I first met. Nate had lost his family in the pandemic and subsequent occupation. He fought to stay alive and ended up hooking up with another group who were making their way to the Base.

Nate was also one of the guys that most of the younger ladies around the Base went gaga over. Honestly, the kid looked a lot like me with naturally tanned skin and a thickly muscled build. The difference was that his hair was a dark brown and his eyes were a pale amber.

"I am not back." I caught his hand in mine and pulled him in for a side hug.

"What do you mean you aren't back?" He frowned at me.

"I am transferring out to the Ranch." I explained to him. "And am no longer head of the Bay. I have been given a new title, head of Alliance Space Craft Mechanics."

"If you are leaving who is going to be the head of the Bay?" He asked with a concerned look.

"You are." I gripped his shoulder proudly.

"Are you serious?" He asked, his voice slightly stunned.

"You earned it. You do the job on my days off and have been doing it for the last weeks while I have been gone." I praised. "And I am just a quick ten minute spaceship flight away if you ever need a hand."

"I don't know, man." He winced, rubbing the back of his neck and looking around the massive Bay filled with lines of various transports. The Bay was at the side of the mountain and had two main entrances. One was for the helicopters to land on and be brought in along with the ground vehicles that used the hidden mountain roads. The other was a large tunnel that ran up at an angle out of the mountain, it was used for the small planes and spaceships to take off and land.

"You got this." I gave his shoulder a shake. "Just make sure to keep on the guys. And listen to them. Report everything and keep the inventory up. Believe me, it fucking sucks when you run out of the shit you need."

"Fuck, ok." Nate nodded slowly his eyes still carrying a wary look.

"Come on, you got me for the day before I head out tomorrow." I walked over and pulled on a set of coveralls.

"I can call you anytime?" He asked nervously.

"Call me, message me. For anything, Nate." I confirmed with a nod.

I spent the morning helping Nate get settled into his new role and fixing some of the backlog.

It was after lunch when I was bent over the hood of one of the all-terrain vehicles that the Farm used when a very attractive red haired head appeared beside mine.

"What are we doing?" Kal asked as he looked over the engine.

"We are putting on some coveralls." I ordered.

"I am way ahead of you." He gestured to his hips where he had the coveralls tied around his waist.

"Hand me that socket wrench." I pointed to the metallic rolling table that was covered with tools.

Kal caught up the tool and flipped it through his fingers before handing it over.

"Lux?" I asked, using the socket wrench to loosen off some bolts.

"Herman put her to work in the Garden." Kal shrugged, taking the bolts I was handing to him.

"I have a new title." I grinned at him, working the cover off the engine so I could find what was burning. "I am now the head of Alliance Space Craft Mechanics and tomorrow I get to see my new office."

"Yeah?" He grinned at me. "Apparently we both get to see our new offices tomorrow. My brother-in-law is in the process of getting that set up for me."

"Are you packed?" I asked him, knowing that I still needed to do that.

"I am and so are you. Lux and I took it upon ourselves to pack your stuff up during lunch today. Your clothes and personal items are all ready for when we leave in the morning." Kal handed me the screwdriver I pointed at.

"Thank you for that." I leaned over and kissed him, adding a little tongue before turning back to the engine.

"So, your crew is all set for your departure?" He questioned.

"As ready as they ever will be." I shrugged, knowing that they would be ok.

"And this new title?" He pressed, watching me work with a set of slowly brightening eyes.

"I am going to be running a garage for Alliance spaceships. The Nordics are bringing in a team of five combat pilots that are going to be based out of the Ranch. The Alliance is going to be training me and Harper on how to maintain both the Nordic crafts and the Andromadan ones." I shared with him.

"It's about damned time the Alliance got off their asses and brought in some real fire power." Kal scoffed.

"They had their reasons." I defended the races that had generously stepped up to help us with the Drako occupation.

"Their reasons were bullshit. You can't support someone by sitting on a fence. You are either in or out." He described with a disappointed shake of his head.

"And what exactly are you all doing?" I pointed out the hypocrisy in his statement.

"There is no fence sitting for us. In this, we are out." He grunted, watching me switch some parts out.

"Is that what you call blowing up the mothership that attacked the Base?" I questioned, knowing of their involvement in that.

"We didn't get permission to do that because of Earth or the Alliance. We got permission because of one very important individual who is going to have a vast effect on the universe as a whole. Someone who will herald a new era." He described. "If it wasn't for that individual's wellbeing we would've stayed out of it."

"That's harsh." I winced at that cold logic.

"Would you like to know what makes it even harsher?" He asked, his eyes darkening with the depth of this conversation. "Asp was in the Base at the time and she's pregnant. Pregnant Pleiadeans can't utilize their energy half so she was stuck there. If the mothership had succeeded in destroying the Base, she would've died right along with the rest of you."

"Neutrality really isn't what they make it out to be." I winced on his behalf, reaching out to grip his shoulder and leaving smears of grease on the pale burnt orange shirt he was wearing.

He was quiet for a long moment as I worked before he cleared his throat. "Thank you for understanding."

"Why wouldn't I understand? I was simply confused as to your actions that night. You explained it to me. As for the rest, I get it. I know that being a juror isn't just a job to you, it's a part of who you are, who your whole race is. You all have to make the hard, heartbreaking decisions, such as standing by and watching you own sister die, so that the rest of us can live and advance. You have to watch as we all live our lives without being able to actually live your own. And you do it knowing that if the investigation you are doing comes up negative, you will also have to watch us be removed. As heart breaking as that shit is, you do it because you know that in the end it's what's best for the universe and every other life that resides in it." I finished explaining my thoughts on it all and turned to take the cover from his slack fingers.

"I love you." He whispered through slack lips.

"For fuck sakes." I snarled, turning to him with a set of frustrated eyes. "I was going to plan this whole thing so I could tell you but you just had to go and blurt it out."

"Just fucking say it." His face cleared of its shock and he rolled his eyes at me. "We can plan something special for Lux."

"I love you too." I caught the back of his neck and brought him in so my lips could show him exactly how much I loved him.

I shivered when he cupped the side of my face and returned that love with every stroke of his tongue.

"Just for curiosities sake, what were you planning?" He asked, his lips brushing along mine, his eyes half lidded.

Hooking my fingers in the side of his tied coveralls, I gave them a pull. "Me, commando in a set of coveralls. Just for you."

"Fuck." He groaned, his head falling back. "I am guessing you were going to get me to tattoo you in front of Lux for her."

"Yup." I nodded, turning back to finish with the engine I was working on.

"Just for curiosities sake, was there any other fantasies you might have?" He asked with a set of eyes gleaming with avarice.

"I don't know." I shrugged. "I haven't really come across anything beyond being with the two of you."

"Ok, let's think about this. I am going to mention something and you picture me or Lux that way and tell me if it arouses you or not." Kal not so subtly pushed.

"Seriously?" I groaned, closing the hood and rolling the table over to the side cupboards to put the tools away. "Why don't I just think about it for a bit and let you know what I come up with?"

"Fine." He rolled his eyes at me.

This was not going to be easy. I wasn't inexperienced when it came to sex, at all, but I never really came across anything that hit me right in the junk. Not like the thought of Kal in glasses did.

"I will say this." I shot him a wicked grin. "If it involves you and Lux, I am definitely on board."

He met my wicked grin with one of his own.

CHAPTER 22

LUX

I had just finished with the poppies and was making my way back to the Garden entrance when I suddenly found myself thrown over a hard shoulder.

If I didn't recognize that ass I would definitely know who it was by the way he appeared out of thin air.

"Hello, Kal." I greeted, bracing my hands on his waist as he walked me down the paths towards the entrance.

"Lux." He greeted back.

"I hope you got the right one. I am pretty sure Malachi won't be happy if he finds out that we are kidnapping strange women." I heard Ambrose call. "Never mind, I recognize that ass."

"I should hope so." I shifted my down hanging head so I could see around Kal's waist. Ambrose was standing near the entrance, waiting for us to reach him. "I recognized Kal's."

"She really did." Kal bragged.

"Hurry up." Ambrose began to frantically gesture us forward. "Herman is coming and he doesn't look happy."

"Fuck." Kal hissed and began to jog.

Ambrose waved at someone I couldn't see as both of men cackled maniacally and raced out of the Garden and down the halls with me still over Kal's shoulder.

"Is there a reason you two are pretending to kidnap me?" I asked as they attempted to sneak me through the busy halls. Ambrose would check to see if the coast was clear before they would both race down the hall.

"It makes things more exciting." Kal gave a wicked laugh.

That was when the emergency tones dropped on our coms followed by an announcement voiced by Marko.

This is only a drill. Repeat this is only a drill. All security personnel please be on the lookout. One Lux Sokolov was taken from the Garden around 4:45 this afternoon by two men. One Ambrose Sokolov and one Kalbeliyas Sokolov. Please be advised that both men may be armed and are definitely having way too much fun.

"Seriously?" I gasped, tilting myself around to eye a laughing Ambrose who was now peeking around a corner. "Is this exciting enough for you?"

"Oh yeah." Kal laughed.

That was when my mind latched onto the other important thing that Marko stated. "You had our names changed?"

"I did." Ambrose confirmed with a proud grin. "Now you will never get away from me."

"Good." I grunted happily. "That's one less thing I have to take care of now."

Ambrose's face flushed with joy as Kal laughed and clapped him on the shoulder.

Ambrose's coms went off with an incoming call. "Ambrose." He answered abruptly.

"Wings is coming from the left so you are going to have to go back and take the other left." River's voice guided.

"Oh, an accessory." Ambrose hummed happily as they backed up and did as she said.

"Do you realize how much security the Base has?" I demanded as they started racing down that hall passed a number of surprised people.

"That's what makes it interesting. Plus, Marko is right, it's honestly a great drill for them to be regularly performing." Ambrose stated, slowing down at the next t-section.

"Marko already has it on the weekly docket." River described in an amused voice. "Straight. Move quick. Bear is coming up that way but is caught in a bottleneck. Go."

The men darting across the hall was followed by Bear yelling for us to stop.

"You are going to have to hide." River hissed out. "Bear is coming in fast with Woody on his heels and Malachi is coming from the other side."

"Here." Kal handed me over to Ambrose and disappeared. One of the doors popped open and Kal was gesturing us inside and shutting the door behind us.

"That was impressive." River claimed as I looked around the occupied but empty suite we were hiding in.

"You haven't seen anything yet." Kal grinned cockily.

"Remember, it's just a drill." River warned.

"Oh, I know. That doesn't mean I can't have any fun." Kal rubbed his hands together.

"What? Noooo, would I do that? No. I have no idea why you can't get into the camera's, must be a glitch of something. No, no, let me do it, you are in the middle of the drill." I heard River's muffled voice echo telling me she was talking to someone else. "They have Carter tracking your scent." She hissed softly into the coms.

"Got it." Ambrose set me down and darted into the bathroom only to return with a bottle that he proceeded to spray all over us.

"That is strong." I winced at the heavy male musk that now covered me.

"Right?" Kal coughed and waved his hand around in front of his face.

"Oh shit." River snarled. "Chriton's in the game."

"Fuck." Ambrose groaned.

"What?" I asked curiously, trying to breathe shallow.

"Chriton can walk through walls. He's probably going from room to room." Kal explained. "Which means we can't hide here indefinitely."

"I have an idea." Ambrose chuckled, his eyes lighting with anticipation.

"This is not going to end well." I groaned, knowing that look.

"It's clear. They are moving to the basement." River's voice had Ambrose levering me over his shoulder.

Kal opened the door and Ambrose led the way down the hall before taking a left down the next followed by another right.

I frowned in confusion when we ducked into the Library and snuck passed a man sitting at a table, fully engrossed in a sudoku book.

The comforting room had a large check out desk set into the wall at one side with stacks of books aisling the other side of the long length of room. The tables started just beyond the desk and extended to the back of the room.

Going straight to the back, we paused outside a door and waited for Kal to do his thing. A loud male yelp of surprise was followed by Kal opening the door.

A blue eyed Andromadan that I recognized as Coren, one of the Guardians, was sitting on the floor beside on overturned office chair. Andromadans, as a race, boasted tall bodies and attractively exotic features that were only accented with their beautiful dark skin and black hair. The Guardians carried bright blue eyes, a familial trait, while the Ancients boasted bright green eyes.

"Oh my God. You are kidnapping a Guardian too?" I exclaimed as Ambrose dropped me down into another chair.

"Hey, we have to fight fire with fire." Ambrose shrugged. "We use one Guardian to control the other."

"It really is very smart." Coren righted his chair and sat down while throwing glares toward the redheaded man blocking the door.

Kal was standing with his arms crossed and his legs braced, his eyes narrowed in warning.

"Now, you are going to be a good little boy and come with us." Kal grinned as Ambrose sprayed Coren down.

"Fuck, that's rank." Coren coughed, turning his head in an attempt to get away from the smell.

"Blame Carter." Kal advised, peeking out the door before taking the bottle and disappearing.

"River, we need a route to the office section." Ambrose explained as he wrote something out on a piece of paper that he handed to Coren.

Coren read the paper and rolled his eyes before holding it up for Ambrose to take a picture.

I laughed when I read the paper.

I have been kidnapped. If I am not found within the next two hours, I am in danger of losing...my supper. Please help me. Fast. I am getting hungry.

"I think I know what you are planning. I wish you luck." River giggled.

Kal returned with a satisfied look on his face and I was once again thrown over a shoulder. Kal eyed the Guardian and rubbed a set of energy cracking fingers together threateningly.

"Time to go." He gave Coren a dark grin.

"All right." Coren shrugged, pushing up from the chair and following Ambrose and I out with Kal bringing up the rear.

As we moved I heard Ambrose type something out and send off a message.

People laughed, really getting into it, as we ran by them to our next stopping place.

"Get the led out, next left. They are making a beeline to the Library." River advised.

"Isn't this cheating?" Coren asked the woman.

"Nope." River quickly denied. "This is having someone on the inside."

"Nice spin." Coren chuckled, pausing to lean against the wall as Kal disappeared right in front of another office.

Another yelp was followed by the door opening to show another angry looking Andromadan. We rushed inside and I was once again set down.

"Hey, Madron." Coren grinned in greeting to the green eyed ancient. "I've been kidnapped."

"Apparently so have I." Madron growled softly, crossing his arms and glaring around at us.

"Your husband is going to be so proud." Kal laughed right before he once again disappeared.

Ambrose wrote out another sign that he handed to Madron.

"For fuck sakes." Madron burst into laughter when he read the sign.

Please help me Wings, you are my only hope. PS. Bring snacks, Coren is hungry.

Ambrose snapped a picture of Madron laughing while holding the sign. Kal returned with the bottle and sprayed him down with that disgusting scent. "Fucking hell." Madron choked.

"Who are we kidnapping now?" River asked causing Madron to started laughing again.

"I am thinking that we need a Nordic or two." Ambrose chuckled gleefully.

"Lysander is three doors down." Madron mentioned.

"Too easy." Ambrose's eyes gleamed as Kal cackled. They really were having a lot of fun.

"The twins share an office at the end of the hall." Coren jabbed his thumb in the direction of the office.

"Let's go while the others are still distracted by the Library." Ambrose caught my hand and we guided the way down the hall to dart into yet another office that Kal helpfully opened for us.

One of the tall Nordic twins, Krishnia, was standing in front of one of the desks, legs braced, arms crossed. The man, like his brother, was extensively scarred. He had blond hair striped with white and boasted one blue eye and one green. His twin, Rashnia, looked exactly the same only opposite. Rashnia's hair was white striped with blond and he had one green eye and one blue.

"I might have to have a talk with Malachi about his security." He stated, his eyebrows rising in surprise at the sight of Coren and Madron.

"Maybe talk to your brother." Kal chuckled as Ambrose made up his sign.

Coren is still hungry. Oh, and if you didn't notice, I too have been kidnapped.

Krishnia calmly held up the sign for Ambrose to take a picture before he was sprayed down like the rest of us.

"You know, once you send those pictures you are going to have to change up the smell. Carter's going to catch on." I mentioned.

"Already taken care of." Kal's arrogant grin told me what he had been doing when he disappeared. Leading Carter on a merry chase.

"Aren't you kidnapped?" Krishnia looked down at me with narrowed eyes.

"Yup." I grinned up at him as Kal circled my waist and pulled me back into his arms.

"I can see why you lot are winning. You have your kidnappee's helping right along with an Operator." Krishnia pointed out as we once again snuck out and headed down the hall, following River's directions.

"Well, to be honest, we don't really need her. We have Kal who can be our scout." Ambrose accurately pointed out.

"I see your point." Krishnia sighed when he realized that we did indeed have an ability laden Pleiadean on our side.

Once we were far enough away from the office section, Ambrose sent out his pictures which sent everyone there while we moved further away. Kal once again disappeared only to reappear minutes later.

We hit Medical, ducked inside, and very obviously snuck passed the confused looking nurse to the back section that housed all of the doctors' offices.

Dr. Luke Graden looked up and grinned maniacally when we walked in. "About damned time. I even made up my own sign."

Luke was a scruffy looking man, similar to Carter, with dark brown hair and grey eyes.

They have come for me. Tell my wife I am going to be late for dinner. Also, Stand, I need you to cover Medical for me.

Ambrose laughed and took his picture before spraying Luke down.

"Fuck, no wonder you all stink." Luke whined, his face looking slightly green.

"Where to next?" Coren asked curiously.

"I know." Kal grinned as he led the way. We slipped down the halls, dodging dozens of security, down to yet another suite.

"I hear you guys are hungry." Ech greeted when Kal opened the door for us.

"We could eat." Coren shrugged as we all walked inside the suite and found places to sit.

"This is fun." I greeted my friend with a hug.

"It certainly sounds like it." Ech laughed, hugging me back. I joined her at the small kitchenette, helping her get some snacks together for everyone. "They are sending out pictures of the new kidnappee's and warnings to watch for the group in question. I am guessing that the residents aren't actually being very helpful on that front."

"Nope. I think they are too amused watching security run around for that." Ambrose chuckled, coming over to lend a hand.

"I have to say, this was a really good idea. Unfortunately, they kind of picked the wrong people to claim as kidnappers. I mean, come on, a Pleiadean?" Luke stated, taking the bowls filled with snacks that Ambrose handed him and setting them out on the coffee table.

"Yeah, they kind of fucked up on that." Madron nodded in agreement, helping himself to some snacks. "Although, it is only a matter of time before Chriton comes across us."

"We can take him." Kal smirked from the chair he was sitting in.

"And Carter?" Coren pointed out, dipping into the snacks.

"Oh, yeah." Luke pointed at Kal.

"I guess we will have to see on that one." Kal shrugged, catching up his own handful.

"I take it we are just waiting for them to track us down now." Krishnia mentioned around a mouthful.

"We could continue kidnapping people." Ambrose shrugged. "But eventually the line of kidnappee's following us down the hall is going to get too long."

"Or." I held up a finger. "We could take pictures hinting at where we are but never really giving it away."

"I like that idea." Luke pointed at me.

"Ok, Luke and Krishnia, stand against that wall and hold each other as if you are scared." Ambrose directed, pointing at the wall.

Both men really got into it, going for pure dramatics as they pretended to be scared. Those pictures were sent into Operations who immediately distributed it to the populace.

The next set was taken in the hall with Coren pretending to be dragged down the hall and Ambrose's hand holding a spreadeagled

Madron face first into the wall. Madron twisted his facial muscles until it looked like he was wailing.

The last was of me hanging over Kal's back, my hand outstretched to the camera.

CHAPTER 23

KALBELIYAS

I t took us half an hour and various more pictures before someone scratched at the door. Ech opened it up for Carter's canine form to come flouncing in. He barked out a greeting and sat down on his butt.

"Busted." Luke laughed.

"Not quite." I grinned as I crossed my arms and leaned back against the door. "He's stuck in canine form and has no way to contact the others."

Carter whined out, his head dropping when he realized that he was just as kidnapped as the rest of us. Ambrose snapped another picture of Carter's dejected form and sent it in. Thirty seconds later Pac appeared, his hooded head landing on me.

"Sit." I ordered my brother with a grin.

Pac shook his head at me but did as I asked, snatching up one of the square covered plates and walking it over to the round table that Ech and Lux were sitting at.

I laughed when Pac fed some of the chips inside the bowl on the table to Carter who was resting his head on Pac's knee.

When another knock came at the door, I opened it up to see a large group of people on the other side.

"Seriously?" Malachi exclaimed, barging into the room with Callden on his heels. "None of you thought to try and free yourselves?"

"Why would we? They have snacks." Coren held up one of those snacks. "Where is Chriton? I am surprised he didn't drop by."

"We didn't want to lose anymore people." Callden crossed his arms and shook his head at the group of snacking people.

"Smart." Ambrose nodded. "Yeah, so, we are going to claim the win."

"As much as I want to argue that I can't." Malachi groaned.

Chriton broke through the group, giving a dramatic sob and racing forward to catch Coren up in his arms. "Thank God, I was so worried. Are you ok? Does your belly hurt? Did they feed you too much?"

"They didn't feed me enough." Coren wailed as they rocked each other.

"Noooo!" Chriton screamed, turning wide, pleading eyes to Callden. "We need to get him supper! Stat!"

Callden groaned and dropped his head into his hands. "They are over a hundred years old."

"If they haven't grown up by now, they never will." Madron noted as he gripped down on Callden's shoulder.

"That's what I am afraid of." Callden exclaimed, his pleading eyes coming up to meet Madron's.

"Why is everyone in my place?" Diad's voice came from the middle of the laughing group still standing in the doorway. "You do know that Catro's place is bigger, right?"

"I thought about that but assumed that they would look for us there." I grinned at Diad who squeezed through and made a beeline straight to Ech for a very long kiss.

"We did." Malachi confirmed with a head nod.

"See." I pointed to Malachi.

"Give me my husband back." Lysander walked inside, grabbing Luke's hand and pulling him towards the door.

"Krish, we have to go get the kids." Rash called from the door.

"Alright, I am out. This has honestly been the funnest kidnapping experience I have ever had." Krish pushed up from the couch and sauntered out the door with a wave.

"Speaking of." Madron looked down at his coms before pushing himself up and bellowing. "Wings!"

"In the back." Wings called back.

"Did you see? I got kidnapped." Madron bragged as he made his way to the back of the group.

"Yeah, you did." Wings stated proudly, catching Madron's hand as they walked off.

"Not to be rude, but unless you are related to me, get." Diad began to shoo everyone out the door. "Maybe work the kinks out of this scenario before trying again."

I laughed and stepped aside as Malachi and the Guardians squeezed out the door and Scope snuck inside.

"Asp and Skylar are coming." He stated as the hall slowly cleared.

Diad held the door open as he waited for the two women to arrive. Skylar was carrying a small bag that she handed to Carter. He gripped the bag in his jaws and strolled into the bathroom.

Skylar snuggled up into Pac's hooded form as his arms surrounded her in a gentle yet protective way. Every movement screamed the love he felt for her.

"All right, supper." Diad rubbed his hands together and began to dig in the fridge and cupboards.

I turned to smile at Ambrose who had Lux tucked back into his chest.

Scope sat down in the living room chair and pulled Asp into his lap. His eyes closed and his face pressed into the side of hers. She was smiling, covering the side of his face with her palm.

Carter came walking out, dressed and carrying the empty bag. "Proper prior planning is important." He claimed.

"It really is." Ambrose chuckled.

"How the hell did this get so blown up?" Diad asked as he cooked.

"Well, we playfully kidnapped Lux from the Garden and apparently Herman reported the incident." Ambrose explained to the group. "I am guessing that they tracked us down on the camera's and when they saw us goofing around they decided to make it into a drill. Once they made that challenge I wanted to see how far we could take it."

"It was fun." Lux tilted her head back and pressed a kiss to the underside of Ambrose's jaw. His eyes warmed and his arm tightened around her.

"You three are heading out tomorrow?" Asp asked from the chair.

"We are." I nodded in confirmation.

"Ela is really excited." Ech smiled happily. "She loves it out there but misses everyone."

"We are looking forward to it." I returned her smile.

"I heard that you got a new title." Diad pointed his spoon towards Ambrose.

"Wings is so jealous that you get to learn about the spaceships and he doesn't." Scope mentioned with an amused look. "Fuck, Madron won't even let Wings mess around with the one he gave him."

"Don't tell Wings but I requested that he be given clearance. But it comes with the caveat that he's not allowed to play without supervision." Ambrose shared.

"He's going to love you for that." Scope laughed, happy for his adopted brother.

"Yeah, well, I can't take the credit for his brilliance." Ambrose shrugged.

Supper was a relaxed affair spent with my family getting to know their new members. Both Ambrose and Lux didn't even blink an eye when Pac finally took his hooded duster off.

When we finally said goodbye and returned to the suite, I was honestly exhausted.

Or at least I was right up until Lux came out of the shower wrapped in nothing but a towel.

I paused for a second on my way in, debating whether I wanted to get clean or dirty the newly cleaned woman. Figuring that I had all night to play, I opted for a shower.

When I came out it was to see Lux spread over the bed with Ambrose's mouth attached to hers. Her hands were buried in his hair, her leg cocked up along his hip. He was shirtless, braced over her on one elbow while his other arm was straight down her torso with his fingers buried between her legs.

"Switch." I ordered, pulling off the towel I had wrapped around my hip and dropping it to the floor.

Ambrose groaned and with one last kiss pushed himself from the beautiful woman underneath him. When he went to walk by me, I caught his wrist and brought his pussy slickened fingers to my lips. Sucking those delicious fingers in, I moaned at Lux's taste. Ambrose's eyes flared with desire as he watched me suck and lick his fingers clean.

"Go." I ordered, releasing him.

He disappeared into the shower while I crawled onto the bed. Lux watched me with pleasure blown eyes and a flushed face. She gave a delightful little gasp when I maneuvered myself over her so that I was straddling her head and my mouth was perfectly positioned to eat her glorious little pussy.

The mouth watering taste of her cream coated my tongue as I licked over her clit. She whimpered, her hands gripping around my upper thighs, her hips rolling up into my mouth, following the pleasure of my sucking lips.

Then I felt the rapturous heat of her mouth slicking over the sensitive tip of my straining cock and pleasure fired through me. Her tongue circled my crown as her cheeks drew on me. That deep suction had my mind stuttering with pleasure and my hips slowly thrusting, dragging my tip over her wicked little tongue.

My body shivered when her hands fisted my length, working up and down with the movements of my hips. As she was torturing my dick with the pleasure of her mouth I was tonguing her pussy, playing with her swollen clit, basking in the taste of her.

A deep groan broke from my chest when she took me deeper into her mouth, gagging when my sensitive tip hit the tight tube at the back of her throat. As much as I wanted to, I didn't push, I let her work her way through learning my length and what she could and couldn't take. I could already tell that deep throating me was not going to be a thing for her, but she definitely made up for it by using her tongue with an eye crossing talent.

Her pussy was soft and pliable under my mouth, her little clit hard, ready to burst.

I hissed when a hand fisted my head and pulled it up. A deliciously hard dick butted into the lips I immediately spread around it. Opening up my throat, I swallowed Ambrose right down to the root. The soft sack of his balls pressed into my chin as my throat worked around him.

He moaned softly, his hips rolling to fuck his length over my rubbing tongue and along the stretch of my esophagus. One of my hands gripped his hip, steadying myself against the push of his crotch into my face.

Between the feeling of Lux's mouth attempting to suck my cock dry and me doing the same to Ambrose, my body was flying high.

Pulling off the saliva soaked dick, I fisted the length and guided it down to rub the deliciously red tip along the wet pussy underneath me. Ambrose hissed and shifted forward on his knees, one of his hands drawing over the smooth spread of Lux's thighs.

Sliding his hard cock down, I notched it into the whimpering woman's entrance. Ambrose's hand gripped down on Lux's thigh as his hips moved, pressing him into her. I licked my lips, my burning eyes watching as her pussy spread around him, opening up as he pressed further and further inside. He kept pushing, slowly breaking her open until he was pressed root deep.

While Ambrose was taking our woman, her lips became more desperate on my dick, sucking even harder. Her mouth vibrated with her cries and her hands tightened. Ambrose slowly drew out, his dick coated in pink tinged cream.

I almost came right then and there.

Rolling myself off of the woman, I gripped down on my rising balls, pulling them down and forestalling my orgasm. My mesmerized eyes stayed locked on the two of them, watching as Ambrose lowered himself over Lux's flushed, breathless body. He braced himself on outstretched arms while Lux's hands came up to move over his flexing chest and grip his sides. His eyes stared into hers as his hips moved, slowly drawing his dick in and out of the tight hold of her pussy. Her hips moved with his, undulating in arching waves. Soft whimpers of pleasure were falling from her lips while his sweat slicked chest breathed hard and fast.

They were such a mind blowing combination of beauty and eroticism that I was having a hard time breathing.

Ambrose growled softly as his hips began to speed up, his strokes becoming faster and harder. Lux's knees rose to grip around his hips, hanging on as he really began to fuck her. She cried out, her body twisting with the pleasure he was driving through her.

There were no words spoken. No words were needed. Their bodies were speaking for them. Ambrose lowered himself even further until they were pressed chest to chest. His knee cocked up giving him more maneuverability for his buffeting body.

His lips found hers, kissing with deep, wet kisses. His arms slid around her, holding her to him as hers did the same. Lux whimpered out into his mouth, their bodies rolling and dancing for long moments. Then Ambrose shifted again, straightening from Lux's hold until he was kneeling back. His hands caught her knees and pushed them up and out, opening her up for my visual pleasure.

This new position had quite the effect on Lux, within a minute she was coming apart right before my eyes. Her voice cried out in rapture as her eyes rolled back in her head. Her body shook and arched in Ambrose's hold. She was coming so hard that I could actually see her pussy sucking on Ambrose's dick.

He snarled and I could see him trying to hold on but wasn't able to. His hips shuddered forward as his head went back. His body tensed, flushing, veins popping, his own pleasure rolling through him.

Once his orgasm slowed, his trembling body dropped down to his outstretched hands. His chest was heaving, his face flushed.

Reaching out, I caught his jaw and turned his eyes to mine. "My turn." I growled.

Ambrose grunted and rolled to the side enabling me to catch up the limp woman against my chest. Her ass rested on my knees, her arms automatically circled my shoulders. My eyes stared into hers as I adjusted her until her entrance was kissing my throbbing dick.

"Kal." She whimpered against my lips.

"I have you, flower." I whispered, my arms tightening around her, lowering her onto the hips I was arching up. I groaned at the rapturous feel of her come slicked pussy spreading around my cockhead. She was tight and scalding hot. Her muscles twitched and pulsed around the muscle I was thrusting into her.

I really tried not to think about the fact that I was fucking through the orgasm that Ambrose deposited inside of her. Their erotically mixed pleasure coating the tender stretch of my skin.

She whimpered into my mouth, her fingers digging into the muscles of my back. My eyes fluttered with pleasure as I sat myself root deep, pausing there to relish in the feel of her channel holding me. With slow strokes, I began to draw my over sensitive flesh through the delightful pull of her pussy.

She cried out when I found her swollen g-spot and made sure to direct my thrusts over that spot. Her body rolled with mine, following my lead as I sped up faster and faster until my overfull balls were slapping into her ass. I could feel my cock hitting her deep, my crown butting into her cervix with every seating.

She didn't seem to mind but kept working her body along mine.

I groaned when her cries turned high pitched and her fingers began to drag over my back, leaving lines of fire behind. Her pussy began to clench on me, pulsing in warning of her incoming orgasm.

Determined to give her more and more pleasure, I kept driving my dick along her g-spot, working her higher and higher until she was coming. Her head fell forward and her lips and teeth found my shoulder. Her pussy sucked and pulled at the cock I kept thrusting through her tightened hold. It felt like her pussy was trying to suck my cock right off as it attempted to strangle my rapture filled muscle.

I didn't know how long I would be able to hold off but I was determined to give her at least one more orgasm. My teeth clenched as I felt my balls already rising. With a quick adjustment, I reached down and pulled them back down, wheezing at the pain of once again pulling my orgasm back from the edge. The more I did it, the more it would hurt and the more intense my pleasure would be when I finally allowed myself to come.

My dick felt like it was on fire, the nerve endings screaming with the pleasure of the friction of her sex. I felt her sex ease around mine. That easing thankfully gave me more maneuverability that I took keen advantage of. My arms tightened around her, holding her still for my hips to slam up into her, fucking her hard and fast. Her body jolted in my hold with my fierce movements, her cries falling from the lips she had pressed to my neck.

Needing to taste her, I pulled her head back and took her mouth with mine, kissing her deep, twining our tongues together. Our lips nipped and sucked, sharing pleasure fueled breathes. Her body was already tensing, her pussy twitching with her incoming orgasm. My balls once again rose, preparing to go right along with her.

A couple more strokes and she was going over. Her eyes rolled back in her head and her body shuddered. Her pussy milked my dick with hard, greedy suctions. I groaned as my hips jerked up. Pure rapture fired through me, stealing my vision and my mind.

My dick flexed as my balls released their built up output. Burning semen rose up my length and spurted out. Stream after stream of come was shot right into her cervix and immediately sucked up into her womb. Ecstasy wracked my body until my straining balls finally emptied everything they had into the woman in my arms.

Released from the hold of my orgasm, I sucked a breath in and collapsed forward to an outstretched arm. I slowly lowered my trembling woman to the bed and carefully withdrew my oversensitive dick from the glorious hold of her body. With one last kiss, I rolled to the side, my body exhausted, my balls aching.

My eyes watched as Ambrose gently cleaned a limp Lux up and coaxed her into a t-shirt before tucking her into bed. She was out within seconds.

"That was interesting." Ambrose noted, his cloth covered hand cleaning my dick and very sore balls.

"Fuck, careful." I groaned, my hips jerking.

"You are going to have to show me that trick." He noted, his hand sliding free of my abused sack.

"It's not for the faint of heart." I warned him. "Your balls will not thank you in the end,"

"Oh, I don't plan on using it on myself." He chuckled, his eyes taking on a wicked gleam. "I quite enjoyed watching you go out of your mind like that."

"I can't say I wasn't warned." I chuckled when he helped me maneuver my naked ass under the blankets. "Thank you." I caught his wrist and pulled him down for a soft kiss.

"Thank you." He returned, his eyes telling me that he truly appreciated being the first to possess our woman.

"You earned it." I ran my fingers over his jaw, guiding his forehead to mine.

"I love you." He whispered, his eyes staring into mine, deep and dark, endless.

"I love you too." I whispered back.

CHAPTER 24

AMBROSE

We woke up early in the morning, got dressed and packed our stuff down to the Bay were Wings met us. The ten minute flight went by quickly and all too soon we were landing down on the upraised landing pad that was just outside the tent village.

Bane Darwish, the head of the Ranch, met us on the landing pad along with Grayson Dodge, the head of Ranch security. Bane had one of his four month old sons riding in a carrier on his chest.

Grayson was a lean, dark haired man with pale hazel eyes who was covered in piercings and colorful tattoos. He was quickly joined by a very happy, indigo colored Pleiadean female who came racing up the path to launch herself into her brother's waiting arms. Kal grinned as he spun Elapidae around before setting her down and introducing us to her. The woman was the spitting image of her other two sisters.

"Ambrose. Your personal tent and Kalbeliyas' office are already setup but we are still getting the equipment in the Aeronautics tent set up." Bane explained, shaking my hand in greeting. "We had to bring in a crew of helpers in order to get it all done in time. Harper is in there now, directing everything."

"Bane." I greeted back. "That's awesome to hear. I am excited to get in there and get my hands dirty."

"He's getting so big." Lux smiled as she tilted her head around until she could see the sleeping boy.

"They both are." Bane chuckled, running a knuckle over the soft cheek of his son.

We said goodbye to Wings and followed the men down the paths that wound through the tents that made up the village. Canvas tents of various sizes.

The village boasted a Cafeteria, a Security tent with cells, a Medical tent, shower and bathroom tents, office and work tents for the various groups of scientists investigating the Ranch, the Equipment tent that housed the vehicles and equipment used. And now the Aeronautics tent.

I caught up Lux's hand, linking our fingers together as we made our way to one of the larger residential tents. It had a number of area rugs covering the floor. A California king bed surrounded by nightstands was set at the back. A large dresser and a number of shelves ran along one wall. Two large trunks were set along the foot of the bed. A couch was sitting facing the front with a coffee table and surrounded by end tables. A small kitchen table was set to the other side with three chairs.

It was fairly spacious and already had Lux's bags set on the bed waiting for her.

We dropped most of our bags off and followed Bane one tent over. A smaller tent that housed a large desk and a number of bookcases already half full of books.

Kal grinned and dropped the bag he hung on to on the desk. I could tell that he was getting ready to dive right in so we left him to it.

"I want to stop at the Botany tent and let the guys know I am back." Lux told me causing Bane to adjust his direction through the paths.

"I know those guys are protective of you but remember that Kal will lose his mind if they touch you." I reminded her of how possessive Kal was.

"I forgot." She cringed, shooting me a worried look.

"I got you." I chuckled, bringing her knuckles up so I could press my lips to them. Bane grinned as we walked into the Botany tent. A large tent with a number of tables and desks that was attached to a greenhouse filled with various plants.

"Lux!" The two botanists that I remembered from weeks ago exclaimed happily as they jumped up and immediately started for Lux. I kept hold of her hand as I stepped in front of her, my body shifting sideways so I could keep an eye on her as well as on them.

Both of them froze when they saw my move, their faces taking on angry looks.

"Who the fuck are you?" The dark haired one demanded.

"I am the man who is about to save your life." I told him, my thumb rubbing over Lux's knuckles.

"Bullshit." The man denied, crossing his arms.

"Not bullshit, reality. I am only one of her men. The other one is very possessive and more deadly than you could imagine." I warned them. "So, this is me doing you a solid and saving your fingers by warning you to keep them off."

"Seriously?" The blond man asked with a scowl.

"He's very serious. Kalbeliyas isn't someone you want to test. At all. Hell, even I refuse to play with that one." Bane backed me up, his body shuddering with horror at the thought of tangling with Kal.

"Fine." The dark haired one growled, still upset but begrudgingly accepting. "I am Ice and this Strayed."

"Ambrose." I nodded in greeting to the guys.

"As in head of the Bay Ambrose?" The dark haired man, Ice, narrowed his eyes on me. "I thought I recognized you. You were abducted with her."

"I was." I nodded. "And I am now head of Alliance Space Craft Mechanics."

"I am guessing that means you and this Kalbeliyas are moving out here with Lux." Ice stated.

"We are." I nodded again, turning to Lux and cupping her face in my hands. "Do you want to stay and work or come with me to check out the Aeronautics tent?"

"I was hoping to get some work done." She gave me a hopeful look, her hands gripping down on my wrists.

"Ok. I will see you at lunch." I hummed, pressing a soft, sucking kiss to her lips. She smiled warmly at me as Bane and I left her there.

"Show me my tent." I ordered, gleefully rubbing my hands together.

"You are like a kid in a candy store." Bane laughed. "Harper is just as excited as you are."

"I just bet. She was the honestly the best mechanic I had and I missed the hell out of her. I am really excited to have her working with me again." I smiled happily.

"I noticed that you said 'with' instead of 'under.'" Bane noted with a set of surprised eyebrows which was interesting considering the one eyed man wore a large black patch over his missing eye.

"Well, it is just the two of us. While I am still her boss I am not seeing our working relationship like that." I shrugged, already knowing that it wouldn't the regular boss, employee relationship.

We walked out of the village and across the newly set cement that made up the new landing area that looked like it boasted a good ten spaces. We made our way over to a huge, brand new tent. Or kind of tent. It was a round topped fabric hanger with large metal doors at the front. It was also erected over a number of heavy cement floor slabs that were placed around drainage gutters.

We walked inside to see about five people maneuvering equipment around as Harper yelled at them. I didn't recognize any of the people telling me that they weren't from the Rocky Mountain Base.

"No! I just said not there! For fuck sakes, go take a break before I lose my fucking mind." She ordered, pointing a finger at the large, opened doors Bane and I were walking through.

"Wildcat." Bane greeted with wicked grin, catching the frustrated woman with his arm and pulling her into his side for a kiss. The child attached to his chest woke up to give a squeak in greeting.

"Ambrose, thank God." She greeted when she caught sight of me, her hassled voice filled with relief. "I don't know how to explain it to these people that if they don't put things in the right spots they are just going to have to move it again."

"I got it." I reassured the frazzled looking woman.

"We have a week to get this shit set up and at this rate it's not going to get done." Harper whined, her head falling into Bane's shoulder.

He gripped the back of her head and pressed his lips to her forehead. "Will a hit of the good stuff make you feel better?"

"Oh, God yes." She crowed, reaching into the carrier and lifting her son out. "Hello, my boy." She crooned, tucking the baby to her chest. The little boy got a two handed grip on her hair and pulled her face down so his toothless gums could gnaw out drooling kisses to her jaw and cheeks.

Harper giggled and kissed the boy's face all over making him giggle and kick his little feet. "Are you being good for daddy?" She asked as she wandered away with the boy, pointing things out to his curious amber eyes with their horizontal oval pupils.

"He slept most of the morning." Bane called after her before turning back to me. "Everything other than the specialized equipment the pilots are bringing in should already be here but let me know if anything is missing."

"I am not going to fully know until I get my training done and the ships arrive." I told him honestly.

"Speaking of." Bane directed me over to a set of desks set in the back corner of the large hanger. "These arrived for you and Harper. She has already dug into hers."

I nodded and set my bag down on the desk before taking the printed out manuals and the strange looking crystal he unlocked from a drawer. As soon as my hand touched the crystal it lit up like a holographic image that ran out horizontally over the top of the desk.

"The manual has directions on how to use the crystal as well as the metallic pad there. The crystal is from the Nordics, the pad is from the Andromadans." Bane explained, tapping a finger beside a metallic pad that was about the size of my hand.

"Ok." I frowned in confusion and began to flip through the pages of the manuals. According to what I found the new elements were to be used on the electronics that the ships boasted. They helped with the programming.

Touching the crystal, I activated the holographic image and used my fingers to manipulate the image or flip through to another page. Besides the programming elements, it also contained manuals on the various Nordic crafts I would be dealing with.

"Why did you show that to him already?" Harper's voice sounded far away. "Now I am going to have to force his ass away so we can get the AT set up."

"AT?" I mindlessly questioned, already deep in the zone of studying the first manual.

"Aeronautics Tent." Harper stated as a set of fingers caught my belt and pulled me away from the crystal, pad, and papers that was efficiently swept back into the locked drawer.

"What..?" I turned to scowl at the woman who was pulling me to the center of the tent and the returning group of helpers.

"Not now. We have more important things to do right now." Harper ordered as Bane laughed. He was on his way out of the AT, his son once again firmly ensconced in the carrier.

"Ok." I turned to the helpers, my arms crossing my chest, my tone brooking no arguments. "You lot are going to put shit where I tell you to put it the first time or I am going to keep you here all night until I am happy with it."

The group stared at me with wide eyes.

"That lift over there, you are moving it to the back section over there, right on the spot that Harper has marked. It needs to be firmly bolted down into the pads and it will be done properly because if it isn't it's going to be your ass the Nordics are going to be taking it out of. Now, move." I got the group going.

Harper marked out the areas and we all started moving the equipment into place.

Within minutes I was highly irritated and yelling. Not only did all of them have issues with their hearing but as a whole they all seemed to really enjoy shortcuts. The issue with that was when it came to installing dangerous equipment like the huge powerlift, there was no shortcuts. The group was a useless pain in my ass and if I didn't need the extra hands I would've sent them all home.

It took us the rest of the day to get the high powered lift set up and firmly bolted down. Thankfully, when I missed lunch, a very sexy redhead came waltzing in with a takeaway bag for me. I made sure to show him my appreciation before allowing him to leave.

That night we got some supper, checked out the showers, and unpacked before falling into bed.

The tent kind of reminded me of our time in the desert only it was a hell of a lot more comfortable. And, for some reason, it felt like home.

CHAPTER 25

LUX

When I woke up in the morning, Ambrose was already gone. I knew that the man was going to be working his ass off for the next week just to get everything ready.

Deciding that I wanted some morning feels, I straddled the man sleeping next to me and ran my hands over the muscular ridges of his torso. My nipples were hard at the thought of his big dick inside of me while my pussy moistened and pulsed demandingly.

"Good morning." Kal smiled up at me when his eyes cracked open. His body gave a deep, shuddering stretch under me before his hands landed on my hips.

"Good morning." I smiled down at him. "Should we talk about how much I love you or would you like to just jump right to the part where I ride you into oblivion?"

"How about we do both?" He shifted my hips forward, catching his fully aroused fat tip at my entrance, and pulling me back, seating that glorious dick deep inside of me.

I cried out, my back arching at the delicious feel of him stretching me, rubbing over all of the nerve laden muscles of my tunnel. I honestly loved having him inside of me. Him and Ambrose. They both knew how to fuck. My hands pulled the t-shirt I wore to bed off as my hips began to rise and fall on him.

The friction of his dick moving was body shivering good. In search of more of that pleasure, I kept riding him, drawing that hard muscle in and out of my tingling sex. I arched back with the fire of my pleasure, his dick hitting that sensitive spot inside me that always got me there. My g-spot.

My hips sped up, rubbing his dick right over that spot. I could feel his pleasure bright eyes watching me, moving over my undulating body and where we were connected.

"I do love you." I whimpered, leaning down and bracing my hands on his pecs. His hands moved up to my shoulders as his hips began to rise and fall with mine.

"I love you too." He rasped, his face flushed, his bright eyes glowing with that love.

Lowering my chest down to his, my hips kept rotating as I kissed him, pouring my love into him. One of his hands burrowed into my hair, holding my lips to his as our tongues licked and danced over one another. I gasped when his other hand gripped my thigh and I suddenly found us flipped over with me on my back and him looming over me.

He had one elbow braced on the bed beside my head while his other hand slid down to my knee and pulled it over the thrusting hips that were drawing his cock through my channel. I cried out into the lips he kept touched to mine, my hands gripping his bicep and the nape of his neck. His eyes stared down into mine, connecting us in that way I loved. Both him and Ambrose did that, looked into my eyes as they dealt out their mind blowing pleasure.

My cries heightened as my pleasure rose higher and higher until I was arching up into him with ecstasy. My pussy began to contract around him as it milked that gloriously hard flesh. It wasn't as intense as the night before but instead was deep and connecting on a whole different level.

His lips groaned into mine as his jerking dick burrowed deep inside me and began to spit out burning heat. His hips shivered and his body tensed, his eyes fluttering with his pleasure. Seeing him like that and feeling him come flooding my pussy only deepened my orgasm until my eyes went blank.

My orgasm abated and I blinked to focus on the sweaty, satisfied face of the man above me.

He smiled down at me and pressed his forehead to mine. "Time to get up."

"Yeah." I breathed, running my hands over his torso.

"I love you, flower." His nose nudged mine as his lips moved.

"I love you too, Kal." I smiled happily, those words echoing in my chest, resounding in a way I knew would last me forever if I needed it to.

We eventually rose from the bed and got going to work.

Ice and Strayed eyed Kal when he dropped me off at the Botany tent. Kal left me with a deep possessive kiss and a look of warning for the guys.

"Ambrose wasn't kidding." Strayed winced.

"He's actually very sweet and easy going until someone oversteps with Ambrose or I." I explained to the men as I moved into the greenhouse to feed and water the plants. "He's a big softy when it comes to his little sisters."

"Who are his sisters?" Ice asked curiously.

"Elapidae is one. Echis and Aspis are the other two. Triplets." I told them around my soft humming.

"Ech is his little sister? She worked with us for a little bit right up until that big assed Andromadan came by and claimed her as his conversance. She was a sweet little thing." Ice smiled warmly in remembrance. "Very high energy."

"She is really sweet. I like her. She is very understanding." I returned his smile with one of my own.

"It's hard to picture that little one being related to that big devil." Ice mentioned.

"If you think Kal is scary you should meet the oldest brother. That guy will turn your hair white. Both of them did everything they could to protect their little sisters and give them a joy filled life." I explained to them.

"Kind of makes me like him, just slightly." Strayed shrugged from the desk he was working at.

"Get to know him and you will really like him." I assured them.

At lunch time, I wandered over to the Cafeteria tent with the two men I worked with and got in line for a burger and some salad.

The huge tent had the actual kitchen in another tent that was attached to the side of it. Along that side was also the buffet area where everyone lined up for their food. Down the other side of the tent was a large number of wooden tables surrounded by benches.

I was heading over to our usual table only to have Grayson and Ela come up behind me and usher me to a table with them. I was just sitting down on the bench across from them when Kal dropped down beside me with a plate filled with two burgers and a mound of fries.

I turned to greet the couple we were sitting with just in time to see Ela's hamburger slide out from between the bun she was holding, bounce off her lap, and splat onto the floor.

"Oh." She pouted sadly down at the burger.

"Here." Ambrose breathed, dropping a new burger onto her plate as he slid in on the other side of Kal. His hair was a mess and he was covered in dirt and grime. "I only have ten minutes." He grunted as he practically inhaled the other burger on his plate in between shoveling in handfuls of fries.

"Thank you." Ela smiled happily, successfully hitting her mouth with the whole burger.

Grayson smiled gratefully at Ambrose who gave the man a nod of acknowledgment.

"Slow down before you choke." I lectured Ambrose.

"Yes, flower." He mumbled around a full mouth.

"I have the afternoon free to help out." Kal shared, eyeing Ambrose. Our poor man looked worn out, frustrated, angry.

Ambrose murmured something intelligible that sounded like an agreement as he pushed the last bite of his burger passed his lips. Within minutes he was up and clearing his tray. I watched as he walked his tray over to the dish bin and dumped it in only to spin around and come darting back. He leaned right over Kal and cupped my face.

"I missed you this morning." He whispered right before his lips covered mine in a long, deep kiss. "I love you." He whispered right before releasing me and walking at a fast clip towards the entrance.

"I am going to kill him." I hissed out, touching the lips he whispered his love against. "He didn't even give me a chance to say it back."

"I will let him know." Kal turned to give me his own kiss before he rose and deposited his empty tray in the bin. "I love you, flower." He called across the tent as he walked out.

"Oh my God, there's two of them." I breathed in shock while Ela giggled and Grayson outright laughed.

"He seems really...busy." Ela noted, referring to Ambrose.

"He's got a lot of work to get done to get the AT set up for the incoming pilots." I explained to her.

"The AT?" Grayson frowned in confusion.

"Oh, that's what they are calling the Aeronautics tent." I informed them.

"Do you think they need more manpower?" Grayson asked, turning to look at the entrance as if he could see all the way to the AT.

"I have no idea." I shrugged. "I do know that they are trying to set it up in a very specific way that will provide the best service to the crafts."

"Smart." Grayson nodded as he turned back and began to type something out on his coms.

"Are you requesting more men?" Ela asked him.

"I am." Grayson nodded. "There is no reason that man should be killing himself trying to get this done."

"Well, he's also trying to get his training on the space crafts done at the same time." I described what Ambrose shared with us last night.

"Yeah, he needs more men." Grayson growled.

"If it helps them out." Ela agreed with Grayson's decision.

Grayson groaned when his coms dinged. "According to Bane he brought people in, the ones that are already helping with the AT set up."

"Maybe there is something Kal can do to help." I sighed.

"Maybe." Ela frowned as she thought. "Although, I don't know if his abilities will be all that helpful in this situation. What we need is a telekinetic and she's out on maternity leave."

"No worries." Grayson lowered his wrist. "Wings is trying to get a group together to come help."

"Good." I nodded, feeling slightly relieved.

CHAPTER 26

KALBELIYAS

I caught up to Ambrose and walked with him back to the AT.

"She is not happy with you right now." I warned him with a smirk. "Mind you she's also not happy with me either."

"What did you do?" He scowled over at me.

"The exact same thing you did. I told her I loved her as I walked out of the Cafeteria tent." I laughed. "Although, I also told her this morning when she told me."

"Good." Ambrose chuckled, gripping my shoulder. "I do plan on giving her the chance to return my sentiment when I have the chance to fully take advantage of it."

"I take it things aren't going well." I took a stab in the dark.

"It's a fucking shit show. We haven't even finished getting the second power lift set up. We still have two more. Not to mention the arms we have to install." He groaned, chewing on his lower lip.

"Arms?" I questioned curiously.

"Mechanical arms that are used to lift heavy parts up. They are usually used for engine installs or removals. These specific ones have been upgraded to deal with the large crafts and are absolute fuckers to install. Just like the lifts they have to be bolted into the cement pads." He sighed as he explained. "It takes a lot of time, especially considering the fact that the people we are working with have never done work like this before and are frankly clueless. And lazy. And idiots."

"Well, you have me now." I reassured him.

"Thank you." He stopped just outside the large metal doors of the AT and turned to me.

"It gives me a chance to work with you." I grinned at him, gripping the nape of his neck and pulling him to my lips for a deep kiss that tasted slight of Lux. "That and seeing you in action is one hell of a turn on."

"Hmmm. I will try to tone down the sexy so you can concentrate on my orders." He breathed against my lips.

"Your orders?" My eyebrows rose in amusement.

"My tent, my rules." He stated firmly, pulling free of my grip and sauntering into the tent.

I laughed as I followed him, willing to allow him to play that card.

Harper was already there, going through a fuck load of tool chests that were set up along a line of metal covered counters. Above the counters were walls of pegboard with the odd tool hanging from it.

I walked over to help Ambrose start inventorying and stocking the cupboards with various containers and parts.

It took about half an hour for the work crew to start straggling in. That was when Ambrose's attitude changed. He became the authority he was and his tone and stance fully reflected that.

He started throwing out orders as we all returned to the half set up power lift.

Everything was going ok until Ambrose and I were in the middle of getting the bottom pad set and Harper frantically yelled out in warning.

Too late.

One of the guys had let go of one of the heavy metal lifting brackets he was bracing before it was fully bolted down.

My heart stopped and my eyes widened in shock and terror at the tall length of hard, sharp metal that flashed through my vision, descending right on us.

As much as time slowed, I still wasn't able to react before the bracket slammed right into Ambrose's arm, knocking him straight down to the pad. He yelled in pained agony, his arm pinned to the ground under the heavy weight of the bracket.

Screams and yells echoed in my ears from the people surrounding us. I ignored them, concentrating on a screaming Ambrose instead. My heart dropped and my chest seized when I saw the blood gushing from where the metallic edge had cut deep into his upper arm. The same bright red blood was splattered all over his side right along with the mat he was pinned to.

"Fuck!" I yelled, frantically dropping to my knees to assess the situation.

It was bad.

The bracket that was almost completely resting on the ground had cut into his arm right in the middle of his bicep. His hand and forearm twitched in a very concerning way before falling limp. My chest hurt and I was having a hard time breathing, my head feeling dizzy at the sight before me.

This was bad.

"Don't move." I caught Ambrose's pale, blood splattered face in my shaking palms and forced him to look at me. "Just look at me. Concentrate on me."

"I can't feel my arm." He swallowed tightly, his gleaming eyes clouded with pain.

"I know." I felt my words sob out before I could catch them. I pushed aside my rising hysteria and concentrated on keeping him with me.

I desperately wanted to fix this but I couldn't. I didn't know what to do.

His chattering teeth clenched and his eyes squeezed shut, tears sliding free. His body was shaking almost violently under my hands, his breathing stuttered.

"Ambrose, look at me." I ordered sharply. I needed to see his eyes, I needed to see the life in them. I needed him to stay awake until help could get here.

His glazed eyes opened to look up at me. I could tell that he was losing it, the severe trauma taking hold.

"I need you to stay awake, stay with me until the doctor gets here." I told him, rubbing my blood stained hands over his pale white and red face in an attempt to keep him awake.

"My arm." He slurred, his glazed eyes taking on a wild look.

"We will get through this. I promise, Ambrose. We will get through this." I rasped, leaning down to press my forehead to his, ignoring the slick feel of his blood sliding between us. "We got through the desert, we can get through this."

"Lux." He whispered brokenly.

"She loves you." I vehemently assured him. "She loves you just as I love you. Which is why you need to stay with me."

"Right here." He slurred, his eyes blinking.

"Move." The greying, brown haired Dr. John James pushed me aside as he knelt down to examine Ambrose's pinned arm. "Fuck." He hissed when he saw the extent of the damage. His light brown eyes moved to mine, silently telling me what I already knew. The arm was gone.

"All right. Bailor, I need you to lift when I tell you too." John ordered Bailor, an equine divergent who was in a triad with Harper and Bane. Bailor was crouched down around the end of the bracket, his hands gripping it. John loaded a needle that he jabbed into Ambrose's free shoulder.

"Kal." Ambrose slurred as the drugs began to take effect.

"Right here, Ambrose. Right here." I reassured him, moving around to take Ambrose's free hand.

"Love." Ambrose breathed right before falling fully unconscious.

"We love you too." I whispered, rubbing his hand between mine.

"He's not going to make it back to Base. We are going to have to do this fast and furious. Bailor is going to lift the bracket off him and I am going to tie the arm off in order to contain the bleeding. The four of us are going to get him on the gurney and onto the transport and straight to the Medical tent." John ordered in fast but efficient manner. "The rest of you need to get the fuck gone and out of the way."

The crowd quickly dispersed, mostly due to Harper screaming at them. The woman was shaking, her face pale with horror and worry.

"Ok. Go." John ordered Bailor.

It happened fast. Bailor lifted the heavy bracket and moved it off of Ambrose while John's hands darted forward and quickly tied a torniquet around Ambrose's upper arm right above the little bit of muscle and skin that was left attaching it to the bottom half.

I wanted to scream at the sight, the pain stabbing through me more agonizing than anything I had ever felt before. Bane was right there, carefully moving the arm with the rest of Ambrose's body as we gently moved him to the gurney. My hands and body were moving on autopilot as my mind spun with horror and my tears slid down my numb face.

We got him strapped down on the gurney and over to the transport.

The drive to the Medical tent was a blur.

The huge tent that we carried Ambrose into had quite the setup and was extremely clean and organized. There was an office desk set in front and just to the side of the door. Three exam chairs ran down the open spaced middle. Along one side were some shelves holding medical tombs and binders, extra scrubs and clothes, different sized

Medi-Pacs, and a coffee center. There was also another desk that was masked behind some cloth room dividers. Along the other side was a length of metal topped, locked cupboards, fridges, and equipment along with a huge sink. In the back was two private rooms with beds that boasted canvas doors that could be opened and closed at will.

We were just settling Ambrose on one of the beds in the back when a pale faced Lux came tearing in. I raced forward to catch her before she could see him, spinning her around so that she was facing the front entrance.

"Ambrose!" She screamed hysterically, fighting me to get to him.

"He's alive, Lux. He's alive." I gave her a shake to get her attention. "But I am not going to let you see him like this."

"What happened, Kal?" Her voice came out high pitched with fear and anxiety.

"One of the powerlift braces fell on him." My shaking voice broke and I needed a moment to continue. "It pinned his arm."

"It pinned his arm?" She asked, her lips quivering, her own tears burning down her cheeks.

"It cut....it cut...his arm." I desperately tried to get the words out.

"It cut off his arm." Lux's face went disturbingly white.

"Yes." I croaked out, feeling my heart completely stop when her face crumpled and her body collapsed against mine.

She sobbed into my shoulder as her hands clutched my arm.

"Move." Dr. Luke Graden came tearing in and raced over to the sink that was set along the side of the tent. The elderly female nurse with him scrubbed up and began to dress him in a set of sterilized protective wear that her gloved hands pulled out. He scrubbed up as she finished dressing him.

"Lux, listen to me." I caught Lux's shaking shoulders and brought her head up to face me. "I need you to go get the Drako first aide kit. We need the liquid inside. You know, the stuff we used on Ambrose's leg."

It took her a moment for her sobbing to stop and for her to be able to focus before she gave me a sharp nod and darted out the tent door.

I turned back to the room and the bed that was now surrounded by doctors. An agonized whimper slid from my throat at the sight of Luke handing Ambrose's lifeless, fully detached arm to John. The arm that once held me, fought for me. The hand that once touched me and showed me how much he loved me.

The sound brought me to the attention of the medical staff and Luke bit something out sharply. The nurse jumped forward and released the canvas walls to close the room to my sight. I felt my strength leave my body as my legs collapsed under me. My burning eyes stared at the closed wall for so long that I barely noticed when Lux came rushing back in.

She raced over to the wall and called to someone inside. I could see her speak to the nurse who ducked her head out as she handed the bottle over. The moment the flap closed Lux stumbled over to me and fell to her knees right in front of me.

"Kal." She whispered, her glistening eyes moving over me, her shaking hands running over my face and torso.

"I was right there." My lips moved without me.

"I know, Kal." Her voice sobbed out. "And now I am right here."

My teeth clenched and my head bowed as I tried to get control over myself. My heartbroken sobs released the moment that Lux's arms surrounded my bowed head and shoulders. My own arms snapped tightly around her, holding her to me as I cried out for Ambrose's pain.

I couldn't stop seeing it, sharp pictures of everything I saw flashing through my mind. His agony and horror, his shock, his blood, his dismembered arm.

I felt her head bowed over mine, her own tears wetting my neck and hair. We held each other as we cried. By the time I finally ran out of tears, I felt numb, lifeless. I picked Lux up off the floor and carried her over to one of the exam chairs where I laid down with her. I needed to hold her, feel the reassurance of her heat against me.

The hours passed slowly as the doctors worked.

My heart jerked wildly and I sat straight up when the wall finally opened and the blood covered trio exited. Luke came right to us, pulling his mask and gloves off. Both Lux and I climbed off the chair and waited to hear the news he had for us.

"As you know, the arm was gone. We finished removing it and got the blood stopped before skinning over the stump. He's in for a long recovery but he's strong and he held on well through the surgery. We are going to keep him out for twenty-four hours to make sure there is no infection. Although, if the stuff you gave us is really as good as you described then that shouldn't be an issue." Luke explained, his eyes carrying a weird mixture of hardness and pained resolve.

"Thank you." My voice rasped out hoarsely, my eyes moving passed the doctor to the gauze covered man that John and the nurse were carefully moving over to the other bed. The one that wasn't covered in blood.

Ambrose's blood.

"Breathe, Kal." Luke gripped my shoulder, bringing my attention back to him. "He is alive."

"He is." I agreed with a slow nod. "Unfortunately, that doesn't diminish the trauma he experienced."

"The trauma you both experienced." Luke expertly pointed out.

"I have seen worse." I informed him numbly.

"Not when it pertains someone you love." Luke grunted, giving my shoulder a shake. "Lean on each other, stay open and honest. Don't let this fuck you up."

"Heard." I nodded slowly, letting the doctor know that I was listening to his words despite my numb appearance.

"Go, sit with him." Luke jerked his head to the set of chairs the nurse was moving over to the side of Ambrose's new, clean bed.

Lux caught my hand and guided me over to the chairs. Instead of letting her sit in her own, I pulled her down into my lap, not ready to lose her touch yet.

"We will get through this." I whispered, my voice slowly filling with determination. I promised Ambrose that we would and that was just what we would do.

"Yes, we will." Lux agreed, her head laying over my chest.

We sat there in silence, watching Ambrose breathe as time passed. John came over a number of times to take Ambrose's vitals and bring us supper. He mostly left us with the tent after that, only coming in every few hours.

I felt Lux fall asleep, her body relaxing into mine.

I didn't sleep. I didn't know if I could with my mind still filled with the images of Ambrose, replaying the incident over and over again.

I did, however, feel a strong presence right before a purplish black cloud of energy darted in and dropped into the seat beside mine.

"How is he?" Pac asked in a low voice, his hood lowered to display his face.

"Armless." I gave a derisive laugh. "But alive."

"How are you?" Pac dropped his next question like the bomb it was.

"Raw, numb, angry, scared, in pain, fucking heartbroken. You name it, I am feeling it." I hissed at him.

"Madron is in the process of ordering a new arm for him. Luke helpfully took the measurements for him." Pac noted in a soft voice, his eyes drawing over Ambrose's unconscious body. "Andromadan replacement arms are frankly amazing."

"They are." I agreed with a nod.

"But they aren't anywhere as good as a Pleiadean replacement." Pac's head turned to me.

"I didn't think it was possible." I shook my head, my brow furrowing. Pleiadean replacement limbs were a feat of ingenuity. They were created from the DNA of the person in need, formed by pure energy. They looked and felt like a real arm. In fact, they were a real arm, just not the original. Beyond the scar the reattachment left behind there was literally no differentiation.

"It isn't." Pac sighed, his eyes delving deep into mine. "Not for a human. But for a human that carries Pleiadean DNA it might very well be possible."

"How the fuck do you purpose to do that?" I demanded, my heart slowly filling with hope.

"Well." He began. "It would begin with you sinking your energy form into him. Deep into every little molecule that makes him up. You would have to coat him in you, share your essence with him. Essentially you would be attaching tiny little bits of your DNA to his. Then we use your DNA to form the arm. Since your DNA will already be a part of him, his body should accept the attachment."

"Let me guess, this is all conjecture?" I guessed.

"Oh, definitely." Pac nodded in confirmation.

"Let's do this." I rose, gently laying an exhausted Lux back in the chair. I was willing to do anything if there was a chance that it would help the man I loved.

"You need to strip down. It has to be pure." Pac guided, rising to stand beside me. "I will help guide you."

"Very well." I agreed, stripping off my clothes until I was fully naked. I took a deep breath in, sending out a prayer that this would work.

Swirling into energy, I laid myself over Ambrose and slowly sank myself into his prone body. While we quite frequently flew through other physical bodies, I had never tried to coat one with my essence before. Sinking deeper and deeper, I carefully stretched my energy out until I was touching every little bit of him, every muscle, every organ, every nerve, every atom and molecule.

"Good." Pac's steady, logical voice guided from above me. "Now, the next step is the same as what you do when you reach out and hook someone else's energy to you, only opposite."

I thought about that for a moment, diagnosing exactly how I used my own energy to pull someone else's in. Then I did as he said, instead of bringing someone to me, I sent waves of my own energy out. I felt Ambrose shiver around me as a groan rumbled out of his chest. It felt extremely disconcerting to feel those bodily actions from the inside.

"More, Kal." Pac directed, bringing my mind back to the task at hand.

I sent more waves out, feeling strands of energy leaving me and attaching to the man I was imbedded in. I sent more and more waves out until Pac finally told me that it was enough. When I drew back, I dropped into physical feeling severely weak and dizzy. Pac was already there, catching me as my legs collapsed under me.

His palm hit my ice cold chest, his own energy pumping into mine, feeding me, strengthening me. When he drew away I felt almost normal. Almost. While my own energy in no way felt diminished it did recognize itself in Ambrose's unconscious body.

"Owe." I jerked when Pac stabbed a needle into my neck, very accurately hitting the vein. He drew out a bunch of tubes of blood before he was satisfied.

"I will be back as soon as I can be." He stated as he swirled into energy and disappeared.

CHAPTER 27

KALBELIYAS

I knew that it would take a couple hours for them to form the arm. I also knew that it took Pac no time at all to traverse long distances such as to the Pleiadean home world.

Using Lux's coms, I typed out a message to Carter, telling him to get prepared to travel out here. I didn't know if we would need a doctor's help with the attachment but if we did Carter was the only one Pac, or even I, would trust with that.

I pulled on a spare lab coat that I found on the shelf and paced the tent as I waited, nervous and feeling as if I was slightly going out of my mind.

Lux woke up and stared at me in confusion. "Are you ok?"

"No." I shook my head. "I did something and now I am terrified that it won't work."

"Come here. Tell me." She held her hands out to me.

I rubbed the back of my sore neck and shuffled over to sit in the chair beside hers. Her hand caught mine and I found my fingers squeezing down.

"Pac came up with something that could make it seem like Ambrose didn't even lose his arm." I whispered to her, keeping my voice low so we weren't overheard. "The Pleiadean's have a way of replacing body parts. A way that involves creating one from the DNA of the person who needs the replacement. Well, that and pure energy. The thing is it won't work for anyone who doesn't carry the Pleiadean energy."

"Ok. So how is this going to help Ambrose?" Lux asked slowly, her eyes narrowing on me.

"Pac and I kind of attached some of my energy DNA to Ambrose so that they can make the arm using my DNA and his body will accept it. At least that's the theory." I winced as I finished explaining.

"And now you are worried that you may have changed him on an elemental level, without his permission I might add, and it won't work." She hammered the nail right on the head.

"Yeah." I breathed out, my anxious eyes coming up to meet hers.

"My beautiful man, stop worrying." She smiled warmly and cupped my face, guiding my forehead to hers. "If it doesn't work, at least you will know that you tried everything to help him."

"You aren't mad?" I felt the tension in my body relax, just slightly.

"Why would I be mad? You gave a part of yourself to him in hopes of giving him his arm back. I am so fucking proud of you." She hissed out, her eyes gleaming with tears. "I honestly love you so much right now that my heart hurts."

"I love him too much not to do whatever I can to help him." I felt those tears returning to my eyes.

"So do I." She whispered, her own tears falling.

The tent flap flipped open and Carter came waltzing in with Skylar's hand in his. "It makes me wonder why my man disappeared in the middle of the night and within half an hour I am being messaged with a demand to get out of my bed and onto a spaceship so that I can fly out to a patient that is not in anyway mine."

"Pac is picking something up for me and he will be back in a couple hours. We might need your expertise when he returns and I kind of want to keep it in the family." I informed him.

"Ah, Pleiadean secure." Carter tapped his temple, turning to the coffee center and starting to fix a pot.

"Here." I walked over and lowered one of the exam chairs until it was practically laying flat. "Lay down, Skylar." I ordered the half asleep woman as I dug out a clean pillow and blanket for her.

"Thank you, Kalbeliyas." Skylar gave me a warm smile as she curled up and drifted off to sleep. I walked over and lowered the lights until the tent was in shadows.

"My sweet man." Lux smiled when I walked over to her with another pillow and blanket that I tucked around her.

"I know you won't sleep but at least you can be a little more comfortable." I whispered to her, pressing a kiss to her forehead before retaking my seat.

Carter brought me over some coffee before wandering over to sit at John's desk. I drank deep of the cup, my body feeling wired and exhausted all at the same time.

The hours passed as the night deepened. It was the early hours of the morning before Pac returned with the new arm attachment.

"Carter." He called softly as he made his way over to the bed. "I need the stitches removed and the stump opened."

Carter scrubbed up as Pac set the energy packaged arm on the bed just below the stump. A masked and gloved Carter came over and expertly unwrapped the stump before snipping the stitches off and opening the end of the stump. Pac unpackaged the attachment and pressed it into the end of Ambrose's arm. The new arm was pale and effervescent, clearly made from my Pleiadean DNA and not Ambrose's human DNA. Although, the measurements completely matched his old arm.

"Kal, I need your energy to seal the attachment." Pac directed. Stripping off the lab coat, I swirled back into energy and surrounded the place where Pac was pressing the attachment into the end of the stump.

"Just like before, Kal." Pac guided.

Sinking myself back into Ambrose, this time concentrating on the connection point I started to pulse out those strands of energy. I felt it, the attachment slowly sealing itself to Ambrose's arm.

"Holy fuck." I heard Lux breathe from above and to the side.

I kept pulsing out more and more of my energy until the arm was completely attached and Pac gave me the ok to back off. Dropping into physical right beside him, he was ready to catch me, his hand already pumping healing energy into my chest. It took more this time as the energy output needed to connect the attachment was massive. It took a couple moments before I felt my strength return.

Lux was there, pulling the lab coat over my shoulders. Once I was stabilized, we all turned to assess Ambrose. The new arm was fully affixed, leaving behind a wicked looking scar that circled his bicep.

"Time to wake up." Pac stated as he set his hand on Ambrose's forehead.

A gentle wave of energy had Ambrose's eyes cracking open. He looked exhausted and dazed but the glazed pain was gone from his eyes. My heart stuttered before racing forward, relief flooding through me to the point that I felt light headed. My eyes stared at him, running over him again and again just to be sure that I didn't see any sign of further injury.

"Fuck." He groaned, shifting in the bed.

Lux's breath sobbed out in amazement when his arm lifted to drag his hand over his exhausted looking face. He froze for a moment and pulled his arm back to study his new hand.

"I feel like I missed something." His voice croaked out and his shocked eyes came to mine. "I was put under with a lost arm yet I seem to have gained a very shiny new one."

"Uh yeah." I winced down at him. "Well, I had to change you a bit to make this possible but this here is your new Pleiadean attachment arm made from my DNA."

"This is going to make jacking off really interesting." Ambrose spoke before frowning at the fact that he overshared in front of people he didn't know all that well. "I think I may still be drugged."

Lux burst into laughter, her shaking hands covering her mouth. "It worked." She practically crawled right on the bed to bend over Ambrose, her hands running over him as if to reassure herself he was alive and once again whole.

"Yes, it did." Pac full out grinned.

"Now, how the fuck do we explain this to everyone?" Carter asked curiously.

"We don't." Pac denied with a set of cold, hard eyes. "The perks of being a Pleiadean. We don't have to explain. As far as everyone else is concerned, Luke was able to save the arm and reattach it using Andromadan technology. It was a miracle that it even worked and it's why the arm looks so different."

"That sounds completely plausible." Carter shrugged in acceptance.

"Let's get our woman home and to bed." Pac walked over to Skylar.

"Use our tent. Get some sleep before calling for pick up." Lux mentioned, pointing in the direction our tent was located. "Here, I will take you."

While she took a moment more with Ambrose, kissing his lips and speaking softly to him, I turned to Pac. "Why?"

"Because he is going to need both his arms." Pac stated. It was simple and to the point.

"Thank you." I held my hand out to him.

He knocked my hand aside and pulled me in for a hug. "It's what big brother's do." His words hit me right in the heart.

"It is. And I might just have the best brother in the universe." I whispered back to him before pulling back.

"No, Kal, I do." He turned and gently picked Skylar up in his arms, following Lux and Carter out of the tent.

"I told you that I would get us through this." I turned to the trembling man who was slowly pushing himself up into a sitting position. Ambrose was still pale, either a left over from the trauma or still in shock.

"Yeah." He chuckled softly, his dark, haunted eyes gratefully watching me approach. "You did. I didn't realize that it would involve you giving a part of yourself to me, in more ways than one."

"I would give everything I had in me to you, to her." I told him, cupping his face in my hands.

"I hope you know that I would do the same." He rasped back, his hands coming up to grip my wrists. "I love you so fucking much."

"I love you too." I whispered back, meeting his lips with mine.

"So, if I use this hand to play with your dick, does that mean you are masturbating?" He asked curiously, his lips twitching up in one corner.

"Yes, it does. And I can honestly say, I am looking forward to my next masturbation session." I laughed, turning to sit down on the bed beside him. "We are going to have to wrap your shoulder up and keep your arm hidden for a week or so. You know, pretend that your original arm was successfully reattached and you are still healing."

"I think I can do that. Although, you might have to help keep an eye on the AT set up for me." He warned, that twitch turning into a playful smile.

"Don't you worry about any of that." I caught his new hand in mine and linked our fingers together. "You know, I think it looks better on you than it does on me."

"Wait until I get it all worked in and covered in callouses." He chuckled, rubbing his thumb over my knuckles. "I cannot ever tell you how much I truly appreciate being able to do this."

"Probably about as much as I appreciate it." I returned, looking down at our linked fingers and frowning.

Raising our link hands up, I studied his fingers. "Is it just me or are your fingers darkening?"

Ambrose shift his whole arm up and we both examined it. The pale skin tone was changing to match his tanned one while still maintaining the Pleiadean effervescent quality. "I am guessing this is my body accepting it as its own."

"Maybe we should test it?" I stated wickedly, waggling my eyebrows at him.

"As much as I want to take you up on that, I am pretty sure John is due in at any moment." Ambrose noted, his eyes going to the tent flap that flipped open for the woman who came rushing in.

Ambrose carefully stood, both of his arms ready to catch Lux against him.

"I love you too." She whispered, gripping the sides of his face and pulling his mouth down to hers. A number of deep kisses were soon broken up by the doctor who came waltzing into the tent only to skid to a stop when his eyes landed on Ambrose.

"What the fuck did I sleep through?" He bellowed out in shock.

"Nothing." I shrugged, walking over to grip the stunned doctor's shoulder. "Don't you remember? You and Luke were able to use Andromadan technology to successfully reattach Ambrose's arm. It really was a fucking miracle."

"Come on." John groaned, his face taking on a look of tearful frustration.

"You will get over it." I reassured him. "And just think of how Luke is going to take it when he is reminded of the miracle he performed."

"Oh, he's going to hate that." John's face brightened. "Ambrose, how do you feel?"

"Like a man whose doctors performed a miracle reattachment." Ambrose grinned from around the woman who was now leaning back in his arms. Lux was running her hands over his new arm, her head tilted to rest the corner of her forehead against his shoulder.

"I see we aren't wavering." John laughed.

"Nope." Ambrose shook his head. "Not when it comes to family."

"Fine." John sighed before his eyes gleamed with avarice. "Not even a hint? My inner doctor is going crazy with curiosity."

"I am sorry for your inner doctor." I patted his shoulder.

"I still want to keep him for while, just to make sure everything is on the up and up." John gestured for Ambrose to return to the bed while he walked over to the sink to wash his hands. "Sit, I want to take your vitals. Then you can get some more sleep. You still look like death warmed over."

CHAPTER 28

AMBROSE

I was feeling focused and strangely pain free but my mind was swirling, still struggling to come to terms with everything that happened.

I sat down on the bed and let John take a look at me.

I still wasn't sure what all went on while I was out but the last thing I remembered before waking was agony. Excruciating agony mixed with the destructive knowledge that my arm was gone. When the brace first fell, it hurt like hell, like someone had punched me in the arm. That punch turned into pure fire that bit over my shoulder and across my torso.

And what was worse was the fact that I couldn't feel the bottom part of my arm. There was no pain there. There was nothing there.

The look in Kal's eyes when he looked at my arm told me the truth. He was horrified, broken looking all at the same time he looked right about to crack with worry. He kept demanding I stay with him, reassuring me that, no matter what, we would get through this.

My mind screamed at my loss while my body screamed at the excruciating pain. Every stuttering breath I was able to draw in only added to that pain. My sliced nerves felt like live wires, firing lightening through my whole body.

The pain was astronomical and was leaving me nauseas and weak. Despite Kal's demands that I stay awake, I was having a hard time. All I wanted to do was sleep.

Thankfully, John arrived and granted that wish, injecting me with something that numbed the mind bending agony and sucked me down into the pain free darkness of unconsciousness.

The next thing I became aware of was the bed in the Medical tent. I was laying there with Kal, Lux, Pacifier, and Carter all staring at me with various looks of hope. Tired, I automatically brought my hand up to rub over my face. It wasn't until Lux sobbed out in relief that I remembered the loss of my arm, the same arm I was using to rub my face.

Upon examination, I realized that it actually wasn't the same arm. It felt like my arm, it worked like my arm, it was even shaped like my arm. But it wasn't.

Kal's explanation had so many different feelings flooding through me. The traumatizing memories of the accident mixed with the knowledge that I did indeed lose my arm. Losing such a vital part of myself like that was a hard pill to swallow. It was just gone.

Then there was the relief and confusion at the sight of the new arm and the realization of how lucky I was that I would still have the same maneuverability I had before the accident. The knowledge of how connected Kal and I now were, was also a struggle, albeit a good one. It felt surreal. He was now a part of me. I big part of me in a very physical way.

What I did know was that I was so thankful to still be able to use two hands to touch, hold the two people I loved with all of my being.

To be honest, I was relieved when John finished his examination and I was able to go back to sleep. Although, I didn't do it alone due to the fact that as soon as I laid back I pulled Lux down with me, needing to feel her close to me.

My arm shivered at the feel of her heat pressing into it, goosebumps flaring over the skin that now looked exactly like mine.

"She's warm." I murmured to Kal, my eyes already drifting closed.

"You both are." Kal whispered, his lips brushing over my forehead. "Sleep."

The next time I woke it was late afternoon. Lux was sprawled over my chest, still fast asleep, while Kal was leaned back in the chair beside the bed, his legs up on the edge. He had his head resting on a pillow, deep in sleep.

I felt rested, more stable. My mind was still struggling with my new circumstances but in a far less erratic way. And my bladder was screaming for release. Carefully maneuvering myself out from under the sleeping woman, I brushed aside the closed canvas door of the back room and stepped out.

A delicate blond Nordic woman with violet eyes, Fain, was standing beside a desk that an adorably tiny human/gray hybrid boy was sitting at. Fain, John's nurse and wife was heavily pregnant. The pointed faced, dark haired boy with huge, dark navy eyes looked to be about three years old. John's youngest son, Tab.

Both of them looked up at me. Fain's eyes widened as they moved over my arm before dropping and moving back to the boy. She seemed to give herself a shake and turned back to me. "Ambrose, how are you feeling?"

"I really have to pee." I winced, looking around for something to cover my torso with. While someone had put me in a set of scrub pants they left my chest bare.

"Uh, ok, let's get that arm wrapped and tied down." Fain rushed over and began to dig out rolls of gauze.

"Fain." I called to the nervous woman. I waited for her to turn back to me before speaking. "It's ok."

She opened her mouth to say something before snapping it closed once again. Her brow furrowed as she thought. It took her moment but eventually she drew in a deep breath and recentered her eyes on me. "It is." She nodded, her body relaxing and her eyes losing that worrisome anxiety.

"There we go." I chuckled and walked over, holding my arm out for her to wrap.

"This is fantastic." She breathed as she ran her eyes over it before rolling the gauze over the scar circling my bicep.

"Right?" I grinned down at her.

She smiled and shook her head in amusement as she finished wrapping my arm and tying it across my torso so it wouldn't move.

"Ok, I think you are good. Just remember, the arm is still healing so you need to be very careful with it." Her eyes twinkled knowingly up at me.

"I got it." I smiled and shuffled out of the tent, teeth clenched, face wincing with pain.

"Oh, you are good." She praised my back.

I gave her thumbs up as I ducked out of the tent.

I shuffled to the nearest bathroom, did my business, and shuffled back. I returned just in time for John to begrudgingly release me into a fully awake Lux and Kal's care. Kal helped me walk down to our tent while Lux's face took on a look of relieved concern.

We had just walked into our tent when Grayson and Elapidae ducked inside.

Elapidae came right over and pulled the gauze on my arm down far enough that she was able to examine the connection point on my arm. "I cannot believe that it actually worked."

"Neither can I." Kal claimed, his arms ready for her incoming hug.

I heard them whispering softly but turned my attention to Grayson who was now studying the arm. "Is it fully functional?" I proved its functionality by flipping him off. "So, that's a yes. How are you doing with it all?"

"It's, uh, very surreal." I winced at him, my eyes darkening with the recent memory of the day before. "As thankful as I am, I am still struggling with what happened."

"And you probably will for a while." Grayson cringed as he stepped forward and gripped my shoulder. "Just know that you aren't alone. You have Kal and Lux, you have us. All of us. And let me tell you, Scope is one hell of a listener."

I couldn't help but laugh at that, yeah, Scope did indeed have a wicked set of ears. The blind sniper could hear a pin drop a mile away. "Thank you, Grayson." I reached up to grip his wrist.

"We are family." He stated, his eyes silently telling me that I was one of them now.

"Yes, I guess we are." I smiled warmly at him, showing him my happiness at his acceptance. "And on that note, I am not the only one who went through hell that day. Kal was right there, he saw everything."

"I am fine." Kal argued, crossing his arms and glaring at me.

"Bullshit." I snapped back at him. "I can still see that haunted look in your eyes. I have no idea what you all saw but I know that none of it was good. And I know those memories are going to try and haunt you. I won't let them."

"Pushy bastard." Kal snarled.

"Maybe, but I am your pushy bastard. I told you that I would do anything for the two of you. And helping you heal from seeing that shit is part of that. Even if I have to jack you off with your own damned hand everyday until it sinks in." I growled fiercely at him.

"Overshare." Elapidae covered her ears as she hummed, her eyes wide. Grayson frowned in confusion before his eyes widened with understanding and he burst into laughter.

"Sorry." I winced at her. "I was in the moment."

Kal's dark eyed glare brightened with desire as he studied my arm.

"Not now." Lux hissed at him, nudging his side with her elbow.

"Ok." Elapidae clapped her hands. "We have our assignments. We need to convince the residents that Ambrose is healing from the miraculous reattachment of his arm as well as help him come to terms with the tragedy that happened to him. We also need to help Kal work through the trauma of seeing the man he loves lose his arm which I am going to say involves a lot of love and cuddles right along with conversations. Then there is finishing the AT which Harper has been working on right along with Wings who arrived this morning to help. Wings might have kidnapped a group of mechanics from the Bay along with the first team for the next two days and they are getting shit done."

"Good." Ambrose nodded.

"As astronomical as your miracle is, the residents and everyone else are going with it. The higher ups are not believing a word of it, especially the Andromadans. The regular residents have seen so many weird and frankly impossible things that they are believing it." Grayson explained what was happening on that front. "I should warn you, though, Diad has shared that Madron is pressing for the truth."

"Madron will have to talk to Pac on that one." Kal stated, his voice firm and unyielding.

"Yes, and that's exactly what Diad told him." Grayson nodded.

"I wish him luck. Pac made it very clear that this stays in the family. Not even the Pleiadeans know. Well, anyone who isn't a Judge as I am sure he would've had to inform them first." Kal explained Pacifier's stance on the matter.

Lux walked over and began to dig clothes out of the dressers. "Shower."

"I agree." I winced in disgust at the blood that I could still feel caked on me. While the doctors cleaned some of it off, there was still a lot on me.

And Kal. His lab coat covered body was liberally stained with rusty, dried blood. All of it from me.

"You are going to need a guard." Grayson mentioned, crossing his arms in a silent offer.

"Thanks, man." Kal shot him a grateful smile.

"Well, I will leave you to it." Elapidae gave her brother one last hug before stopping for a kiss from Grayson on her way out.

The group helped me out of the tent and we shuffled slowly down to the closest showers while I kept my head bent down. We walked inside the canvas tented area to see a set of shower stalls that came up to my upper torso. They were built out of wood and canvas and boasted hooks and shelves to hang your stuff. A set of long benches ran along the back wall. A set of sinks built into wooden countertops were set along the same side that boasted an open doorway that led to a number of porta potties.

The showers were thankfully empty at this time of day which made it easy for Grayson to stand guard outside.

Lux helped unwrap the gauze, her dark eyes moving over me, her hands warm and gentle. When she was done, she set the gauze down on the countertop and pressed soft kisses along the connection scar. "I love you." She whispered, her soothing touch sending tingles over my arm and body.

"I love you too, flower." My other hand reached up to protectively cover the back of her head. "I was so scared that I wouldn't be able to properly hold you every again, to show you how much I truly love you."

"Even if you didn't get this, I would still feel it." She whispered against my new arm. "Just feeling your heart against mine, your lips on mine, is all I ever need to feel your love."

I felt my heart swell painfully at those words. I didn't think I could ever love her more in that moment.

"Shower." Kal reminded us, naked and already strolling into one of the stalls with his shower supplies.

My eyes automatically caught on the flexing cheeks of his muscular ass. When the stall closed, cutting off my view, my gaze turned to see Lux's eyes trained right where mine were.

"Shower, Lux." I laughed, walking over to the bench and shucking the scrub bottoms. Catching up my own supplies I walked over and took the stall beside Kal's.

Concentrating on cleaning myself, I found that at least blood was a hell of a lot easier to wash off than sand was.

It was only when I was done that I stole a peek over the stall wall and down Lux's gloriously lush, naked body. My dick immediately jerked to life and snapped up into my abdomen with a very distinctive slap.

Kal froze in his drying off and slowly turned to eye me knowingly.

"She's wet and naked." I shrugged, using my own towel to dry off as I walked over to the bench and my clean, dry clothes.

Kal's eyes dropped to my bobbing dick, his own sleeping sex waking with its own thumping slap. I chuckled and pulled on my underwear and sweatpants, forcing my arousal down the side of my leg. Teeth and hair brushed, deodorant on, I leaned back against the cupboard with Kal at my side and we both watched Lux dry off and get dressed. That was almost as erotic as watching her undress.

Kal rewrapped my shoulder and tied my arm to my torso while she finished her toiletry. Then he helped me pull on a t-shirt. We packed everything back in our bags and I shuffled out with Kal's help.

"Thanks, man." Kal clapped Grayson on the shoulder as we passed him.

"Let me know for next time." Grayson flicked a couple fingers at us over his shoulder as he walked away.

CHAPTER 29

AMBROSE

W e returned to the tent and the moment Kal zipped the door shut I was pulling the shirt off and yanking at the gauze.

"Calm down, what's the rush?" Lux walked over to help me just in time for me to get free.

My arm circled her under her ass, catching her up against my chest. I was expecting some sort of pain with the use of my newly connected arm but there was absolutely nothing. No strain, no pain. Nothing but the feel of hot woman.

"Ambrose!" She gasped, her arms circling my neck as her legs circled my waist.

"It's fine, Lux." I reassured her, pulling her lips down to mine. My mouth feasted on hers as I walked her to the bed and lowered her down underneath me. "It's perfectly fine."

My hands moved, stripping her top off while my lips and tongue hungrily feasted on every inch of flesh I uncovered. She whimpered and undulated under my manipulations, her legs spread around my kneeling form, her fingers gripping my shoulders.

I shivered when a set of firm hands glided over my back, a hard body pressing into mine.

"My turn." Kal breathed in my ear, one of those hands delving into the hair at the back of my scalp and yanking my head back into his shoulder.

"What's your plan here, big boy?" I hissed out, my eyes still trained on the diamond hard nipple I just had in my mouth. I chewed on my bottom lip, my tongue tingling to feel that nipple against it.

"I am going to fuck this sexy ass of yours." Kal's erotic words had my ass clenching and my dick twitching in anticipation. "And while I do that." He reached around me to glide his fingers over the underwear covered folds of Lux's spread pussy. "You are going to fuck this tight little pussy."

"You think so, do you?" I growled out my question, my eye watching him dip his digits beneath the band to play. Lux cried out and arched up into his stroking fingers.

"No, Ambrose, I know so." His glistening fingers came out and up to brush over my lips.

My mouth automatically opened and I moaned as I sucked those fingers in, licking them clean of the divine taste coating them.

"Why don't we get those panties off so this dick can feel how hot and wet she is?" His hand dropped down to grip the dick I still had tucked down the leg of my pants.

I hissed, my hips jerking at how good his hand felt.

"Best idea." I pushed him back so I could do just that.

His hands caught at the waistband of my pants and underwear, pushing them down as I pulled Lux's wet panties off. Her aroused eyes hungrily moved over me, avidly watching my movements, her gaze catching on the flesh Kal was revealing. Her little tongue licked over her lips when my demanding dick popped out to smack up into my abdomen.

My mouth started watering at the sight of her juicy pussy. The head of my throbbing dick began to leak precum in preparation of filling that pussy with everything I had.

"Fuck." I breathed, relishing in the beauty spread before me. "You are so fucking beautiful." My new hand landed on her neck and glided down her torso, feeling over every inch of that smooth, soft skin.

"So are you." She whispered, catching my hand and adjusting my index finger out as she pulled it into her the heated suction of her mouth.

I felt that suction deep in my dick. Catching her hip, I gripped down as I slicked the head of my dick through her pussy down to her entrance and thrust inside. Her muscles rapturously tugged and pulled at the sensitive flesh of my dick.

Kal's hand gripping on my hip had me pausing, my dick fully buried in Lux. Moving my hands so that I was braced over her on my outstretched arms, my eyes stared down into hers, needing that connection.

I hissed softly when Kal's knees spread my legs and his lube slicked fingers pressed between the cheeks of my ass to rub over the crinkled hole. Sharp pain sliced as his fingers pushed through the right ring at the entrance of my asshole. That pain quickly turned to pleasure when his fingers drew along the sensitive muscles of my bowels. He worked me open, stretching my ass at the same time he lubed it up.

It had been a long, long time since the last time I allowed someone to fuck me. The unfortunate fact was that while I loved dick, I wasn't a big fan of having one inside of me. If it didn't hurt, it felt raw and uncomfortable. It honestly didn't feel good to me. But with Kal, I was totally willing to give it up for him whenever he needed no matter how raw it felt.

For some reason, whatever Kal was doing back there felt a hell of a lot better than anything I ever felt before. It actually felt good. Really good. Then those wicked fingers found the swell of my prostate. My breath wheezed in and my hips jerked when he stroked over that nerve laden spot. Fire raced up my spine and my dick somehow hardened even further.

"Oh my." Lux breathed, her hands moving over my arms and chest, her hips grinding against mine, stirring my dick inside of her.

"Fuck." I grated out between my clenched teeth. That grate turned into a high pitched squeak when I felt him maneuver something tight over my balls, a thick and rubbery band that successfully held my balls down and stopping any orgasm I might have wished to have. "Fucking hell."

"We wouldn't want you to go off too fast." Kal crooned in my ear, his slickened dick pressing into my asshole.

As loose as his fingers had worked me, his dick was a hell of a lot bigger than those digits. I bit back my groan of pain and concentrated on the way Lux was erotically swirling my dick around the fist tight channel of her pussy.

That pain flared when his crown popped inside then, like with his fingers, that turned to pure pleasure. His thick cock and its bulbous head stroked right over my nerve laden prostate as he seated himself inside my ass. He felt huge. I could feel my ass squeezing around him, investigating over him.

Kal groaned as he drew out before snapping his hips forward, slapping them off my ass and his balls off of mine.

My own hips started moving, fucking my dick through Lux's glorious pussy. Rapturous friction. The delicious drag of flesh gliding along flesh.

My fingers dug into the blankets below me as my dick found Lux's g-spot, driving over that spot over and over again. Her pleasure fueled cries echoed in my ears, her fingers digging into my forearms. The sensations rolling through me were mind boggling intense.

I could already feel my pleasure building and building with every stoke. Every erotic glide and roll of sweat slicked bodies. My hips sped up, slamming my dick into Lux while Kal pounded his dick into my ass.

Lux's pussy started to rhythmically tighten around me, her hips shuddering with pleasure. Her face was flushed, her eyes glazed. That rhythm soon changed into hard orgasmic contractions. She cried out, her body shaking, her eyes rolling back in head. Her pussy grabbed greedily at my cock, sucking at it so hard I swore she wanted to keep it.

My own pleasure rose sharply, my balls attempting to rise. My eyes widened when Kal's expert manipulations of my prostate actually worked and I felt my body orgasming without actually coming. My ass contracted around Kal's dick as my own dick flexed dryly, my testicles aching for release. My tensed body bowed back, shuddering from the intensity of the ecstasy blazing through me.

"What?" I gasped when my orgasm abated enough for me to breathe.

"Dry, prostate induced orgasm." Kal huffed, his dick still pounding its way through my tingling bowels.

"Fuck." I growled, my hips once again finding their rhythm and pumping my dick with hard strokes. Lux, her face flushed with her recent orgasm, whimpered as my dick stabbed through the slick muscles of her pussy.

Seeing her like that, lost in her pleasure, I couldn't resist lowering my torso down so I could taste her swollen lips. Her hands dug into my hair, holding me to her as our lips slid together and our tongues licked. Kal's hands caressed up my back to grip my shoulders.

My hips took on a rotating grind that had Lux crying out and tightening around me. It also did wonderous things for the sensations happening in my ass. It was mere moments before Lux was coming again, her pussy milking my cock, the muscles massaging my sensitive skin.

My teeth clenched as I road out her orgasm, my eyes watching her come apart in my arms. My sweat slicked body tensed tightly when I felt another one of those intensely dry orgasms rising. Lux's hands caressed over my face, her eyes intent on me.

I hissed out as that orgasm bit deep and I was the one coming apart in her arms. Blindingly intense. This time when I was done my balls felt almost hard, painful with the sperm building up in them and my dick felt oversensitive. The tip felt like it was splitting open, the hole burning.

"Kal." I moaned, my husky voice filled with desperation.

"Soon." Kal growled out and proceeded to force two more orgasms from me and three from Lux.

My body was shaking, my dick and balls on fire, my prostate hugely swollen. I could hardly think with the rapture that was constantly flaring through me. Waves of pure ecstasy tempered with low humming pleasure.

Lux's unfocused eyes rolled back in her head with another orgasm and my dick screamed for relief. That was when Kal finally pulled the band from my straining balls and releasing the pent up sperm built inside. They immediately and painfully snapped up and began to violently contract. Mind destroying ecstasy screamed through me.

I buried my face in the pillow beside Lux's head in order to muffle the high pitched scream that ripped from my throat. The deep burn of semen fired up the length of my dick and right out of the yawning tip. Over and over again.

My eyes went blind as my body seized. Ecstasy stole my mind and darkened the world around me.

I vaguely felt Kal's dick jerk inside of me and my bowels being filled with scalding heat.

My balls continued their hard contractions, pulsing more and more come out of me. Right when I thought I was finished they started up all over again. I couldn't think, I couldn't breathe. There was only pleasure. My fingers clawed and tore at the bedding as my highly sensitized dick spat out stream after stream of the body shuddering orgasm that seemed to never end.

I lost count of how much I deposited inside of the straining woman under me. Everything turned into pure sensation, pain and pleasure.

CHAPTER 30

AMBROSE

When my balls finally ran dry and my orgasm slowed, my mind stuttered into focus enough to realize that I was collapsed on top of Lux. My body was shaking almost violently, my balls aching painfully, my dick and ass tingling, raw with overuse. The rawness in my ass was only compounded by the warm cloth that was running over it, cleaning it.

"I think he's done, back." Lux voiced, her hands soothing over my limp face and body.

"Yeah." I gasped in, chewing on my lower lip.

"Come on." Kal caught my shoulders and helped me roll my aching body to the side of Lux.

I groaned softly when he carefully cleaned my dick before turning that cloth to the river leaking from Lux's pussy. She whimpered and attempted to close her legs on his hands, clearly feeling just as raw as I did.

"That was intense." She mentioned when Kal turned to toss the dirty cloth into the laundry basket.

"I have no words for what that was." I rubbed my hands over my face. "My dick and balls hurt and I think I fucking came enough for a week of fucking."

"It's intense but not usually that intense." Kal winced on my behalf as he laid down on my other side, propped up on an elbow, soothing his hand over my heaving torso. "You ended up having multiples."

"No kidding." I rolled my eyes at him, fully aware of that fact.

My arm circled the woman who curled into my side and rested her head on my chest. My hand came up to sooth through her silky hair.

"I say we grab some food from the Cafeteria tent and bring it back here." She stated, pressing soft kisses over my pec.

"I am not supposed to be out and about too much anyways." I shrugged, too comfortable and weak with satisfaction to move. Then there was the fact that I had my woman in my arms. My beautiful Lux.

"Yes." Lux maddeningly hopped off the bed and began to pull on her clothes.

"I will help you." Kal pulled on his own clothes and caught her hand in his as they left.

I winced as I rose from the bed and walked over to pull my sweatpants back on. I was just about to return to the bed when I heard Harper's voice calling from outside.

I pulled on a zip up hoody, zipping it up over the arm I kept tucked inside. Walking over to the couch, I relaxed back against the cushions.

"Come in, Harper." I made sure my voice was a pained rasp when I called out to her.

Harper unzipped the door and peeked her head in. She shot a glare behind her when someone pushed her inside.

"I, uh, brought your training supplies." She patted the bag she had hanging off her arm.

"Thank you." I nodded gratefully to her, my eyes turning to see Bane and Bailor stepping in behind her. Each of the men had a baby attached to their torso.

"How, uh, how are you doing?" Harper asked as she set the bag down on the coffee table and sat on the edge of the couch.

"I will be ok." I told her, not technically lying.

"I was so relieved to hear that they were able to successfully reattach your arm. And frankly amazed." She gave me a shaky smile.

"We are living in amazing times." I returned her smile, adding a grimacing element.

"Seriously, though?" Bane narrowed his eyes on me.

"Seriously." I nodded. "I will be ok."

"You know damned well that isn't what I am referring to." His voice came out as a frustrated clip.

"It's the only answer you are going to get." I told him, my voice firm, my eyes hard.

"For fuck sakes. These secrets.." Bane snarled.

"Aren't yours." I cut him off. "They aren't even mine. And you cannot tell me that you wouldn't do the same for the ones you love."

Bane's eye flashed with understanding before he nodded slowly. "Yeah."

"All you need to know is that the only person who was physically hurt, was me. And as I said, I will be ok." I reassured him. "As for the trauma that anyone else experienced that day, that is unfortunate but it honestly has nothing to do with the fact that I still have an arm."

"The workers were unfortunately brought in from other bases to help with the AT build. Most of them signed on in the hopes of being offered a permanent position here. We have filed incident reports on all of them. Copies of those reports have been sent to their home bases just as all of them have been sent packing. Their security clearances have been revoked and they are now denied any future access to any Rocky Mountain Base Property." Bane explained. "As for what happened, the man holding the brace erroneously assumed that it was fully bolted down when he let go."

"I assumed as much. To be honest, I am not surprised. The team was already having a hard time with the work and seemed to just want to get it done. They didn't seem to, uh, understand most of our orders and we had to force them to redo a lot as it was usually not done to the specifications needed." I described the struggles we were having. "Even when I explained the safety reasons for all of it they just seemed to ignore it."

"Harper shared all of that when the reports were made." Bane nodded as a wicked grin crossed Bailor's face. "She also shared the debriefing she had with them right after the incident."

"It was fucking phenomenal." Bailor laughed, bringing up his wrist and tapping over his coms. "I recorded it."

A number of different voices echoed out, the only one I recognized was Harper's.

Oh my God! Oh my God!

What the fuck happened? Harper yelled.

I thought it was bolted. I swear, it thought it was bolted.

No! I told you that I almost had it. Almost.

I didn't hear you say almost!

Probably because you were too busy telling me to hurry up.

You know what, fuck you!

Enough! Harper again. *Throwing the fucking blame. This is on each and every one of you. That man in there lost his fucking arm if not his fucking life, all because you dumb fucks couldn't fucking listen. You all were too busy fucking around and complaining about the bosses to care if someone ended up hurt. How many fucking times did we tell you dickheads to pay attention to what you are doing? To not rush? To do the fucking job properly? We told you that someone could end up severely hurt. And guess what? Someone did. Someone who didn't fucking deserve it. Someone who was too worried about your fucking safety when he should've been worried about his own.*

You can't blame this on us. It was an accident.

Yes! I fucking can! Because I just had to watch a good man, a man I respect, a man I consider a good friend, have his arm severed because you fucking idiots couldn't fucking slow down and fucking listen! It was pure fucking negligence and if this was the real world you would be fucking charged and thrown in jail. And you damned well know it. I fucking hope this haunts each and every one of you. I hope you have nightmares about it. I hope it fucking plays over and over again in your mind until you get it through your thick fucking skulls to stop being lazy fucking selfish assholes and actually think about the safety of others.

That's a little harsh.

No! There is no harsh in this fucking situation. There is only blood and agony, the loss of limb and maybe life. None of which any of you are forced to endure. This is a situation that never should've fucking happened in the first place and wouldn't have if you all had pulled your empty fucking heads out of your fucking asses. It is purely because of you that one man has been severely injured. And what's worse is that it happened right in front of one of his partners. You pricks didn't just ruin one life today, you ruined at least three, and that isn't counting the other family members. You do realize that the redhead that was in there, the one who was sobbing over Ambrose's body, terrified that he will lose the man he loves, is Grayson's brother-in-law. He's also Scope's brother-in-law and that isn't mentioning the fucking Andromadan Ancient who is also a brother-in-law.

It was silent for a long moment before Harper began to speak again.

Yeah. You better pray that Ambrose survives, because if he doesn't it's not going to be good for any of you. If I were you, I would be completely honest when delivering your incident reports and fully acknowledge your fuck ups. I would also think long and hard about your actions and how they can inadvertently effect others. As for what happened today, I suggest you all pack your bags, because there is no way any of you are staying on Rocky Mountain Base property.

That's it! You are just going to send us home! We worked our asses off for you!

You fucking dismembered a man! When are you going to get that through you fucking head? Or are you too fucking stupid to understand words? Maybe I should cut your arm off and fucking beat a brain cell into that empty fucking head of yours with it!

Ok, Harper. That was Bailor's voice. *If they don't understand what their actions caused by now then they will never understand it.*

"Yeah, some of them did try to lie on their reports. Unfortunately for them, we also sent every single report made of the incidents to their home bases so their heads know exactly what happened despite their lies." Bane described with his own smirk. "Needless to say, the heads of those bases were not impressed and have apologized on behalf of their residents. They are very worried how this will affect their relationship with the Rocky Mountain Base. Malachi and Lysander are currently in review with them and are now instituting a full DNA security check on any visitor or resident that comes in from an outside base."

"Good." I nodded, happy with that. The security checks that the Base used for their residents were very intensive and intrusive but for good reason. Too many times someone who ended up being a threat to the Base had slipped through.

"We will leave you to your recovery." Harper gave me a warm smile as she rose from the couch. "If you are feeling up to it tomorrow you should come out to see what the group Wings brought in has accomplished. It's frankly amazing."

"Will do." I gave her nod and watched as the group slipped out the door.

CHAPTER 31

LUX

Ice and Strayed understood when I let them know I wouldn't be back for another day or two, wanting to spend time with Ambrose after the accident.

My heart literally stopped when I heard the news that Ambrose had been in an accident. I didn't know what had happened other than that he had been severely injured and was being taken to the Medical tent. When I reached the Medical tent it was to see Ambrose, unconscious and covered in blood. I caught the quickest glance before a blood coated Kal caught me and spun me away from seeing anything more.

When Kal told me what had happened, I lost it. All I could think of was the horrifying pain Ambrose had to be in. I was so grateful when Kal gave me something to do, going to get the Drako first aid kit, it gave me a chance to steady myself and get my mind on straight. My heart bled for Ambrose and his loss, but at least he would live. Anything else we could and would deal with, together.

As for his new arm, I was so grateful that it worked. I didn't care that it wasn't actually his, I was just so happy that he wouldn't be in pain any longer.

And he wasn't.

That night I slept with my ear pressed to his chest, listening to the heavy rhythm of his heart. Kal fell asleep on Ambrose's other side, his hand firmly pressed to Ambrose's chest right beside my head, feeling that beat. We both needed that reassurance that he was still alive and right beside us.

The next morning, Kal got up early and took a trip to the Cafeteria tent to snag us breakfast and coffee. Then we got dressed with Ambrose once again tying down his new arm with the gauze and pulling a long sleeved t-shirt over it.

Ready for the day, Kal helped Ambrose shuffle down to the AT so we could check on the work that was being done. I was frankly amazed to see what had all been accomplished within the span of a day.

I was also horror-struck at the sight of the blood that still stained the cement floor around the powerlift they had been working on that day. So much blood and all of it proof of Ambrose's pain.

My eyes began to burn as my mind pictured how it must've been for him being trapped against that floor, the knowledge of the loss of his arm screaming through his mind. A sob caught in my chest when my eyes caught on a perfect handprint that was pressed right beside that stain. Kal's hand. My heart hurt so bad seeing that, knowing that Kal saw every second of it and stayed right with Ambrose the whole time.

Hard hands caught my waist and spun me into an equally hard chest.

"I am so sorry, Kal." I whispered, my hands fisting in his shirt. "I am so sorry."

"You have nothing to be sorry for." Kal's chest rumbled while his arms tightened around me and his hand stroked through my hair.

"You are so beautiful." I cried, drawing my head back and gripping the sides of his face to bring his forehead down to mine. "So fucking beautiful. You stayed with him through all of it. And I know, I know that had to kill you. And I am sorry because it never should've happened."

"You are right. It shouldn't have happened. But don't tell me that you wouldn't have done the same if it had been you here and not me." Kal growled softly, his red eyes dark.

"I just, I need you to know how much I love you." I whispered to him.

"I know, flower. I know." He whispered back.

Slowly drawing from him, I wiped away my tears and turned to find my other man. Ambrose was talking with Wings, Scope, and Harper.

"He seems like he is doing good." I emphasized the 'seems'.

"While he is still trying to come to terms with everything he is doing good. He's strong." Kal confirmed what I was feeling coming from Ambrose. "He told me that this place is now fully his because he has put his blood, sweat, and tears into it. He only jokes like that when things aren't serious and his mind is in a good place."

"Or when he's drugged." I pointed out with a smile.

"Yeah, I was slightly shocked at that one. But it also told me that while the new arm was a shock, he was ok with it." Kal chuckled.

"He just needs to get it worn in, get some grease on it, then it will start to feel like his." I smiled, my eyes turning to watch Ambrose shake his head and glare at Wings as the man gestured. "Come on, let's go save Wings."

"Yup." Kal nodded, his hand finding the small of my back as we walked over to Ambrose.

"No, Wings." Ambrose bit out. "We want them parked along the side by the tool chests because it will make it easier to do emergency quick fixes. If we need them up on the powerlifts or under the arms then we are doing maintenance and big fixes, that's where the rolling tables come in. The center has to remain clear for the flight paths. I have gone over it numerous times and this is the best way to set this up."

Wings frowned as he looked around before finally nodding in agreement. "Ok, ok, it makes sense now."

"Thank you." Ambrose rolled his eyes.

"Kal, how's it hanging?" Wings nodded in greeting.

"Do you really want me to answer that?" Kal expertly turned the question around on him.

"Side stepping the double entendre here..." Wings shot Kal a quick smirk before his face turned serious. "I wouldn't have asked if I didn't want to know. You are a good friend, pretty muchly family, and it's been a rough couple days for you all."

"We are healing, slowly." Kal told Wings, his eyes warming with appreciation.

"Well, let us know. Scope is pretty good at handling loss and traumatizing accidents." Wings clapped Scope on the back causing the redhead to roll his eyes.

"Fortunately, I didn't actually lose anything like Scope did." Ambrose gestured to the lump under his shirt.

"Yes, the miracle of a successful reattachment." Wings nodded with a sly smile kicking up at the corner of his lips.

"It truly was a miracle." Ambrose agreed softly.

"Madron is going crazy wanting to know. Him and Callden. Especially since Diad knows. I even broke down and asked Scope but he doesn't know anything about it." Wings chuckled.

"I told Asp that I didn't want to know." Scope stated, crossing his arms. "Then I am not keeping secrets from Wings."

"Good call." Kal chuckled. "Madron is just going to have to live without knowing."

"Are you going to hang around and criticize everything we do?" Wings asked Ambrose with sly grin.

"No, I will leave you to it." Ambrose shook his head and gave a very believable wince. "I think it's time to go."

With that, Kal caught Ambrose's good arm and helped him shuffle out while I walked beside them.

"Hold up." Scope called as he jogged up to join us.

"I thought you didn't want to know?" Kal asked him.

"I don't. This is about something else." Scope shook his head slowly. "Diad, Grayson, and I were talking about everything you have done for us and the girls."

"And?" Kal frowned at him.

"And, we all just want you to know that we are here for you. For whatever you need. It's one of the reasons Wings collected as many people as he could to bring out here and get the AT done. It was honestly the least we could do." Scope explained as we stopped at the large, opened, metal doors.

"I appreciate that." Kal stated, frowning at the man.

"The thing is, you aren't just the triplet's brother, but you are ours as well." Scope continued. "Just like Ambrose is now our brother."

"Nope." I shook my head in denial. "Both Kal and Ambrose cannot be brothers. That is just wrong."

Scope burst into laugher. "Ok, maybe I didn't phrase that right. What I am trying to say is that we consider Ambrose and Lux just as much a part of the family as you consider us to be. So, whatever this is, we have your back."

"Thank you, Scope." Kal nodded, reaching out to grip the man's shoulder for a moment.

"Ambrose, Lux, I am really looking forward to getting to know both of you better. From everything I have heard the three of you make one hell of a team." Scope nodded at us before turning back into the AT and yelling for Wings.

"I like him." Ambrose grunted. "I always have."

"Should I be worried?" Kal joked as we shuffled back to our tent.

"No, redheads aren't my thing." Ambrose ducked his head down to hide his mischievous grin. I could stop myself from giggling at the astonished look Kal shot him. "What? It's true. Right up until the moment you were dragged into my life I was all about delicate little brunettes with deep, dark eyes who spent their days singing to plants."

"You say the sweetest things." Kal laughed.

"He really does." I smiled, feeling my cheeks warm with those words.

We reached the tent and Ambrose settled at the kitchen table with his training supplies while Kal disappeared for awhile. I relaxed back on the bed with a book. The morning passed with a comforting silence. At lunch time, I walked down and picked up lunch for us.

Kal returned in the early afternoon and dumped a whole host of large, square black bags on the coffee table. Curious, I wandered over to see that he had tracked down tattooing supplies. A gun, needles, ink, tracing paper, sterilization equipment, gloves, aftercare products. My heart jumped with anticipation, my sex already waking.

"I have an idea that I want to draw out before you make your final decision." Kal told the man who was watching from the kitchen table.

"What are you thinking?" Ambrose asked, just as curious as I was.

"Something to cover the scar." Kal grunted, pulling out a sketch pad and some pens. "Give me an hour."

Ambrose shrugged and returned to his studies while I returned to my book.

It was about an hour later when Kal called us over.

I was astonished at what my talented man had drawn. A ripped skin design that went all the way around the bicep displaying mechanics underneath. The mechanics were made from roughened, grease streaked engine parts. Long vines were laced through the ripped skin, in the process of stitching it back together again. The vines flowered up his bicep to his shoulder and down to his elbow. The flowers were a bright red and the vines carried an eerily glowing red shadow.

It clearly displayed the inner strength Ambrose carried being boosted by Kal and I. We were all there.

"This is my final decision." Ambrose breathed in shock, running a fingertip over the drawing. "It's all of us, together."

"It's beautiful." I felt tears pop in my eyes.

Kal's lips stretched into this warm, soft smile that hit me right in the heart.

Ambrose stripped out of his shirt and pulled off the gauze before laying down on the surprisingly sturdy coffee table. I helpfully pulled one of the end tables over so Kal could set up his stuff.

With Ambrose's arm stretched out, resting on his knee, Kal began. I knelt at Ambrose's other side and keenly watched as Kal worked. Ambrose's muscles twitched under the needle as it drew over his skin. My hand rested over Ambrose's hard, stretched chest, feeling the slight trembling moving through him.

Kal's eyes concentrated on what he was doing, a line or shadow of ink was followed by a cleaning swipe of a towel.

I couldn't stop my mesmerized eyes from devouring the sight in front of me. There was just something about watching this, the whole process of the needle moving, sinking the ink deep into the skin. I couldn't lie, it was frankly arousing.

My hand stroked, feeling over bulging muscles, ridges, hard nipples. Before I could stop myself I found my lips moving over his shoulder.

"You aren't helping." Ambrose's flushed face turned to me.

"Are you sure?" I asked with a sly grin, nibbling on his salty, deliciousness.

"I need to stay still." He growled softly, his voice carrying an element of warning.

"You really do, don't you?" I licked along the side of his pec.

Kal chuckled, his amused red eyes tipping up to mine from his bent head. "Did you know that when men get tattoos done on their cocks, it is recommended that they aren't aroused?"

"Really?" I turned a set of questioning eyes to Ambrose.

"Fuck no." He immediately shot that hope down. "There is no way. Can you imaging how long I would have to wait for it to heal before I can have sex again."

"Oh, yeah, not worth it." I vehemently agreed while Kal laughed. "Aren't you glad that the same rule doesn't apply right now?"

"Lux." Ambrose grunted. "If I have to keep it in my pants, so do you."

"Fine." I rolled my eyes at him and laid my chin down on his shoulder.

His hand curled up to grip the back of my head as his lips pressed into my forehead.

While it only took Kal an hour to draw the design out, it took a lot longer for him to ink it. First came the outline that went all the way around Ambrose's arm which had him shifting around so Kal could reach the back. Then came the color and shading. The last was the very fine details.

Watching Kal work was a weird mix of arousing and hypnotizing. His strong fingers pinched down on the gun, the tendons and bones of his hand flexing and rolling right along with the tendons in his forearm. It honestly amazed me how wickedly talented he was.

By the time he was done, setting the needle aside to be cleaned and cleaning the ink off of Ambrose's shoulder. It was beautiful, the muted colors somehow blending seamlessly with his skin in a way that made it look so realistic.

"Woah." I breathed softly as Kal slathered antibiotic ointment on it before covering it with transparent tattoo film.

"Keep it on for a couple hours." Kal ordered. "After that it should be mostly healed."

"Yeah." Ambrose nodded, siting up, still examining the tattoo. With a wicked fast movement, he caught the back of Kal's neck and yanked him in.

Lips met, pressing, sliding. Tongues flashed, licking. Jaws moved, eating.

I truly loved watching them kiss.

"It's beautiful, thank you." Ambrose breathed when he finally pulled away, resting his forehead against Kal's.

"Anytime." Kal grinned with a mixture of pride and anticipation. "You are a great canvas."

CHAPTER 32

LUX

The next week passed with Ambrose pretending to slowly get better while doing his training and keeping an eye on the AT set up. The two day push that Wings and the group he brought in successfully got all of the heavy equipment set up leaving the small stuff left for Harper and Ambrose to handle.

I was walking into the AT one afternoon to see Harper standing between a kneeling Ambrose and the open doorway. She jumped in guilty surprise when she saw me walk in. I couldn't help but laugh when I got close enough that she was able to see that it was me and she immediately deflated with relief.

Ambrose was kneeling at the bottom of an air compressor with a socket wrench on the ground beside him. He had been adjusting his shirt over the arm he was still hiding under it, but stopped the moment he saw that it was me.

"How long has this been happening?" I raised a set of questioning eyebrows and pointed my finger between the two guilty looking people.

"Since Wings left." Harper cringed while Ambrose pushed to his feet and grinned at me.

"I so knew you wouldn't be able to resist." I laughed, catching the front of Ambrose's shirt and yanking his smiling self in for a kiss. "Sneaky man."

"Hmm." He hummed as his lips playfully nipped mine open for his tongue to get its taste.

Sliding my hand under his shirt, my spread fingers glided up the ridges of his abdomen to find that hand, I pulled it out the bottom. I couldn't help but laugh at the grime smeared over his fingers.

"I knew I felt some callouses building on these." I rubbed my fingers over the ones he was successfully roughening up.

"You like my callouses." He whispered into my forehead.

"That's not true. I don't like your callouses, I love them." I whispered back, loving the sight of the grime on those talented digits. "It's you. And I love you. Every little part of you."

"Flower." He breathed, his fingers tightening on mine.

A familiar humming sound had all three of us looking to the entrance of AT. We weren't expecting an order.

Ambrose pulled his hand back into his shirt and caught my hand in his other one as he guided us to the door.

We stepped out to see five black ships shaped like open ended triangles.

"The pilots are here." Harper grinned excitedly.

"They are early." Ambrose frowned as the ships hovered above the protective energy Dome that circled the Ranch.

"Fuck! Fuck! Fuck!" Grayson came barging down the path with Bane right on his heels. "What do you mean they haven't cleared security? We have them right the fuck here, Marko!"

"I am working on it, Grayson." Marko's voice snapped out. "They literally just sent in their ship profiles."

"Are their DNA profiles done at least?" Bane asked as the two men skidded to a stop right beside us.

"Yes. Thank God they sent those in when they first signed on." Marko growled, the usually calm man clearly frustrated. "For fuck sakes, we asked for these profiles when they first took off so that we could be ready for them."

"This is fucking ridiculous." Grayson growled.

"Give us some fucking time, Grayson. We are working as fast as we can but they are going to have to wait until Wings gets there and scans them." Marko stated, his voice clipped.

"Where is he?" Bane questioned.

"They are just lifting off now. Lysander and Malachi are with them." Marko informed us.

"Can you get me a line of communication to the head craft?" Ambrose asked.

"Yeah, uh..." Marko fell silent for a couple seconds before Ambrose's coms dinged with an incoming call.

Ambrose tapped on his coms and began to speak. "November Charlie 1 this is Romeo Alpha Tango, Alpha Sierra Charlie Mike 1, please confirm."

"Romeo Alpha Tango, Alpha Sierra Charlie Mike 1 this November Charlie 1, Sierra Charlie Papa 1, reading." A low masculine, grating voice came over the line.

"Confirmed, welcome." Ambrose greeted. "Please await security confirmation."

"Patience is a virtue, RAT ASCM1. We are cognizant of our advanced arrival and am apologetic of it. Unfortunately, we were forced to employ extreme combat maneuvers during our journey. NC2 and NC5 have taken some damage." The voice returned somehow becoming even raspier as it continued to speak.

"Heard, SCP1, we are prepared for damage control." Ambrose reassured him. "Any injuries to report?"

"Nothing life threatening." SCP1 returned.

"Heard. Staff doctor is available." Ambrose stated as Bane quickly typed something out on his coms.

It took a couple minutes before John came ambling up the path with a Medi-Pac in his hand. He also had two little boys walking beside him. While his sons were usually with him in the Medical tent, he rarely took them with him on outside calls like this. Fain, his wife usually had the boys during those times, but Fain gave birth to their daughter the day before and was currently recovering in their tent.

"Our appreciations." The voice came back just as another ship appeared, this one Wings' Andromadan ship.

The line fell silent as Wings scanned each ship and one by one they finally descended through the Dome to land on the large landing pad just outside the AT. The last to descend was Wings. Lysander and Malachi immediately disembarked to meet up with the disembarking pilots. They were all wearing dark silvery uniforms that slicked over their bodies, some sort of silvery, flexible boots, and black gloves.

After a couple minutes the group started walking our way. Some of them did indeed have blood staining them.

John immediately stepped forward to take a look at those ones. I couldn't help but notice how they all smiled at the adorable boys who were helping their father.

"ASCM1?" One of the pilots stepped forward speaking in the voice from Ambrose's coms.

The man was wickedly tall and lean with wide shoulders and a slim waist. The sharp muscles of his body clearly outlined by the suit he was wearing. Eerie pale grey eyes looked out from under dark brows. Dark blond hair was cut close to his head showing numerous scars. One of those scars was fairly deep, curving along his cheek, around his ear to curve around to the back of his skull. There was another distinctive one that started on his Adam's apple and ran across one side his neck to curl down and disappear under his suit.

"SCP1." Ambrose released my hand to hold his hand out to the man.

"Ragel." The man nodded, shaking Ambrose's hand. "I guess we are going to be working fairly close with one another."

"Ambrose." Ambrose smiled. "My woman, Lux. My second, ASCM2, Harper. And yes, we will be."

Ragel gave me and Harper a nod in greeting before turning back to Ambrose. "I have heard some phenomenal things about you and am looking forward to seeing you in action."

"Thank you." Ambrose's teeth caught his lower lip.

"My team." Ragel turned to the other four pilots. "My second, SCP2, Xaxa."

The blond woman had white gauze tapped to the side of her head. Her long, pale blond hair was braided down her back. Her eyes were a clear, pale blue. She looked very strong and flexible.

"SCP3, Noriel." Another male, shorter yet bulkier than Ragel with a shock of hair boasting an interesting mix of shades. He had aqua eyes.

"SCP4, Erus." A male of similar height to Noriel with a sharper build that looked more built for speed than strength.

"SCP5, Vorhalla." A female with jagged shoulder length hair and a slim, willowy build. Her eyes were a greyish green.

"SCP's I would like to introduce you to Bane Darwish and Grayson Dodge, code name Reaper." Lysander stepped forward to introduce. "Bane is the resident head of the Ranch and Grayson is head of Ranch Security. Grayson is also Malachi's second. They are the ones who will be keeping you all in line and keeping your asses safe."

Handshakes went around as the group greeted one another.

"We have tents already set up for you. If there is anything else you require just place an order and if possible it will be found and delivered." Bane started his spiel. "You all should've received the security packet with the procedures and regulations and will be assigned coms."

"Yes, it was...a lot." Xaxa noted, her brow furrowing slightly.

"It is, but we have found that being overly cautious saves lives and makes living here better for everyone." Bane explained. "We take our safety and security very serious. But that doesn't mean we don't find ways to de-stress and have fun."

"That is understandable." Ragel shot Xaxa a punishing look that caused her to immediately drop her head.

"Look, I know it seems like a lot, but there is a reason a high number of people apply to live out here." Grayson reassured the group.

"I am looking forward to it." Erus grinned.

"Why don't you get your crafts parked in the AT and Harper and I will give them a once over while you all get settled in and familiar with the place." Ambrose gestured to the tent village.

"We have equipment to unload." Ragel shook his head in denial.

"You can grab your stuff but leave the equipment to us." Ambrose directed. "It's been a long trip for you and not an easy one. Take tonight."

"Are you sure?" Ragel frowned at Ambrose, his eyes landing on the lump in Ambrose's shirt.

"We got this." Ambrose reassured him.

With that everyone started moving. I left them to it as I wandered down the path to Kal's office tent. I couldn't help but giggle at the sight of him sitting at his desk with a baby strapped to his chest.

"Where is Sabastian?" I asked, pulling Dominic free and tucking the happily gurgling boy to my chest.

"With Ela." Kal murmured, his eyes trained down on the mess in front of him. "Bailor got called out to one of the sites."

"That was not easy." Elapidae exclaimed, walking in with Sabastian attached to her chest and a cringe on her face.

"Oh?" I questioned, running my hand over Dominic's tiny back.

"I had to pee." She explained.

"Oh." I cringed on her behalf.

"Our new residents arrived." She hinted, sitting down in one of the chairs in front of Kal's desk.

"They have. It's going to be an adjustment but their commander, Ragel, seems to have a firm handle on them." I described for her.

"Good." She sighed softly, her eyes taking on a relieved look. "Everyone has been so on edge since the incident, and with these newcomers..."

"They have nothing to do with us." Kal mumbled, scrawling something out on a piece of paper.

"God, I love watching him work." I noted, bending my head down to breathe in the womb clenching scent of baby.

"What are you doing?" He frowned up at me.

"Breathing baby." I hummed happily.

"Right?" Elapidae exclaimed, getting her own whiff off of Sabastian. "Yeah, that's the stuff."

"You two are weird." He shook his head and returned to his work.

Swaying over to him, I bent down until my lips were brushing his ear. "What if I told you that I was ovulating?"

His head snapped up and bright red eyes found mine. "Yeah." I smirked down at him. "That's exactly what it's like for us."

His eyes dropped to the baby in my arms before returning to mine. "Heard." He grunted, returning back to his work.

That was right about when Dominic started searching, his soft gurgles turning into angry grunts.

"Now what are you going to do?" Kal chuckled, his eyes flashing with amusement.

"Now I am going to do what anyone would do and wander down to this little guy's tent to get him a bottle." I rolled my eyes at Kal, turning to walk out the door. "We will be back."

"Wait, I might as well come. They tend to have the same eating patterns so Sabastian is going to get hungry right away." Elapidae followed me out.

"He's going to be such a good dad." I smiled warmly down at the boy who was sniffling, his face still searching over my collarbone.

"He really is." Elapidae agreed. "He did such a good job with us."

"He did." I agreed, fully aware that Kal ended up being not just a brother but a father figure to the girls growing up. "You all turned out so awesome."

"Honestly, I have no idea how we would've turned out if he never stepped up." Elapidae explained with a sad look on her face. "He was always there for us and, as much as I hate to say it, we frequently took him for granted. When he went missing for those weeks, it was kind of a wake up call for all of us. We all started remembering everything he did for us. Everything he gave up for all of us, including Pac. He gave up having a normal childhood so he could take care of us and give us the childhood he was missing out on. He took care of us, watched over us, supported and loved us. All without one single complaint."

"You know when he talks about his childhood it's mostly good things, happy things. I know that you all are regretting how your may or may not have treated him, but please don't. He doesn't regret one single moment of it and I really don't think he would want you to regret it either." I reassured her with a warm smile.

"Oh no, we don't regret our time with him, we regret that we took him for granted." She cringed.

"I hate to break it to but that isn't an uncommon thing when it comes to a parental figure. Youngsters always just assume that they will always be around. They fight and argue with them, they get mad at them. All of those things that seem to resonate when the loss of that parental figure is presented. But all of that means that they were doing their job, guiding and protecting, giving the youngster a safe place where they can be happy." I explained to her.

Ela chuckled softly. "You know, I have been to so many worlds and seen so many different familial relationships but I have never heard it described so accurately before."

We reached the tent and ducked inside to head to the minifridge and the bottles. We got them prepared and sat down on the couch to pop them in a couple hungry mouths.

"I have noticed that all of you have been trying so hard to show how much you appreciate him. I mean Pacifier has stopped by to spend time with Kal at least once a day." I gave her a smile. "And Kal loves that, he always loves spending time with all of you, but he did say that he hopes it isn't affecting your day to day lives. He just really wants you all to be happy."

"Well, speaking for myself, it isn't." She laughed. "And we want him to be just as happy as we are. Which is where you and Ambrose are nailing it."

"I totally caught Ambrose cheating today. Harper was covering for him." I shared with her, pulling the bottle free to burp a little boy. Dominic showed that he was an expert at that. Sabastian, not so much.

"I told Grayson he wouldn't be able to keep his 'hand' to himself." Elapidae laughed.

"Right? Stubborn man." I rolled my eyes at how stubborn Ambrose was. Well, both him and Kal.

"Grayson is the same." Elapidae shared.

"Is there a reason you are in my tent?" Bailor demanded when he strolled inside only to stop in surprise.

"Feeding time." I gestured to the bottle that Dominic was hungrily devouring.

"Valid." He nodded, walking over to crouch beside the couch and smile down at his boys. "I can take them now."

"Kal still has the other carrier." I pointed out.

"That's ok, I am going to attach the back carrier and have one on each side." He smiled happily.

We finished feeding the boys but quickly abandoned them to their father when a very aromatic odour began to rise from them.

"Thanks." Bailor yelled sarcastically after us, his arms full of babies.

"Anytime." I called back as Elapidae and I raced off, laughing our asses off.

"Hello." A deep male voice greeted from the group we inadvertently ended up walking into.

"Yeah, no." Grayson clipped out at Erus as he stepped forward to stand in front of Elapidae.

"Yours?" Erus asked, trying to peek around Grayson.

"All mine." Grayson claimed, his hand tightening around the one Elapidae slid into it. "My wife."

"Interesting." One of the men frowned.

"Lysander." Grayson turned to the man.

"Nope." Lysander shook his head. "We are waiting to hear back."

"Then I will leave you to it." Grayson guided Elapidae and I away, ignoring the curious looks we were getting.

Once we reached Kal's office tent, we ducked inside and headed straight to Kal.

CHAPTER 33

KALBELIYAS

I walked into the Cafeteria tent behind Lux that night for supper and ignored the wide eyed looks I got from the new combat pilots. Being a myth was hard work sometimes.

Ambrose was missing, telling me that I would need to pick up supper for him. I was kind of looking forward to delivering it to him, but first Lux and I would need to get changed.

We just sat down with our meals and the bag of takeaway for Ambrose when a man with multi shaded blond hair sat down across from me.

"Hello." The man greeted, his eyes narrowed on me.

Pausing in my eating, I tipped my eyes up to the man and met his eyes with mine. I stared at him, reading the feel of his energy. Strength, trauma, intelligence. There was an edge of darkness swirling around him, anger, distrust, pain. A familiar feeling, one I felt from so many others. This man had been abused and had never been given the chance to heal.

And this was the reason he was sitting with me, his silent way of attempting to intimidate me into giving him answers he felt like he needed. I was pretty sure it would have worked if I wasn't who I was.

I felt Ela and Grayson pause at the end of our table. "Shit." Ela hissed.

"Up we go." Grayson caught the man's shoulders and pulled him up. The man tensed tightly for a bare second, coiling to strike, before relaxing. The movement was so quick it would've been missed by anyone else other than me.

"I was just being polite." The man excused.

"Pick someone else." Grayson cringed, passing the man off to a very concerned looking Bane who appeared at his side.

"Come, Noriel, you can sit with me and my family." Bane attempted to pull Noriel away only for the man to suddenly freeze solid, becoming an immovable wall.

"I know who you are." Noriel hissed down at me, almost silently. "Both of you."

"No, you really don't." Bane growled out just as silently, his voice filled with warning.

Noriel stared at him for a long moment before once again turning his gaze to mine.

"You have been warned, Nordic." I stated coldly, rising from the bench with the takeaway and bringing Lux with me.

"I thought the woman was with Ambrose." The man noted, his curious eyes falling to Lux.

"She has a name. And she is also mine. They both are." I warned him in a crooning voice, reaching up to run a threatening fingertip over his chin. "You may think you know who we are...Noriel...but you really have no idea."

His eyes flashed with fear before dropping from the intensity of mine, his gaze moving blindly around the tent as his jaw clenched under my ominous caress. Leaning in, I whispered right next to his ear, feeling the shiver of terror that ran through his body. "Fuck around, Noriel, and find out."

Noriel's face paled right before he was suddenly yanked back by a very tall, scared man who had a hand on the neck of his dark silver uniform. The man hauled Noriel all the way down the path to a table that the rest of the pilots were occupying. Leaving them to that, I guided Lux out of the tent, passed the four other shocked looking pilots. I chuckled softly as we walked down the path, heading back to our tent.

"You really enjoyed that." Lux giggled, rubbing her face over my shoulder.

"I did." I shot her a knowing grin. "He may have come across one of my race before but he hasn't come across a juror or a Judge. We would never have allowed him to see us. Plus, his disrespect rubbed me the wrong way."

"Understandable." She agreed.

We changed and were walking to the AT when a robed, hooded figure appeared right beside me. "I hear the Ranch has some new guests." Pac stated by way of greeting.

"I am surprised it took you this long to show up." I grunted at my brother.

"I have been here since Lux and Ela amused the hell out of me by leaving a set of very odorous children with Bailor. He was not a happy camper when he unpacked those loads." Pac chuckled darkly.

"Bad?" Lux grinned with amusement, the takeaway bag swinging from her arm.

"All the way up the backs. Both of them. He had to haul the kids down to the showers to clean them properly." Pac described.

"You know, we really shouldn't laugh. I mean, someday that will be us." Lux very accurately pointed out.

"If the day every comes that I have to shower my kid off because they overloaded, I am going to be laughing the whole time." Pac shrugged, a warm, hopeful smile crossing his face.

"What is the plan here?" I asked curiously, wondering what his play was.

"After that confrontation, we wait. They can sit on their assumptions." Pac declared firmly.

"Keep me posted." I told him.

"Now that we have that out of the way should we talk about these new looks you two are rocking?" Pac gestured a black tipped finger over us.

"Date night." Lux smiled excitedly.

Pac studied us for a long moment before shrugging. "Looks interesting."

"Oh, it will be." I grinned with anticipation.

All three of us slowed to a stop as we crossed the path of the tall, scarred pilot who seemed to be in charge. The man slowed to stop and eyed us warily.

"Fuck." His deep voice grated out in way that told me that he'd had his vocal cords damaged at some point.

Pac head slowly and ominously tilted to the side as he studied the man.

"He has trust issues." The man held his hands up in surrender as he attempted to defend his pilot.

"So do you, so that defense is mute." I stated coldly.

"He needs to learn." Pac's voice circled out and around the man.

"I will keep him in line." The man promised.

"We will see." Pac's voice had the man's body tensing.

"You will." The man nodded sharply. "Uh, my name is Ragel."

Both Pac and I simply nodded in return. This man and his team would have to earn the right to our names.

"I, uh, really am looking forward to working with Ambrose. I heard a lot of good things about him." Ragel's eyes dropped to Lux as if speaking to her. "And I heard what happened with his arm. I am frankly amazed at his fortitude."

"He has been looking forward to working with you as well. Although, we got very little information on you and your team." Lux explained politely to him.

"Lysander explained that. The Ministry was supposed to send all of that information ahead of time and I am not quite sure what happened. They should be getting our personal profiles soon." Ragel explained.

"That's good." Lux nodded.

"Well, I will leave you to your evening." Ragel bowed his head to us before sliding around us and continuing on his way.

"He has a chance." Pac murmured as we continued on our own way.

"Pac." I started speaking as we approached the AT. "As much as I love you, you might want to bow out now before things get detailed in a way that will probably haunt you."

"Yep." Pac nodded. "I am going to go find out if Carter looks good in glasses."

With that he swirled into energy and disappeared.

Lux giggled as she tiptoed up and pressed a kiss to my lips before swaying into the open doors. The heels of her stilettos clicked loudly on the cement with her firm steps. Her knee length, skintight black skirt showed off the delicious sway of her panty less ass. Sheer stockings slicked up her legs and under her skirt where I knew they were tied to the black garter belt she was wearing. Her blouse was unbuttoned far enough to give a peek of the lacy black bra that was pushing her beautiful breasts up and out. Her hair was up in a smooth French twist and a set of black rimmed glasses were perched on her nose.

As for me, I was dressed in a set of black slacks and a vest with a white dress shirt that was opened right down to the top of the vest. My sleeves were rolled up and I had my own set of black rimmed glasses on my face. In my hand was a wooden pointer.

I couldn't stop myself from grinning when I heard Lux's voice snap out. "Mr. Sokolov!"

"Uh?" Ambrose emoted in confusion.

"I have received some very disturbing reports from your professor. You have been a very disobedient boy." Her voice clipped out coldly.

"I am sorry, Mrs. Sokolov." Ambrose's voice sounded huskily amused. "I meant no harm."

"Be that as it may, we do not condone that type of behaviour." She stated right before gasping. "Mr. Sokolov."

"Well, if I am already in trouble." His voice came out huskily.

Swirling into energy, I shot inside to drop down into physical right behind the man who had Lux pressed back into the edge of his desk. His head was ducked down to her, his mouth was firmly attached to the smooth arch of her neck.

"Tisk, tisk, Mr. Sokolov." The pointer in my hand snapped up to press into the underside of his jaw, pushing his head up and back. "Is that the way you react when the Dean confronts you on your highly erroneous behaviour?"

"Professor." His Adams apple moved as he swallowed, his teeth gnawing on his lower lip. "Would you be so kind as to inform me on my wrong doings?"

"Very well." The pointer snapped down to crack over his ass causing him to jump in surprise. "This ass is a tease."

He chuckled softly right before he spun around. The pointed was ripped from my hands and snapped in half before it was tossed over his shoulder. "It isn't my ass that is the tease, Professor." His voice came out dark, husky, his eyes devouring over me.

I snarled when his hand found my vest and yanked me forward, taking full control of the situation. My already aroused cock twitched wildly as it was flooded with even more blood. "But you are right, I am a very bad boy. And I am about to show you exactly how bad I am."

"Mr. Sokolov." I gasped as if in outrage.

"Very, very bad." He crooned in my ear sending shivers through my body. I groaned when his other hand slid down my chest to grip down on my aching dick. "Don't even think about, Mrs. Sokolov." He growled back to the woman who was attempting to slide out from between him and the desk.

"Mr. Sokolov, I really must protest." She cried out, her hands attempting to move him.

"You are going to protest even more before I am done with you." Ambrose stated, the hand gripping my vest and shirt ripping them right down the center. Buttons popped free, pinging everywhere as the material parted to reveal my chest.

"Look at that, Professor." He hissed, running his hand over my chest, pausing to play with one of my hard nipples. The hand gripping my cock felt over the sensitive muscle, sending pleasure flaring through me. "This feels really good but I am thinking that I should see what I am playing with. After all, that is the best way I learn."

"Mr. Sokolov, this is highly unadvisable." I slapped his hands away and attempted backed up.

His hands came right back, one at my neck, the other to my belt, yanking me right back into him. My hands followed, gripping down on his wrists in an attempt to stop him. He held me still, his dark eyes burning into mine as he yanked open the belt and began to work on the front of my pants.

I felt that look deep inside. Something about when he took control like this really got to me. That is not saying that I didn't like taking control myself when I felt the need. But seeing him like this got me so aroused that it felt like my dick would crack in half with the slightest pressure.

His eyes flared when he read the clear enjoyment in my eyes. His lips tilted up in a smirk and his hand dipped into my pants to palm my cock. "Naughty, Professor. No underwear."

"Fuck." I moaned as his deliciously hard hand stroked up and down my dick, pulling up my aching length to milk over the tip.

"Tell me, Professor, if this is so wrong how come you are so deliciously hard?" He leaned in a whispered in my ear.

"It's an automatically bodily reaction to stimulation." I lied to him. If anyone else but him or Lux pulled this shit on me there was no way I would be aroused let along this hard. Instead, I would be beating their ass.

"Bullshit." He growled, twisting around to press me to the desk beside a highly aroused Lux.

She was doing well at keeping her face serious but the flush covering her face and the glint in her eyes gave her away.

"Mr. Sokolov!" Her voice snapped out. "That is enough!"

"Not even close." Ambrose bit out, his hand releasing my neck to grip her jaw. "I am betting that despite all of your protestations that sweet little pussy of yours is soaking fucking wet."

She glared at him as she tried to pull her face free only for his fingers to tighten. "Nuh uh." He denied. "Professor, why don't you do all of us a favor and check that for us?"

When all I did was glare at him his hand tightened threatening on my cock. "Now."

With a sneer, I turned to the woman beside me and snaked a hand up her skirt to finger her pussy. My sexy little Dean was indeed wet, very wet. Lux gasped, her legs automatically spreading as far as they could go in that skirt, her hips arching up into the stroke of my fingers.

"Tell me." Ambrose released my cock to grip the back of my neck.

"She's soaked." I shared with him.

"Yeah? A gentleman would offer to help her clean that up." He guided me over to stand in front of Lux. "Pull that sexy little skirt up."

My greedy dick spurted a line of precum as my hands did as he asked, working her skirt up her thighs and over her ass.

"Fuck, that's a juicy little pussy." He growled. "Help her up onto the desk, Professor, and clean up that mess."

"How the fuck do you want me to do that, Mr. Sokolov?" I demanded in a harsh voice, my hands helping Lux up onto the desk while my body pulled against his hold.

"With your dirty mouth, Professor." His hand caught the back of my neck and pushed my head down. "Spread her legs nice and wide so you can really get your tongue in there."

I growled as I was bent over, my hands finding Lux's thighs and spreading her legs up and out. My hungry mouth fell on her delicious pussy, my tongue already sweeping up her taste. My eyes rolled with pleasure, my hips rolling, fucking my desperate dick through the air.

"Undo the blouse and bra, Mrs. Sokolov." Ambrose's next order had the whimpering and undulating woman in my hold flicking open the buttons of her shirt and opening the front clasp of her bra. Her luscious breasts popped out, nipples gloriously hard and begging for attention.

"Now isn't that pretty." Ambrose crooned, his hands pushing my loosened slacks all the way off my hips to pool around my ankles.

I shivered when his hands stroked over my ass, guiding my hips back and tilting my ass up even further.

"Make sure you get all of that juicy mess cleaned up." He ordered, his voice husky.

A deep groan broke from my chest and vibrated over the pulsing clit I was sucking on when one of his slickened fingers found my asshole and pushed inside.

"She keeps producing more." I hissed around her delectable flesh.

"Then maybe you should plug that leak with something long and thick." His hand caught the back of my hair and pulled me up at the same time the hand on my hip shoved me forward. I fell over Lux's sprawled from, my hands hitting the desk beside her head, my dick gliding through the heated folds of her pussy.

"Oops, we missed." Ambrose chuckled darkly, his hard hand helpfully finding my straining cock and pressing it right where it was screaming to be. My hips shuddered as his hold on my hip pushed me deeper and deeper, forcing my dick through the straining muscles of Lux's twitching pussy.

"Fuck." I groaned with pleasure at the same time Lux gripped my shoulders and cried out with orgasmic ecstasy. "Kal!"

Her hips snapped up, completely seating me as she came all over my cock. Her greedy little pussy gripped and milked my cock, doing everything it could to suck out my sperm. My teeth clenched and my body tensed as I did everything I could to stop myself from following her right into that ecstasy.

I was just getting a grip on myself when a hard dick pushed into my ass. My fingers scrabbled over the top of the desk as that rapturous dick glided right over my prostate until hips hit the cheeks of my ass.

"How does it feel, Professor, having my big dick buried deep in your tight ass?" Ambrose breathed in my ear, his teeth nipping at the lobe. His lips moved to my back as his hand pushed me down until my chest was pressed to Lux's. Her hands moved from my arms and chest to my shoulders and face.

"Fuck." I groaned, unable to emote anything comprehensive. The pleasure rolling through me was successfully stealing any thoughts my brain was struggling to produce.

"That's right, Professor." Ambrose growled, his hips pulling that glorious cock out only to slam it back inside of me.

Every movement he made had my own hips moving, fucking my dick along the mind blowing tight hold of Lux's pussy. My eyes stared down into Lux's, connecting with her, my lips brushing over hers. Our breathes mixed just as our rapture fueled cries did.

"Kal." She whimpered, her body dancing with mine, her hips rising under the fall of mine.

"Fucking Ambrose." I snarled, feeling my pleasure rising and rising.

"Fucking, indeed." Ambrose kissed over my back. "I love this. I love you both for doing this."

"I love you too." Lux cried as my pleasure slacked lips could only groan.

"Shit, fuck. I am not going to last long." Ambrose groaned just as Lux's body tightened around mine once again. Her eyes rolled up in her head as her body shook. The mind boggling contractions tightening her sex around mine had my ass automatically tightening around Ambrose's rapture inducing dick.

The friction of him moving through my bowels, rubbing up and down my prostate mixed with Lux's pussy sucking at my dick had my mind blanking with the ecstasy that fired up my spine. My drawn balls began to contract and my dick flexed as my come fountained out, firing deep into Lux's womb. As I was coming, I felt scalding heat filling my ass. Ambrose's lips mouthed over my back, moans vibrating from his chest.

"I love you." My voice stammered when my orgasm finally abated enough that I could finally think.

Ambrose pressed soft kisses over my back. "That was so fucking hot."

"Oh my God." Lux breathed, her body still trembling in the aftermath of her pleasure.

I chuckled softly, soothing my hand over the side of her face to catch her chin and hold her still for my lips. She moaned softly and dug her hands into my hair as I kissed her deeply.

I winced when a warm cloth soothed over my raw, well used ass, cleaning up the come dripping down my balls. In that moment I felt so full, in more ways than one.

Drawing back, I took the cloth that Ambrose handed me, pausing to take part in the kiss he generously doled out. With one last nip, I turned back to use the cloth to clean the mess I made of our woman.

"How did I get so lucky?" Lux smiled up at us warmly.

"What do you mean you?" Ambrose frowned down at her. "I am the lucky one. I have the love of the most beautiful girl in the whole universe and the sexiest man alive."

"I am going to have to disagree with both of you." I bent down to pull my pants up, zipping them closed before helping Lux down. "I am the winner in all of this."

Lux giggled and circled my shoulders when I lifted her down from the desk and helped her adjust her clothes. "I honestly cannot state how much I love the both of you. The day that we were all kidnapped by the Drako's was the day my life truly began."

"I can't argue with that logic." Ambrose dropped his arm over my shoulder, his new arm once again tucked inside his shirt.

"Me neither." Lux caught Ambrose's shirt and tugged him down for a kiss.

With that we shut the AT down and locked it for the night before returning to our tent.

Our home.

My home.

EPILOGUE

KALBELIYAS

I looked across the carpet covered path to Ambrose's shining eyes. His face carried the same look that I was sure mine did. Anxiety mixed with anticipation and joy. His lower lip was firmly tucked in his worrying teeth, his gaze darting around wildly. At least it was until it met mine. Then he seemed to steady.

His black suited chest rose with his heavy, rhythmic breathing, his hands tucked together in front of his pressed, black slacks.

Like me he was dressed in a black, double breasted suit and vest. Our hair was done, our face's clean shaven.

The men who stood at our sides were similarly dressed. Scope, Diad, and Grayson stood in a line descending outwards from Ambrose while Pacifier and Carter stood at my side.

We were as ready as we would ever be.

The music changed and our eyes moved straight down the flower strewn aisle that was surrounded by wooden chairs filled with guests.

The first to come walking down was Skylar. Her hair was curled and laced with flowers. She was glowing radiantly in her strapless purple gown. She walked up to stand between Pac and Carter.

Asp was next, gorgeous in blue. Her distinctively pregnant stomach leading her way to Scope who helpfully stepped forward to help her make it all the way up to the line.

Then came the beauty that was Ela, her hair similarly done to the other two women with curls and flowers, her dress indigo. She had a soft, secretive look on her face.

Ech was last, her orange dress showcasing the slight swell of her growing stomach. She skipped up the aisle to stand beside a smiling Diad.

It was only then that my racing heart skittered to a stop.

Lux.

Her long white mermaid gown, sleeveless with a sweetheart neckline, slicked over her beautiful body. Her face was flushed, glowing with happiness. Her hair was curled down her back with a crown of flowers circling her head and flowing down those dark curls.

She was the most beautiful thing I had ever laid my gaze on.

My eyes feasted on her as she walked down the aisle towards us, a soft smile playing on her lips. Ambrose and I both raised our hands to her at the same time. I chuckled and slid him an amused look as he waited patiently for me to relieve her of her bouquet so I could take her hand.

We helped her step forward until we were all standing in front of the flower covered arch that Malachi was standing under.

"Hey." He greeted when we all turned our waiting gazes to him.

"Hey." Ambrose and I greeted back as Lux giggled.

"We have all gathered here in order to celebrate." Malachi's voice rose to reach the audience as he spoke. "A rare thing for us as we haven't had much to celebrate over the last five years. I don't know about the rest of you, but I am truly grateful to be given these rare chances, chances to come together and share our joys. In the three years we have welcomed new friends, new family, new children. We have seen life being born and life miraculously surviving through extreme odds. So many beautiful miracles that shine like beacons in the darkness that is shadowing our world. It shows us the undying strength that love can have and it gives all of us hope for the future."

"Today, we are here to celebrate the joining of one of those families. We are going to help three people scream their love out to the universe. And maybe, just maybe, someone out there, feeling lost and hopeless, will hear our screams and maybe it will help light up the darkness of their world." Malachi paused and turned to us. "Ambrose, do you take Lux and Kalbeliyas to be your partners in life? To have and to hold, to love and to cherish until death parts you?"

"I do." Ambrose's voice was over loud and slightly breathless.

"Kalbeliyas, do you take Lux and Ambrose...?" Malachi started only for me to cut him.

"Yes." I winced, my face flushing when I realized that I jumped the gun. Ambrose chuckled while Lux brought my knuckles up to her smiling lips. "Uh, I do."

"Ok. Lux, do you take Kalbeliyas and Ambrose to be your partners in life? To have and to hold, to love and to cherish until death parts you?"

"I do." Lux whispered so softly that I barely heard her.

My hand jerked before tightening on hers, my heart filling so full that tears popped into my eyes.

"Awesome." Malachi grinned. "Now the rings. Find a finger and decorate it."

I shook my head in amusement as I caught Ambrose's hand and pushed the dark, metallic band made from Pleiadean minerals onto his finger. Once his hand was free, he guided a smaller version of the same band onto Lux's finger. She smiled as she turned to me and guided the twin of Ambrose's ring onto my finger.

When we turned back to Malachi, he turned to the waiting crowd. "I now pronounce you married. Kiss each other. And make it good."

I wasn't about to argue with that order. And neither was Ambrose as he spun to catch Lux's face in his palms so that he could kiss her, hard and deep. When he drew back his eyes were shining, glowing with amazement and love.

"I love you," He rasped against her lips.

"I love you too." She whispered back, her hand caressing over the side of his face and along his jaw.

Lux turned to me only to find my lips right there. My hand gripped the back of her head, holding her mouth to mine as I sealed our vows. Drawing back, I stared deeply into her beautiful dark eyes. "I love you." My voice was husky.

"I love you too." She smiled up at me, her hand gripping the edge of my jacket.

She carefully stepped back and my eyes came up to Ambrose's. My eyes widened when I saw the gleam there. A gasp broke out of my chest when he grabbed me and spun me around in a dip at the same time his lips found mine.

I could hear Lux's laughter joining the crowds as our lips fed from one another. Pure love filled our kiss.

I laughed when I suddenly found myself returned to my spot, straight and slightly mussed.

Ambrose grinned proudly and we all turned to the cheering audience. Lux yelped when I bent and threw her over my shoulder. Ambrose led the way as I carried our woman down the aisle and over to the tables and dance floor that had been set up on the old landing pad.

Setting Lux down in the middle of the dance floor, I circled her waist with one arm while my other hand reached over to grip Ambrose's shoulder. His arm circled the other side of Lux's waist and his hand circled around her to grip my shoulder.

Lux laid her hands on my chest and her head on Ambrose's chest as we danced to the music.

Married, connected.

Home.

———— ✕✕✕✕ ————

LUX

I WAS NEVER DOING THIS again.

Never.

"Carter." My hand snapped forward to grab his lab coat and yank him forward until my sweating face was right in his. "If you don't get these things out of me right now I will yank every single piece of scruffy hair out of your face, one at a time."

"Ok, Lux, flower." Kal crooned as he reached over the leg he was holding so that his fingers could carefully pry my fist open and release his brother-in-law from my hold.

My breath sucked in with a fierce snarl as my body bowed back with the pain that radiated through my stomach and over my back.

"Threats aside, you are now at ten centimeters. If you want them out so bad, Lux, I would advice pushing." Carter maddeningly grunted, returning back to the stool he was seated on between my blanket covered, cocked up legs.

"You push!" I screamed as I felt my vagina spreading with pure fire.

"You got this, Lux." Ambrose praised, rubbing his hand up and down the leg he was bracing up for me.

"Fuck!" I screamed as my torso bent up, automatically trying to dispel the ripping pain from my body.

"One more, Lux." Carter guided, his yellow eyes trained between my legs.

"Don't fucking lie to me." I snarled right before I was forced to push again.

"It's a boy." Carter crowed happily.

Both Ambrose and Kal looked around the sheet that was barely covering my lap and to where Carter's hands were working. My burning eyes caught on the tiny, goop covered being that Carter was handing over to Fain. She expertly caught our boy in her blanket covered hands. Little hands and arms jerked around above the blanket. So small and tiny.

My eyes followed Fain as she took my son to the counter in order to check him over only to bear down with another wave of pain.

"And here comes number two." Carter stated.

"Thank you, Captain Obvious." I growled around the agony of my vagina once again being forced wide.

Two pushes later and I was once again able to breathe. My whole torso radiated with pain, my vagina was on fire, fuck, even my asshole hurt.

"Another boy." My lightheaded brain heard Carter claim. My dazed eyes turned to watch the next goopy boy, this one shrieking angrily, be handed off to a ready John.

I wanted to cry when that band of pain once again tightened and that excruciating agony once again tore through me. I didn't even have the energy to scream as my exhausted body attempted to push the next child out.

"Push, flower." Kal demanded while Ambrose's arm caught around my back and helped me bear down.

The world spun and my vision darkened as I pushed and pushed and pushed. My breath finally wheezed in when the next child finally slithered free.

"A girl." Carter exclaimed.

"No more." I slurred, my weak body collapsing back to the raised back of the bed I was sitting on.

"No more." Ambrose agreed, his hands moving over my sweaty face, his worried eyes staring into mine. "You did beautifully, Lux."

"Tell that to my vagina." I mumbled, my shaking hands coming up to grip around his wrists, my forehead moving over the one he had pressed down.

"Maybe this will help." Kal's voice had Ambrose drawing back and both of us turning to the bundle he was carefully laying on my chest.

My chest gave a sob at the feel of that warm, tiny body against mine. With shaking fingers, I carefully moved the blanket so I could look down on our son. Dark blue eyes darted around as he snuffled and whimpered. Tears rolled down my eyes and my fingers drew down the baby soft cheek that had Pleiadean metallic marks drawn over it.

The little boy on my chest was soon joined by two more screaming, red faced babies who looked almost exactly the same. My men sat down at the edges of the bed and rested their hands on small backs. Their eyes were glowing with amazement and joy. And love. So much love that it hurt the heart that was screaming it's love right back at them.

Our triplets were beautiful.

And hungry.

AMBROSE

"DADDY!" MY THREE YEAR old daughter dropped out of energy in mid air right above my head.

My heart stopped as my hands frantically darted out to catch my falling daughter, tucking her little body safely into my chest. Attempting to get my racing heart under control, I slid down from the craft I was working on to land on my braced legs.

"Velana, my girl, where is your dadda?" I asked, my chest straining for breath.

Velana, like her aunts, was a triplet. She was delicate little thing, like her mother, with naturally tanned skin and the Pleiadean metallic markings. She had bright red hair just like her dad. Her brothers, Amon and Slater, looked almost exactly the same only Amon had purple hair and Slater had indigo.

All of them carried dark blue eyes.

"Dadda." Velana pointed just as Kal appeared in front of us with Amon over one shoulder and Slater curled under the opposite arm.

"Sorry, she darted off the moment we landed." Kal narrowed his eyes on our giggling daughter.

"So, I see." I turned my own serious eyes down to our mischievously adorable daughter. "Velana, we talked about energy safety."

"Yes, daddy." Her little voice lisped as her little hand tucked into my chest and her eyes turned sad. "Sorry, daddy, dadda."

"Daddy!" Amon's little legs kicked wildly right before he disappeared.

"Amon!" Kal bit out as his eyes tracked our son's energy.

"Daddy." My free arm was thankfully ready, catching Amon against my back when the boy dropped there.

"Daddy." Slater voiced, his little head tipped up to me, his hands reaching for me.

Kal sighed and shifted the boy upright as he carried Slater forward so our son could join his brother and sister in my arms. The kids were shifted around until I had all three safely tucked to my chest, my neck surrounded by strangling little arms.

"Missed you, daddy." Amon rubbed his face over my chest.

"Daddy." Velana smiled, pressing little kisses over my face.

"Love you, daddy." Slater laid his head on my shoulder.

"I missed all of you and love you too. I am so glad you are home." I breathed, my heart feeling just as full as my arms.

Lux came racing in, her worried eyes darting over the AT before landing on us and filling with relief. That relief quickly changed to joy and she was once again running.

With a quick exchange, Kal got the kids transferred just in time for me to catch their mother. Lux and Kal had been at the Base for the last couple of days with the kids while I had to stay behind to work on some of the crafts.

It was so quiet without them around, empty in a way that I hated.

I caught Lux up, my arms circling her as her legs and arms circled me. My hand caught the back of her head in order to deepen the kiss she placed on me.

"I missed you, flower." I whispered against her lips, holding her forehead to mine as I stared deep into her eyes.

"I missed you too, Ambrose." She whispered back, her dark eyes filled with so much love that it hurt my heart.

"Dadda, how come you not greet daddy like momma?" Slater asked curiously.

"I already have the best part of your dad in my arms, you guys." Kal pressed his forehead to Slater's.

"No, dadda, hug daddy." Velana crossed her arms and glared demandingly at Kal.

"Fine." Kal rolled his eyes as he set the kids down.

Lux dropped from my arms in order to run herd on the triplets as Kal backed up. I shook my head in amusement and braced myself knowing what was coming.

Once he got far enough back, Kal stopped and his red eyes met mine. A sly smirk pulled at the side of his lips as he rubbed his gleeful hands together.

He raced forward and my arms reached out to catch the body he was barreling towards me.

He hit me like a battering ram.

I was honestly surprised that I was able to keep my feet, only stumbling back a couple steps when his legs circled my waist and his arms my neck. Hugging him tightly, I grinned and spun him around. He laughed and arched back with his arms out.

It was only when I put him down that I realized the whole AT was stomping and cheering for us.

"Thank you." I grinned proudly while Kal and I bowed to our audience.

Kal laughed and turned to me, catching the back of my neck and pulling me in for his own kiss. "I hate being away from you."

"It's too damned empty." I vehemently agreed with him.

"I am done for the day." I called to the crew as I chased after my kids, catching their giggling forms up one by one and carrying them out of the AT.

Lux and Kal followed us out, their hands linked together, their eyes warm with joy.

I couldn't stop my smile from crossing my face as my kids curled themselves into me, just as happy to be home as I was to have them home.

Don't miss out!

Visit the website below and you can sign up to receive emails whenever T. M. Kuefler publishes a new book. There's no charge and no obligation.

https://books2read.com/r/B-A-WJAP-LEOKC

BOOKS 2 READ

Connecting independent readers to independent writers.

Did you love *Red Skies*? Then you should read *Runaway*[1] by T. M. Kuefler!

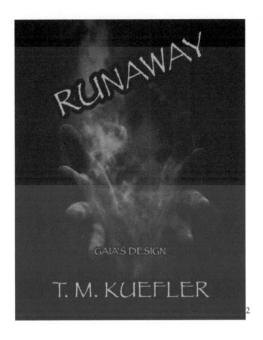

[2]

The president of the Gods Defenders and Poseidon's warlock extraordinary, Aster, has spent months helping Princes. But now, he is the one who needs help tracking down the one woman who he hurt. Sarah, Juno, Calypso. So many names and identities, all for one reason, to hide who she was from a world that was doing everything it could to tear her down. Her enemies have finally tracked her down. Them and one very demanding ex-boyfriend. Aster hurt her more than anyone when he spent weeks cheating on her with another woman. While she was the one who walked away, she did it broken in a way that left her with the inability to trust. Anyone. Even the ex

---

1. https://books2read.com/u/bzKEv9

2. https://books2read.com/u/bzKEv9

who is doing everything he can to drive her insane as he places her in his protective custody and hauls her back to the Specter.

Also by T. M. Kuefler

Extra Elements Series
Connection Bound
Detected Conversance
Triumvirate Protagonism
Ambrosia Realized
Fairy Girl
Unchained Backdraft
Buck Off!
Flight Plan
Rational Existence
Endangered Essence
Persuading Cynicism
Blind Luck
Astral Fusion
Stirring Pieces
Opaque Equilibrium
Red Skies

Gaia's Design
Grrrr!
Half Life
Pursuit

Runaway

Knights Five
Cracked Tableau
Extracted Tableau
Disintegrating Tableau

Standalone
Sunshine
Father

About the Author

An avid book lover and keen psychology student, Canadian T.M. decided it was time to pull up her big girl panties and put fingers to keyboard. During this time, the alarm on the phone gets a big work out, just so that T. M. remembers to pull her head out of the literary dreamland and back into reality.

Milton Keynes UK
Ingram Content Group UK Ltd.
UKHW040653191023
430917UK00001B/80